MRS. MIRACLE

Also by Debbie Macomber

Family Affair
Touched by Angels
Angels Everywhere
Christmas Angels
Mrs. Miracle
Sooner or Later
Someday Soon
The Trouble With Angels
One Night
A Season of Angels
Morning Comes Softly

DEBBIE MACOMBER

MRS. MIRACLE

WILLIAM MORROW
An Imprint of HarperCollinsPublishers

MRS. MIRACLE. Copyright © 1996 by Debbie Macomber. All rights reserved. Printed in the United States of America. No part of this book may be used or reproduced in any manner whatsoever without written permission except in the case of brief quotations embodied in critical articles and reviews. For information, address HarperCollins Publishers, 195 Broadway, New York, NY 10007.

HarperCollins books may be purchased for educational, business, or sales promotional use. For information, please email the Special Markets Department at SPsales@harpercollins.com.

FIRST WILLIAM MORROW PAPERBACK EDITION PUBLISHED 2017.
FIRST AVON BOOKS PAPERBACK EDITION PUBLISHED 2005.
FIRST HARPERCOLLINS PAPERBACK EDITION PUBLISHED 1996.

Library of Congress Cataloging-in-Publication Data has been applied for.

ISBN 978-0-06-269390-7

17 18 19 20 21 LSC 10 9 8 7 6 5 4 3

To Renate Roth,
the world's best assistant,
for the everyday miracles she worked in my life.
Happy Retirement!

Be not forgetful
To entertain *strangers*
For thereby some have entertained
angels unawares.

—HEBREWS 13:2

MRS. MIRACLE

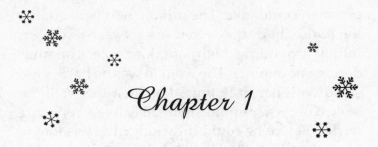

Chapter 1

A lot of people want to serve God,
but only in an advisory capacity.

—Mrs. Miracle

"I told you not to swear, you little turd." Seth Webster grabbed his sons by the scruffs of their necks in order to keep his squirming twins apart. It demanded all his strength to keep the two, fists flying, from attacking each other.

"Mr. Webster!" Mrs. Hampston, his housekeeper, the third in as many months, stood with her hands braced against her hips, her mouth thinned with disapproval. "That's hardly the example to be giving your children."

Truth be known, Seth couldn't have agreed with her more, but there was a limit to just how much one man could take. The minute he'd walked into the house, he'd discovered his six-year-old twins rolling around the bedroom floor, intent on murdering one another. The woman was no help. She'd stood with her back braced against the wall and barked orders, sounding incredibly like a Yorkshire terrier. Before he could fully judge the wisdom of his actions, Seth had entered the fray. Within seconds his patience was shot.

Judd swore. Seth swore. Mrs. Hampston gasped, shocked to the very tips of her toes. Jason stuck his tongue out at his brother and looked well pleased with himself.

Judd retaliated, his tongue resembling that of a Gila monster.

"Judd. Jason. Stop that this instant."

Both children squirmed. The fight went out of Judd first, and his shoulders slumped forward. "I'm sorry, Daddy." His son scuffed the toe of his Nike against the bedroom carpet, his gaze lowered to the floor.

The love Seth felt for his children tightened a band around his heart.

"I was wrong, too," he admitted, affectionately mussing the boy's brownish red hair. The last few months had been a trial for all three of them. His in-laws had raised the twins for the past four years following Pamela's death. Judd and Jason had been toddlers at the time of the traffic accident, needy and demanding. Seth couldn't care for them properly and maintain his engineering position with Boeing. Having the two move in with Sharon and Jerry had seemed the perfect solution. His own parents traveled extensively and were unable to help. With time and effort the twins had adjusted to life without their mother—something Seth had yet to manage.

"I need to talk to you privately following dinner," Mrs. Hampston announced stiffly as she walked past him on her way back into the kitchen.

"She's gonna quit," Jason announced as soon as the housekeeper was out of sight.

"The same way Mrs. Cooper quit," Judd added.

"And Mrs. Larson."

And everyone else, Seth added silently. He felt as if the entire world had quit on him. It'd all started when Sharon had phoned last July and abruptly announced it was time the twins moved back with him. It was long past time, Seth suspected, but he'd grown comfortable leaving the responsibility for the care of his children with his in-laws, comfortable in his role of weekend "Disney" dad. With Judd and Jason due to start first grade in the fall, the time for transition was now. In the months since, Seth wondered if he was ever meant to be a father.

He appreciated his in-laws' help. They'd done more for him and the twins than he'd ever be able to repay. But Jerry had recently retired, and the two had already sacrificed four years of their lives. Their help had gotten Seth through the worst of the child-rearing years, or so he believed. He'd taken a crash course in this parenting business and discovered it wasn't nearly as easy as it sounded.

It shocked Seth how short his patience could be. Within five minutes of promising himself to set a good example, he'd referred to his own son as a turd. Unfortunately the term fit Judd to a tee. The lad was full of vinegar, into everything. Nothing was sacred. Jason was the follower. On his own he was quiet and shy, but with his brother forging ahead, he was quick to follow.

It had been much easier to consider himself a decent father when he was separated by a thousand miles. He called often, mailed the kids letters, and spent as much time with them as his schedule would allow. The lessons had come swiftly and sharply that summer when Judd and Jason had moved back in with him. The quick succession of live-in housekeepers was testimony to exactly how much of a failure he'd been.

"Are you gonna wash my mouth out with soap?" Judd asked, making a face as though he could already taste the unpleasantness.

Seth sat down on the edge of the bottom bunk bed and weighed the decision.

"He can't," Jason assured his twin, flopping

down on the mattress beside him. "Dad said the *T* word."

"Is the *F* word worse than the *T* word?" Jason looked to Seth for the answer.

"The hell if I know."

Judd's eyes widened with warning and he whispered, "Watch it, Dad, Mrs. Hampston doesn't approve of the *H* word, either."

"It don't matter 'cause she's gonna quit anyway." This bit of wisdom came from Jason. The kid was probably right, too.

Sitting back against the wall, Seth draped an arm around each of his children's shoulders and released a jagged sigh.

"What are we going to do now?" Judd asked.

"We need a housekeeper," Jason added.

His son turned dark, round eyes to Seth, looking for him to supply the answers.

"Hey, she hasn't quit yet." Seth tried to sound optimistic but doubted that he convinced anyone. They'd seen it all too often before not to recognize the symptoms. The housekeeper wanted out.

"We tried to be good."

"I know." Seth was sympathetic. He'd done his best too and had repeatedly fallen short.

Earlier that week, Seth had stopped off at the grade school for a parent-teacher conference and learned that his children's behavior wasn't that much different in school from what it was at home. The term their teacher had used to describe Judd was "high-spirited," which was later translated as "disorderly, disruptive, ill-behaved, and stubborn." His brother was a willing accomplice.

The woman assured him there was nothing malicious about their behavior, but the twins tended to be . . . affectionate troublemakers. It wasn't as if Seth hadn't noticed.

On a conscious level he realized the kids' behavior had a great deal to do with the recent upheaval in their young lives. They'd been indulged by Sharon and Jerry and had been thrust back into life with a father who'd buried his grief in his job. Following Pamela's accident, Seth had steadily climbed the ladder of success within the Boeing Airplane Company. He was the youngest senior engineer in the company's history. To further complicate matters, he'd recently been assigned to the Firecracker Project. It wasn't uncommon for him to put in fifty to sixty hours a week on the top-secret project Boeing was developing for the Department of Defense. With the arrival of the twins, Seth felt fortunate to get in a regular eight-hour day. His work had suffered, along with his health, his disposition, and just about everything else.

"I better go see if I can smooth the waters with Mrs. Hampston," he said, inhaling deeply. This wouldn't be fun. The middle-aged woman possessed all the tact of a Sherman tank. She lived and breathed discipline. Not that Seth was opposed to a little order. Anyone who could bring harmony to the chaos that had taken control of his life was welcome indeed. Mrs. Hampston, however, was better suited to whipping raw recruits into shape than dealing with two six-year-olds and one insecure dad.

He'd say one thing for the woman, she'd lasted twice as long as any of the previous housekeepers. One woman had left after only two nights. Another, an older, more mature grandmotherly type, had stayed as long as two weeks. In Mrs. Hampston's case it had been an entire six weeks. He'd never been fond of the crotchety old biddy, but then Seth suspected Mrs. Hampston knew that. The fact was, she'd probably gain a good deal of satisfaction in leaving him in the lurch.

Crow had never been one of his favorite dishes, and knowing Mrs. Hampston, she'd enjoy serving it to him on a dome-covered silver platter. Taking a few moments to compose his thoughts, Seth stepped into his study and slumped onto the leather wing-backed chair next to the fireplace.

It wasn't supposed to happen like this. What the kids really needed was someone who would enjoy their boisterous nature. A woman who would appreciate their creativity and spontaneity. Someone who would laugh with them instead of trying to stuff them into a mold.

A mother.

His head fell forward at the weight of his burden. Seth remembered the day he and Pamela had gone into the doctor for the ultrasound that had revealed two tiny but distinct babies. Seth's first reaction had been sheer wonder and an incredible, breathtaking sense of excitement and joy. Twins. They were having twins. Only later had the weight of the responsibility overtaken him. He'd been able to hide his fears from Pamela. He'd even managed to sweep them aside himself . . . until after Judd and Jason's birth. It helped that Pamela was a natural mother. Loving and patient. Perfect.

Then without warning Seth's flawless world had shattered on a rain-slick street when his wife's car had slid out of control and she'd slammed into a telephone pole. Her death, Seth had been told, had been instantaneous. The children, tucked securely in their car seats, didn't receive so much as a scratch. But in those tragic seconds, his wife was gone. His wife and his very heart. His life was as ruined as the twisted metal that had once been her vehicle.

In retrospect it might have been easier to deal with Pamela's death had there been someone to blame. A drunk driver. A speeder. Anyone to focus his anger and frustration upon. But there had been no one. In the beginning, he'd sought to blame God. He'd longed to shake his fist at the sky for stealing away his very heart.

For a time anger had consumed Seth's soul. Shortly after her funeral, he had sold the piano. Now, four years later, it seemed a bit dramatic to have given up his music, but he'd simply lost the desire for it. Music was something he'd shared with Pamela. His world had felt devoid of all that had once brought joy, and in his pain he'd destroyed everything that had connected him with his dead wife. It was his way of telling God to "take that."

Seth's gaze fell across the room to a row of bookcases. The hardbound version of C. S. Lewis's *The Lion, the Witch and the Wardrobe* captured his attention. The well-read, much-loved book had been Pamela's favorite, one she'd treasured since childhood. From the moment they'd learned she was pregnant, she'd talked of one day sitting with her children at her side and reading them the story she loved so much.

Seth ran a hand down his face and closed his eyes as he dealt with a fresh wave of pain. Not for the first time he wondered if it'd ever get better. If he'd always feel this raw-edged anguish when he remembered Pamela. The years hadn't eased it. Having the children with him hadn't lessened his sense of loss. If anything, their arrival increased his awareness of what he would never have. He carried his grief with him the way some men toted around a briefcase. How different his life would be if Pamela had lived. In many ways it would have been kinder if they'd buried him along with his wife.

He walked over to the oak bookcase and slowly removed the book by C. S. Lewis. The edge of the spine was tattered by love and time. Carefully he laid open the novel in his palm. Inside, a six-year-old Pamela had carefully printed her name in large square letters. The twins were six.

The sharp pain clenched Seth's heart. He'd done such an effective job of burying his grief that when it bubbled to the surface it almost always caught him unaware.

Instead of replacing the book back inside the oak bookcase, Seth carried it to the desk and set it carefully in a bottom drawer. He couldn't explain why. He didn't want to be sucker-punched a second time by glancing across the room and finding Pamela's favorite childhood book in his face. He had enough to deal with.

Unsure how to handle the situation with Mrs. Hampston, Seth walked into the kitchen. "You wanted to talk to me." He struck a casual pose and leaned against the counter.

Mrs. Hampston didn't possess an ounce of fat.

Everything about her was severe, right down to the polish on her black, spit-shined shoes. Disapproval radiated from her the way fire warmed a room.

"As you might have guessed," she announced primly, "I find my services to be neither appreciated nor—"

"That isn't so. The kids and I think you're wonderful," Seth countered quickly, hoping God would forgive him the lie. "I couldn't be more grateful for your help, and—"

"I beg to differ, Mr. Webster."

No amount of coaxing had persuaded her to call Seth by his first name. But then, he'd never been able to think of her as "Bertha," either.

"It seems apparent to me, if to no one else," she continued stiffly, "that I can no longer stay."

"But you're wrong, we'd—"

"Please, don't attempt to sway me. My mind is made up."

"I'd be willing to offer you a substantial raise," Seth said, attempting to sound contrite and appreciative and failing, he feared, on both counts.

Mrs. Hampston hesitated, then cocked her chin and gave him a look of mild disgust, as if she'd been deeply insulted by the mere suggestion that she could be seduced with money.

"I'd appreciate it if you'd stay until after the holidays," he added, growing more desperate.

"Mr. Webster, apparently you didn't understand me. When I said I'd reached this decision, I wasn't looking for you to change my mind. I refuse to be bribed."

"Bribed." Seth did his best to sound confused.

"Exactly."

If her nose got any closer to the ceiling, she'd be in serious danger of having a bird roosting on it.

"I can't tell you how sorry I am." Seth sincerely hoped he sounded regretful, but he doubted he'd be any more successful in pulling the wool over this woman's eyes than he was with his own children.

"I'm afraid I don't share your regrets. Of all the positions I've held in my fifteen-year history of domestic service, I can never remember having to deal with a worse pair of undisciplined children. I understood when I accepted the position that the twins were considered a handful, but this is ridiculous."

"They're only six."

"Exactly. Six going on thirteen. I don't have a moment's peace from dawn to dusk. Those two are constantly underfoot. They're savages, I tell you. Savages."

"I've already explained to the kids that goldfish can't live in Jell-O," Seth said. "I realize it was a shock to open the refrigerator and find the goldfish bowl filled with lemon Jell-O and three small fish."

"The problem with the goldfish was the tip of the iceberg," she responded, and grimaced.

"Okay, okay, so maybe those water bazookas weren't such a good idea. I didn't think they'd turn them on you." By sheer willpower, Seth managed to squelch a smile. One gloriously sunny autumn afternoon, he had been washing the car while the twins raced across kingdom come, soaking each other with their fancy water guns. When Mrs. Hampston stepped onto the porch Judd and Jason had guilelessly turned their weapons on her. To put it mildly, the housekeeper had not been amused. To Seth's way of thinking, a little water never hurt anyone.

"It isn't the Jell-O incident or the water bazookas. It isn't even having to routinely dig little green army men out of the bathtub drain. It's you."

"Me?" Seth demanded defensively. He'd bent over backward to keep the peace with Mrs. Hampston, and now she was accusing him!

"You know absolutely nothing about being a father."

Seth's mouth snapped shut. Like all good military strategists, she attacked his weakest point. He had no argument.

"The twins are your children, Mr. Webster, not

your friends, and not cute pets. They need a firm, guiding hand. As far as I can see, you're no example for them. None whatsoever. Swearing is one thing, but to put it bluntly, you're a slob."

Seth knew she was right. He was an absent-minded professor, his head filled with work, the kids, and everything else. He didn't mean to be untidy, it just happened that way. He constantly lost and found himself. Mundane things like remembering to fill up the car with gas escaped him. The other morning, to her disgust, Mrs. Hampston had found his shoes in the refrigerator. Seth vaguely recalled putting them there.

"If you'd be willing to give me another chance . . ."

"I've already assured you I won't."

"Yes, but finding another housekeeper might prove difficult just now."

"I'm sure it will be, but that isn't my problem."

Seth leaned against the door, wondering where to turn to next. Mrs. Hampston had been his last hope. The agency didn't have anyone else to send. He didn't know what he would do, where he would turn.

"Frankly, Mr. Webster," the woman stated smugly, "it isn't a housekeeper you need, it's a miracle."

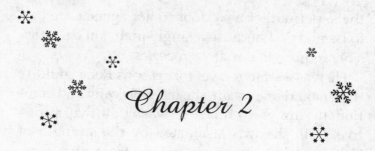

Chapter 2

The best way to get even is to forget.

—Mrs. Miracle

"Reba, there's a call for you on line one."

Reba Maxwell's gaze remained fixed on the parking lot outside the strip mall where her travel agency was located. She saw him again, the mystery man who'd dominated her thoughts for weeks. The one who made her smile. Half the time she wondered if he knew where he was. He'd climb out of the car and then stare at the storefront as though attempting to remember what he was supposed to buy.

She knew nothing about him. Not his name. Or if he was married. Where he worked or lived. Nothing. He stopped off two or three times a week at the supermarket next door to her agency. He had to be married because a single man couldn't possibly require that many groceries.

He was a stranger, yet for reasons Reba couldn't understand or explain, she felt physically and emotionally drawn to him. He wasn't all that attractive. Still, she was fascinated by the strength of character that seemed to radiate from him. Even from a distance she noted that his jaw was strong, his cheekbones high and pronounced, and his lips full. He wasn't especially tall, and he didn't possess any of the other attributes that generally interested a woman. Nevertheless she waited day after day, hoping to catch a glimpse of him.

He wasn't even her type, she reasoned, impatient with herself. She'd learned her lesson long ago and avoided those high-powered executives. Always so crisp and formal. Always in control.

"Reba, line one," Jayne Preston reminded her.

She pulled her attention away from the window and reached for the phone. "This is Reba," she answered in a businesslike tone.

"Hello, dahlin'."

Her mother. "Hello, Mom," she answered, keeping her voice even and unemotional. She knew what was coming, had been expecting it, and dreaded the confrontation and all that was sure to follow.

"How are you feeling?"

Her mother sounded as if Reba had recently recovered from a life-threatening illness, as if she suffered with impossibly fragile health—if not physically, then emotionally, which was a greater insult. She gritted her teeth and prayed for patience before she answered.

"I'm fine. I suppose you want to talk about Christmas." No need delaying the inevitable. She preferred to deal with the unpleasantness now and be done with it.

"Well, yes . . ." Joan Maxwell said, and hesitated, her frustration grating through the telephone lines. "I would really like it if we could have a family Christmas this year. With your aunt Gerty and uncle Bill coming, it'd be so awkward with you and your sister . . ."

Reba's jaw tensed. "We can have a real Christmas."

"Oh, Reba, does that mean you're willing to put aside your differences with Vicki and—"

"We can have a family Christmas," she repeated without emotion. "We'll do exactly as we have for the last four years. Vicki and her husband can choose to spend either Christmas Eve or Christmas Day with you, Aunt Gerty, and Uncle Bill. Then I'll be free to join you and everyone else when they aren't there."

Her mother's disappointment was palpable. "I see."

"I don't have to come home for Christmas, Mother," Reba returned, unwilling to be manipulated by her parent or anyone else. Really it was ridiculous, seeing that she lived in the same south-end community of Seattle. Reba visited her parents on a routine basis. It wasn't as if she'd saved the holidays for her annual pilgrimage home. Despite the differences with her older sister, Reba made an effort to stop by her parents' at least every other month. With one condition: She'd go as long as Vicki wasn't there.

"Not come home for Christmas?" her mother echoed. "Your father and I would be so disappointed. . . . It's just that, well, your dad hasn't been feeling well lately, and it would do us both a world of good if you and your sister would—"

"Mom, stop." This wasn't a topic Reba wished to discuss, not when she'd already been through it a million times. "We both know what Vicki did, and—"

"You don't know everything."

"Listen," Reba returned, irritated that her mother insisted on pursuing the issue, insisted on taking her sister's side. "I've told you this before and I meant it. If you're going to phone me to talk about Vicki, then I'll hang up. I've got a business to run."

"But it's been four years."

"Four and a half," Reba amended. It wouldn't take much effort for her to calculate it right down to the minute. A lifetime would pass away and she'd never forget what her sister, her own flesh and blood, had done to her. She wasn't going to forget, not ever. God help them both, but she wasn't willing to forgive her sister, either. To her credit, Vicki had attempted to repair the damage, but it was too little, too late. Three times her sister had come to her seeking forgiveness. Three times Reba had rejected her apology. What Vicki had done was unforgivable. It had been so hurtful and cruel that whatever closeness they'd once shared had forever been destroyed.

Even as youngsters the two sisters had been competitive. Because she was almost two years older, Vicki had the advantage when it came to sports. But that didn't keep Reba from trying. She made the varsity basketball team, was a high school cheerleader and track star the same as Vicki, but she'd worked hard for those accomplishments. Unlike Vicki, who was naturally athletic.

Over the course of her high school and college career, Reba had nearly killed herself in an effort to keep pace with her sister's accomplishments. Both girls were evenly paired in the academic realm. Each had been offered full scholarships to the University of Washington.

Their rivalry, although often keen, had always been friendly. Reba liked to think that they brought out the best in one another. Each challenged the other to give one hundred percent to their individual endeavors.

Until Reba started dating John Goddard.

Even saying his name mentally produced a hard lump in her throat. Briefly Reba closed her eyes until the pain and bitterness passed.

In retrospect she was willing to admit, albeit grudgingly, that part of John's attraction had been that Vicki had been attracted to him, too. Her sister had joked that she'd been the one to see John first. Her teasing had taken on a decidedly sharp tone as Reba and John's relationship turned more serious.

Later, when Reba was head over heels in love with John, she suspected Vicki's feelings for the architect went beyond "sisterly" love. She didn't realize how accurate that impression was until—

"I do so wish you girls would settle your differences."

"It's settled, Mother," Reba said starkly, emphatically. "As settled as it's going to get."

"But Vicki's your sister."

"Not anymore."

"Reba, sweetheart, why do you continue to carry this grudge when John is out of your life? Out of Vicki's. He's married to someone else now. Neither one of you has talked to the man in years, and yet you continue to wage war with your sister."

Reba closed her eyes, hating it when her mother

insisted on dredging up the past. For her part, she was perfectly content to leave matters as they were.

"You can't go on like this." It was the same argument, second verse. Her mother played the familiar warped record each Christmas. Frankly, Reba didn't want to hear it. Nothing her mother said or did would ever cancel the heartache and pain her own sister had brought into her life.

What she said was true. John was out of the picture, but the blame for what had happened fell squarely, solidly, on Vicki's shoulders.

Reba had wiped both Vicki and John from her life. The two deserved each other. She'd fully expected Vicki to take advantage of the situation and marry John herself when she stepped aside. It had come as something of a surprise when her sister had married Doug Minder a year later. But then, it really wasn't much of a puzzle. Vicki hadn't truly been interested in John. She just hadn't wanted Reba to have him. Her sister had achieved what she'd set out to do, and that was to ruin any chance Reba had of finding happiness.

"I do wish you'd reconsider," her mother said, breaking into her thoughts once more. "If you won't do it for your father or me, then do it for your aunt and uncle. They think the world of you and Vicki."

"I can't," she said, and because she knew her

response was an invitation to argue, she added, "I won't." She did feel a certain amount of regret, but she refused to turn back time. Nothing her sister said or did now would make up for the bitterness of her betrayal. They might have been competitive, but they were still sisters. Flesh and blood didn't do what Vicki had done to her.

The silence stretched until it felt as if the tension would snap.

"It'd mean so much to your father and me."

Reba closed her eyes. "Mom, please stop."

"Don't you realize how difficult this is on us?" her mother whispered. "We love you both."

"I know, Mom, and I'm sorry, I really am, but I can't share the holidays with you if Vicki's there, too. Not the season of love, peace, and goodwill. My presence would be a lie. I'm sure Vicki and her family would be more comfortable without me."

Again Reba felt her mother's disappointment, but she saw no reason to give her parents hope. As far as she was concerned, she had no sister.

He was back.

Reba's gaze followed the man she'd seen a moment earlier. He'd gone into the grocery store and now walked out carrying a single bag. He paused, scratched the side of his head, and continued toward the parking lot. If she didn't know better, she'd think he'd forgotten where he'd parked his car. He was just what she needed, Reba mused. Comic relief.

"But, Reba . . ."

Her mother was unwilling to drop the subject of Christmas. This was bound to be the first of many such conversations.

"Mom, don't. This is hard enough. Let me know if Vicki wants to come Christmas Eve or Christmas Day and I'll be there when she won't. If that isn't agreeable, I'll simply skip Christmas this year." The holidays weren't that important to her. Not any longer.

"You can't do that."

"Just let me know when Vicki plans on being at the house, all right?"

Her mother's sigh was deep and heartfelt, heavy with defeat and sadness. "Tell me, what would it take to heal this rift between you and your sister?"

Reba didn't hesitate. Not for a moment. "The answer's simple. It would take a miracle."

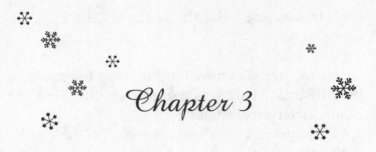

Chapter 3

*Feed your faith and your
doubts will starve to death.*

—Mrs. Miracle

The doorbell jingled at the worst possible moment. Seth was trying his hardest to get dinner on the table. Cooking had never been his forte. Try as he might, he couldn't manage a simple casserole without forgetting one ingredient. It was already past seven, and everyone was cranky and hungry. The house was a disaster, which was no surprise, and he was in no frame of mind to deal with the Avon lady.

Jason had taken it upon himself to help him by pouring the milk. Seth had tried to tell him he was too small to manage a gallon container, but Jason wouldn't listen. By the time he turned to stop him, it was too late.

"I'll get it," Judd shouted, tossing aside the Nintendo game as he rushed to the front door. Two seconds later he glanced over his shoulder and yelled at the top of his lungs, "It's for you. . . . Some lady."

Seth jerked off the apron, set aside the milk-soaked sponge, and stalked to the front door.

"Yes?" he muttered impatiently without looking. He never did understand why salespeople found it convenient to call during the dinner hour. Surely research would tell them how irritating it was to have a meal disrupted.

"Mr. Webster?" An older, grandmotherly type stood under the golden ray of the porch light. Her eyes were warm and kind, her smile wide and friendly. She carried a wicker basket under one arm and waited expectantly for him to respond.

Seth couldn't take his eyes off her. The porch light appeared to enshrine her, as if she were the source of the light, which of course was ludicrous. She was the storybook image of—he hated to say it—Mother Goose. She was round and soft, her gray hair pinned into a loose bun, with dimples and the most loving eyes he could ever remember seeing.

"I'm Seth Webster," he said after an awkward moment.

"I thought you must be. I'm Emily Merkle. The agency sent me."

The agency. Seth couldn't believe his good fortune. There was a God, and He was willing to overlook Seth's bungling attempts at fatherhood. Willing to give him one last chance to redeem himself.

Before she could find an excuse to leave, he grabbed the new housekeeper by the arm and dragged her inside the house. Apparently Mrs. Hampston hadn't had time to complete the complaint sheet against him. In the past week he'd telephoned the employment agency a dozen times, only to be told he'd already gone through every domestic employee the company handled. He wasn't about to question his good fortune now.

"Welcome, welcome." No truer words had ever been spoken.

She glanced about, a look of shock on her face. "Oh, my."

Seth viewed the room with fresh eyes. A load of clean laundry littered the sofa. Jason had attempted to fold the towels and had decided to iron them first. Seth had discovered it just in time to prevent him from burning down the house. As a result, three fluffy yellow bath towels showed the charred black imprint of an iron. While Seth had been occupied cooking dinner, Judd decided to help his brother fold clothes. Unfortunately his assistance consisted of hauling out the drawers from every dresser in the house. By the time Seth had discovered what the two were doing, clothes cluttered the carpet and furniture until the room resembled Filene's Basement during the biggest sale of the year.

"Dinner's ready. You'll join us, won't you?" Seth said quickly, fearing his new housekeeper would turn tail and run before he could convince her to stay. On second thought, canned tomato soup and toasted cheese sandwiches would reveal exactly how desperate he was for help.

"I realize it's inconvenient for me to arrive at the dinner hour. . . ."

"Inconvenient? No way," he countered swiftly. By now she must have guessed the truth. "You're welcome any time." Judd stood beside him, but Jason had wrapped his arms around his leg and held on with the strength of a boa constrictor.

Walking was a shade difficult with Jason attached to his thigh, but Seth managed to pretend nothing was amiss. He wanted it to look as though he often loped across the house with a six-year-old connected to his leg.

"I hope you don't mind, but I decided to bring dinner along with me."

Seth's gaze dropped to the Red Riding Hood–style basket draped over her arm. A tantalizing scent of rosemary and sage wafted lazily toward him.

"It's a specialty of mine, chicken pot pie." She advanced into the kitchen and set the basket on the only clear spot available on eight feet of counter-top.

If the living room was in mild disarray, the kitchen was in chaos. Spilled milk splashed across the tabletop looked like a work of modern art. What had managed to seep through pooled on the floor beneath.

Dirty dishes filled the sink, and the groceries he'd purchased two days earlier cluttered the countertops, along with discarded remnants from breakfast. No one had bothered to tell him milk-soaked cereal that dried onto the sides of a bowl required a blow torch to remove.

"I'll have this mess cleaned up before you know it," he promised.

Mrs. Merkle dismissed his offer with a brisk hand gesture and turned her head, but Seth thought he might have seen her roll her eyes. "You're Judd and this must be Jason," she said, grinning at the children. She removed the hatpin from her no-nonsense hat and set it aside.

The children were either mesmerized or terri-fied, Seth couldn't decide which. They stared up at her with their mouths hanging open.

"Children, you can help by setting the table," Mrs. Merkle instructed as she casually unfastened the large round buttons of her dark wool coat. She slipped it from her arms and carried it into the living room along with her hat and purse and laid them over the back of the sofa.

While she was out of the room, Seth dumped the tomato-paste-consistency soup down the sink, watching it gurgle like thick toxic waste as the pipe sucked it down. He whirled around guiltily when Mrs. Merkle returned, forgetting for the moment that Jason was clamped to his leg. His weight, although slight, nearly knocked him off-balance, and he caught himself by gripping hold of the edge of the counter.

Seeming not to notice either him or the twins, Mrs. Merkle went about readying dinner. She appeared to be grumbling under her breath. She placed the chicken pot pie in the oven to warm, wiped the table free of milk, and organized the kitchen with a skill and dexterity that left Seth astonished. He wanted to help, wanted to prove he wasn't entirely worthless, but he couldn't stop staring. The housekeeper moved with an effortless ease about the room while he stood with the children, watching her with his mouth gaping open in sheer wonder. After what seemed less than five minutes, she had dinner on a clean table, in a near spotless kitchen.

"Dinner's ready," she announced, turning to face him and the children.

"It's a miracle," Seth mused. It wasn't until he

heard the sound of his own voice that he realized he'd spoken aloud.

"Are you a miracle?" Judd asked the housekeeper outright.

Mrs. Merkle chuckled softly. "Now that, my fine fellow, is a matter of opinion."

"Mrs. Miracle," Jason announced, offering the new housekeeper a shy smile.

As far as Seth was concerned, the woman's arrival couldn't have been anything but divine providence. Mrs. Hampston had left a week earlier. Seven days, and as far as Seth was concerned the Middle Ages had passed faster.

He'd tried to work a regular forty-hour week, but his involvement with the Firecracker Project required far more of his time and effort than that allowed in a routine schedule. He'd been bringing what he could home with him and working until all hours of the morning, overdosing on caffeine and managing on four or five hours' sleep a night. As a result he'd shortchanged his children and his employer, and he was killing himself in the process. Another week of this and he'd be a candidate for the loony bin.

Judd and Jason didn't need to be encouraged to take their places at the table. His children weren't fools. Dinner, especially one not cooked by their father, put them on their best behavior.

Once everyone was seated, Mrs. Merkle opened the oven door and brought out the hot, bubbling chicken pot pie. The crust was browned to perfection, and the tantalizing gravy leaked up through the sides. The scent all but made his knees go weak. Seth didn't need to be urged to place his napkin in his lap and grip hold of his fork in eager anticipation.

"Wow," Judd whispered, and looked to his dad. His tongue moistened his lips, and his eyes sparkled with eager anticipation.

Afterward Seth would have been hard-pressed to say when he'd enjoyed a meal more. He supposed he should be asking his new housekeeper for references, but he was too busy enjoying his dinner to take the time. She had a kind, honest face, but he'd been fooled before. Then again, she could well be the good-hearted, generous soul he'd requested from the beginning.

Frankly, he wasn't keen on the agency's placement tactics. They'd waited until he was at his wits' end before sending him a new housekeeper. Since he was paying top dollar, one would think they'd want to please him.

"This is good," Seth said, and helped himself to seconds.

"It's an old family recipe that I've updated."

Seth would have polished off a third slice of the

succulent pie, but he was already stuffed. Placing his hands on his stomach, he excused himself and scooted back his chair.

"I'll help Mrs. Mirkl . . . Mrs. Meeraki . . . Mrs. Miracle," Jason burst forth triumphantly.

"I'll help, too," Judd insisted. Always before, his chauvinistic sons had insisted dishes were woman's work. Even when Seth was up to his armpits in suds, risking dishwater hands, they had refused to help. This attitude, Seth suspected, was the result of living with their grandparents for the last several years. Jerry Palmer's outdated views of what was and wasn't fitting work for the male population had unfortunately rubbed off on his grandsons.

"You can both help," Mrs. Merkle decided, pushing up her sleeves.

"When we're finished, will you read to us?"

One dinner after a week of his cooking was all it took to win over his children, Seth noticed.

"You read, too?" To hear Jason talk, the woman's talents were unlimited.

Seth had tried reading to his children before bed, but the only one he put to sleep was himself. He'd get warm and comfortable, and before he knew it, his eyes would start to droop and his head would nod. The next thing he knew, the twins would slip away silently and decide to help him by rewiring the house or turning the washer into a breadmaking machine.

"Will you be taking your coffee in the family room, Mr. Webster?" she asked.

"Yes, please." It wasn't until he was seated on the leather recliner that Seth wondered how it was his new housekeeper knew he routinely drank a cup of coffee with the evening newspaper following dinner. But then, it wasn't such an unusual habit. Seth suspected half the male population read the evening paper over a cup of freshly brewed coffee.

Mrs. Merkle carried a steaming mug in to him a few minutes later. "I imagine you have a number of questions you'd like me to answer," she said as she set the mug on the coaster. "If you don't mind, I'd like to wait until I've tidied up in the kitchen and gotten the children down for the night."

"Of course." She was right; he should have a long list of questions, important ones. Naturally he'd want to read her references. These were his children, his own flesh and blood, his very reason for living. He'd need to be sure he wasn't entrusting the twins to the care of a serial murderer.

Mrs. Merkle? Naw. A woman who could cook up a chicken pot pie that good was a gift from God. And who was he to question a miracle? Oh, he'd make a few basic inquiries, listen to her answers,

but it would all be for show. The employment
agency routinely screened their applicants. They
would have already completed a background
check and handled the necessary paperwork. Besides, any questions he might have about the suit-
ability of a housekeeper concerned that old biddy
Hampston. He never had cared for the woman,
and it was all too apparent she'd been similarly
inclined to dislike him. Although her leaving had
been an inconvenience, it was for the best.

Seth dozed off while reading the sports section
and woke to the sound of giggles and laughter.
With his eyes closed he tried to picture what his
life would have been like had Pamela lived. Surely
he would feel this contented, this relaxed. Resting
after a long day at the office, his stomach full, his
wife at his side, with the sound of his children's
laughter echoing through the house.

The picture was almost complete, except that he
felt so desperately alone. Pamela was forever
gone. His mother-in-law was right: it had been
time to send the children back to him. He hadn't
realized how much he'd missed the twins. For
four years he'd buried his grief and his loss in his
job and reaped large financial rewards. The time
had come for him to break out of his shell, if not
for his own sake, then for those of his children.

Seth straightened, shocked to see that the
laundry fiasco had disappeared. Other than the

newspaper, which had slipped out of his hands and onto the carpet while he napped, the area resembled a furniture showroom. Inviting, cozy, tempting.

How Emily Merkle and his two rambunctious children had managed to clear away a truckload of clothes without him hearing was short of another supernatural event. Either that or he was more tired than he'd realized.

His interlude was interrupted by the sound of footsteps racing down the hallway. Seth lowered the footrest and stood. He found Jason, cheeks rosy red from the bath, wrapped in a large towel.

"As soon as you're into your pajamas, I'll get my book," the new housekeeper offered.

"You won't fall asleep, will you?" The inquiry came from Judd, who glanced meaningfully toward Seth.

"Don't be so hard on your father. He needs to catch up on his sleep."

The woman was not only a marvel in the kitchen, she was also a born mind-reader.

"Isn't that right, Mr. Webster?"

He managed a nod, wondering how she knew he'd been burning the candle at both ends.

"Did you need me to carry in your luggage?"

"Luggage?" she repeated, and a look of surprise flashed in and out of her eyes. "Not to worry, I'll get it myself."

"I insist." It was the least he could do.

"All right." Again he noticed her hesitation. "I believe it should be on the porch. . . . That's right, I left everything on the porch. I was so pleased when I learned of this new assignment that I packed as fast as I could."

Seth prayed his twins wouldn't give her reason to alter her opinion.

Humming what sounded surprisingly like a hymn, she returned to the children, ushering them like a mother hen out of the room.

Seth couldn't remember a time Judd and Jason had taken so quickly to anyone. With every other housekeeper it had demanded the better part of a week before they'd been comfortable enough to address the woman. But then no housekeeper had arrived with a meal fit for a king. The vegetables had been so well disguised that neither Judd nor Jason had noticed.

"Mrs. Miracle . . ."

"Mrs. Miracle . . ."

Laughter erupted as the twins roared out of the bedroom, dressed in their pajamas, their wet hair combed away from their faces. Seth paused, seeing the joy and excitement in their eyes. It was something he'd viewed only on rare occasions since they'd moved back in with him.

A warmth seeped into his heart. For the first time in a very long while, he had hope for the future.

Country Pot Pie

1 stewing chicken—make it easy and buy canned chicken; they'll never know the difference

⅓ cup butter

⅛ cup flour (more if necessary)

1 teaspoon salt

¼ teaspoon pepper

½ teaspoon thyme

½ teaspoon rosemary

2 cups chicken broth

1 piecrust—the kind you buy in the refrigerator section of the local grocery works great

1 potato, cubed and boiled until tender

2 carrots, sliced and boiled until tender

1 cup light cream (evaporated milk works in a pinch)

1 small can onions

1 small can peas

Preheat oven to 450 degrees. Simmer chicken in water to cover for 45 minutes, or until tender. Remove meat from bones and reserve stock. Melt butter in saucepan and stir in flour, salt, pepper, thyme, and rosemary to make gravy. Gradually add broth and cream and cook over medium heat, stirring frequently until thickened and bubbly. Add the cubed chicken and vegetables to the gravy. Prepare the pie crust. Line a 13x9x2-inch pan or 2-quart casserole dish with ⅔ of the pie crust. Put the filling in the dough-lined pan, top with remaining crust and bake 15 minutes, or until crust is golden and the filling is bubbling.

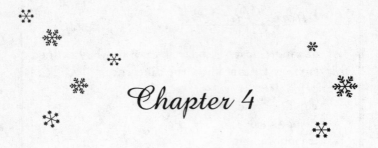

Chapter 4

God wants spiritual fruit, not religious nuts.

—Mrs. Miracle

Harriett Foster prayed with one eye open as she studied the older, retired women in the Tuesday morning Martha and Mary Circle. She zeroed her prayer request toward Ruth Darling. Harriett had seen the way the sixty-year-old had been eyeing the new man in church. A married woman, mind you. Why, it was nothing short of scandalous. It was difficult enough for a widow like herself to find a new husband without having to compete with a married woman.

"Dear Lord," Harriett said loudly, making sure her voice carried, "I'm selling my sewing machine. My Singer, Lord, with five separate attachments.

Why, Lord, a person could embroider names on the thickest of towels with this machine. Hemming skirts at the proper length, of course, would be no problem, nor would it be difficult to attach buttons. Those of us suffering arthritis can appreciate a sewing machine with all those built-in extras." She paused and surveyed the group once more. "This modern marvel was reconditioned only six months ago. I'm a reasonable woman, Lord, and you and I both know that my Singer, although ten years old, is well worth the hundred-dollar asking price. You've placed that figure upon my heart, and I don't feel I can let it go for a penny less. You know that I'd gladly tithe my ten percent of that sales price, too.

"Now, I feel, Lord, that there's someone in this very group of women who could use this machine. Theirs may be out of date, or in disrepair, whatever the reason, they need this machine. I ask, Father, that you lay it upon that person's mind to buy my beautiful, looks-almost-new, Singer sewing machine." She breathed in deeply and peeked at Ruth Darling to see if the group's leader revealed any interest. To her disappointment, she saw nothing. Discouraged, Harriett murmured, "Amen."

A low murmur of "Amens" followed.

Slowly the women opened their eyes and raised their heads.

"We'll meet again next week, same time, same place," Ruth Darling announced.

Harriett noticed a smile wobbling at the edges of Ruth's mouth and wondered what it was that the group's leader found amusing.

Ruth zipped up the pouch around her Bible and placed it inside her bag along with the study guide for the Book of Philippians.

"I don't suppose you'd be interested in buying my Singer, would you?" Harriett asked, cornering Ruth. Sometimes a hint just wasn't strong enough. If ever a woman needed something to occupy her time, it was Ruth. Naturally it'd be considered unkind to mention that she'd noticed Ruth's roving eye, although Harriett was certain she wasn't the only member of the Martha and Mary Circle to recognize what was happening. Personally Harriett wondered if Fred Darling had wind of it. Fred wasn't the kind of man who would tolerate any hanky-panky from his wife.

Ruth glanced up. "I have a sewing machine."

"New?" Harriett pressed.

"Fairly new."

"I thought you said yours was ten years old?"

This came from Barbara Newton, and Harriett didn't appreciate it. "It is, but as I said earlier, it's been reconditioned."

"My daughter might be interested."

Harriett spun around. "Really?"

The door opened and the church secretary, Joanne Lawton, burst into the room. "Oh, good, you haven't left yet. Ladies," she said, clearly distressed, "I just got off the phone with Milly Waters. Joe's been transferred. . . . It's all rather sudden, and they're leaving within the next two weeks."

"Milly and Joe are moving?"

"Oh, dear, we're going to miss them."

A chorus of voices echoed, mixed with excitement and regrets. Joe and Milly were church favorites. Milly's sunny disposition made her a popular Sunday school teacher, and the children loved her. Joe had been the Sunday school superintendent for several years running. They would both be sorely missed.

"What about the Christmas program?" Barbara Newton asked.

The mood of the room went into a tailspin. Milly had been working with the children for weeks, laying the groundwork for the Christmas pageant. Someone stepping in with just a month to go would have big shoes to fill.

Harriett took one step backward, not wanting to give the impression she might be interested. Not her. She'd served as a deaconess for three years, washing the communion cups after worship service, acting as a greeter. She'd sung with the choir twenty years or better and played piano for more Sunday evening services than she could count. Over the years she'd done it all and more. Her days of volunteering were over. Some might say she was resting on her laurels, and she'd let them.

The last thing she wanted or needed was to direct a group of loud, ungrateful schoolchildren. That was a task for the young, someone with more patience than she. Children, even her niece's two girls, were more of a handful than she could take, other than in small doses.

Never having borne children of her own, Harriett fawned over Jayne, her only sister's child. She didn't see Jayne as often as she would have liked, but then young people didn't respect their elders the way they should these days.

Ever since Jayne had started working at that travel agency with . . . Oh dear, she forgot the woman's name now. She'd met her once or twice. Reba, that was it. Reba Maxwell. Since Jayne had started working with Reba, she hadn't seen near enough of her, or Suzie and Cindy. The five- and seven-year-olds were as close to having grandchildren as Harriett was likely to get.

The others in the Martha and Mary Circle were busy discussing Milly and Joe's move. A low buzz filled the room as speculation arose as to who would assume the director's role for the Christmas program. Finding someone, anyone, at this late date would be difficult.

"Sally couldn't possibly do it," Ruth Darling was telling Joanne. "She's started back to college."

"Oh, dear, you're right."

"What about Lillian Munson?"

"She and Larry have already made vacation plans for the holidays," someone responded.

Harriett waited until the possibilities were exhausted and a pregnant pause followed. "I know who could do it," she said. Every eye turned to her. She waited until she had the group's attention. This was almost as good as if she were volunteering herself. "My niece."

"Jayne?"

"I'll talk to her myself," Harriett promised. "I'm sure she'd love the opportunity to step in at the last minute like this. Jayne's the type of woman who thrives on a challenge."

"But I thought she just started a new job." Ruth, of all people, looked skeptically toward Harriett.

"That shouldn't be any problem," Harriett returned confidently. "I know my niece. She's going to leap at the chance to help out like this. She's a lot like me, you know. A lot like me."

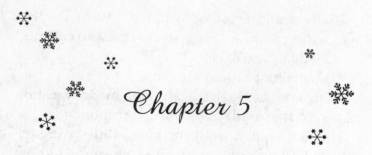

Chapter 5

Some folks wear their halos much too tight.

—Mrs. Miracle

"*Y*ou did what?"

Reba Maxwell watched as her friend Jayne Preston vaulted upright out of her chair, sending it shooting backward into the filing cabinet. Jayne's face reflected her outrage.

"Aunt Harriett, how could you possibly volunteer me? . . ." She clamped her mouth shut. Apparently the news didn't get better, because Jayne leaned against the poster of Mickey Mouse, arms extended, inviting everyone who entered the Way to Go Travel Agency to explore Disney World.

Reba had heard the stories about Jayne's aunt from the time she'd hired her latest employee. Apparently Auntie was a holier-than-thou type. Personally, Reba got a chuckle hearing about Jayne's infamous aunt. She felt more at home attending church services when she realized there were others beside herself whose lives weren't in shipshape order. According to Jayne, her aunt Harriett had been a thorn in her side most of her life. Reba could hardly wait to hear what the woman had done this time.

Reba had hired Jayne a few months back. She knew her from church, but only by sight, not by name. Her own attendance had been sporadic at best, although she enjoyed Pastor Lovelace's sermons.

After breaking off the relationship with her sister, Reba had avoided church. She wasn't sure what had prompted her to attend at all. Habit, she suspected. Her mother faithfully observed the Lord's day, and both Reba and her sister had tagged along. While in high school, Reba had gotten involved in the church youth group and played on the church volleyball team. The summer between high school and college she'd served as a camp counselor, and she remembered those times fondly.

As an adult, she found herself feeling restless and bored Sunday mornings, so she'd begun to stop by the local community church. She didn't go often. Every time she was tempted to become more involved, the pastor would preach some stirring message about forgiveness. It stopped her cold.

Few people understood that some wrongs could never be forgiven. Or righted. This was a sermon she didn't want to hear. A message she chose to ignore. It'd taken her the better part of four months to return after one such sermon.

Even at that she'd come to recognize a few people, Jayne being one of them. She'd hired the young mother because she was a familiar face, someone she knew and wanted to know better.

"I can't believe it," Jayne cried as she replaced the telephone receiver. She wrapped one arm around her middle as if protecting herself. "Aunt Harriett's done it again." She slapped her side with her free hand.

"What's she up to this time?"

"Without consulting me, without so much as asking, she volunteered me to take over the job of coordinator for the Christmas program. Milly Waters was doing it, but apparently Joe's gotten transferred to Oregon. With the move and everything, Milly had to resign."

"So good ol' Jayne's willing to step in?"

Jayne plopped herself down on her chair once again. "Not this time. I can't, Reba. Surely you realize that. Steve's working overtime every night, and no one realizes that when Steve works overtime so do I. The girls miss their father and don't understand why he's gone so much. I've been having discipline problems with them. And now my lovely, interfering aunt assumes that I'll take on the pressure of organizing and producing a Christmas pageant. I refuse to be emotionally blackmailed. Not this time!"

"You don't need to convince me."

"You don't know my aunt Harriett." Jayne wiped the hair off her forehead. "She's like a pit bull. I've never seen anything like it. She gets hold of an idea and won't let go. She's going to needle away at me, push all my buttons, and remind me of everything she's ever done for me, and before I know how it happened I'll give in."

"Will you really?" Reba was more sympathetic than she sounded. In a number of ways Jayne's aunt Harriett reminded her of her own mother. Ever since her falling-out with Vicki—although that was putting it mildly—Reba's mother had hounded her to mend fences with her sister. Like Jayne's aunt Harriett, Joan Maxwell didn't give up easily, either.

Jayne glanced anxiously toward Reba. "Come to church with me on Sunday, will you?"

"Me?" If Jayne couldn't dissuade good ol' Aunt Harriett, it was unlikely Reba would do a better job.

"Steve won't be able to come—he's worked every Sunday for the last month, and Aunt Harriett is sure to corner me, especially with Steve not there. She has a way of getting to me."

"And you want me there to ward her off?"

"No . . . well, yes. You don't know my aunt Harriett. Before I can help it, she'll have me backed up against a wall."

Reba hesitated. "Maybe deep down you're secretly dying to take over the Christmas pageant."

Jayne mocked her with an abrupt laugh. "Read my lips. I refuse to do this just because my aunt Harriett thinks I should." Her eyes softened and she looked imploringly at Reba. "You'll come, won't you?"

Reba didn't refuse. This could prove to be downright entertaining. Besides, she'd like to formally meet Harriett. "I'll be there."

"Don't let me down," Jayne pleaded.

"I wouldn't think of it." Smiling to herself, Reba returned to the task at hand.

The phone pealed again, and since her other two employees were on their lunch break, and Jayne remained shaken after the confrontation with her aunt, Reba answered it herself. "Way to Go Travel."

"Hello, sweetheart."

"Hi, Mom." So Reba was due to face her own nemesis. It must be the day for it, she reflected.

"I hate to pester you at the office. You're not busy, are you?"

She opened her mouth to say that she was in the middle of something important. Her mother didn't need to know it was merely alphabetizing her Rolodex cards. She wasn't given the chance.

"I promise to only keep you a moment."

"Mom . . ."

"It's about Christmas."

"Haven't we already been through this?"

"No," her mother denied. "Sweetheart, it's less than a month away."

Her mother held true to course: hurt, anger, guilt, in that precise order. It astonished Reba how the routine didn't waver. Year after year, battle after battle.

Reba replaced the telephone receiver and released a pent-up sigh.

"Your mother?" Jayne asked.

She nodded. A part of her wanted to explain what had happened, but she bit her tongue. Few people truly understood, and deep down she feared Jayne would be like all the rest. She didn't want advice, didn't want to hear that it would be far wiser to settle her differences with Vicki. Nor was she seeking pity. All she wanted was for someone to recognize that she'd been wronged.

"I need to run some errands," she announced suddenly. "Will you be all right by yourself?" What Reba really needed was a few minutes alone to compose herself.

"Sure," Jayne assured her, although they both knew it wasn't true. Office procedure stated that no employee should be left alone to deal with both the phone and the foot traffic.

"I'll be back shortly," Reba promised on her way out the door.

"Take however long you need."

Sunday morning Reba arrived for the worship service ten minutes early, knowing Jayne would be waiting anxiously for her. She stood inside the vestibule as the organ music filled the small sanctuary.

She didn't have long to wait. Jayne, with her two daughters in tow, arrived shortly.

"Thank goodness you're here."

"Have you met up with Aunt Harriet?"

"Not yet. I managed to escape her just now in the hallway outside the girls' Sunday school classroom. I pretended not to hear her."

"Mom, can I sit with Becky?" Seven-year-old Suzie tugged at Jayne's sleeve.

"Even my daughter's looking for a way of avoiding my aunt," Jayne whispered out of the corner of her mouth.

"Can I, Mom?"

"All right, but no talking, understand?"

Suzie was off like a shot.

"Let's take a seat," Jayne urged, glancing over her shoulder. She accepted a bulletin from one of the deaconesses who acted as a greeter and slithered up the side aisle, seeking, Reba assumed, the one spot in the entire church where her aunt wasn't likely to see her.

Not that Jayne had much chance of escaping the inevitable, Reba suspected.

"Oh, good," Jayne muttered after they were seated. Cindy sat between them on the hard wooden pew.

"What?" Reba whispered.

"Aunt Harriett's playing the organ."

Reba's gaze sought out the middle-aged woman sitting at the organ. She didn't mean to smile, but she would have been able to pick out Jayne's aunt Harriett from a police lineup. The woman wore a dress that seemed to suggest anything fashionable must surely be a sin. Her glasses rode down on her nose so far, they threatened to glide right off. Her pinched lips made her look as if it required a substantial effort to smile.

"Do you see her?" Jayne asked, leaning her head close to Reba's.

"Shh . . ." Six-year-old Cindy pressed her finger to her lips and glared accusingly at the two adults.

Smiling to herself, Reba straightened and focused her attention straight ahead. She'd come for the express purpose of lending her friend moral support, but she was glad she'd come. The music, even if played by Aunt Harriett, was wonderful.

An older woman entered the church, a round portly soul, grandmotherly and kind looking. She paused, her gaze gentle yet focused as she looked squarely in Reba's direction and smiled as if she'd known Reba her entire life. The directness of the stare caught her unaware. The older woman's eyes brightened, and she nodded as if acknowledging someone.

Reba supposed her face was new and the woman was making an effort to welcome her. She responded with a smile.

To puzzle her further, the woman glanced pointedly over her shoulder at a man with two small children at his side. Reba's gaze followed the woman's.

It was him. *Him.* The man she'd seen so often at the grocery outside the strip mall. The very one who'd captured her attention weeks earlier. The one she found herself looking for day after day. The one who seemed as needy as she was herself. Another lost soul in a world full of the walking wounded.

"Who's that?" she asked, gripping Jayne's sleeve in the same urgent manner in which her young daughter had earlier.

"Who?" Jayne asked, tilting her head closer to Reba's.

"The man with the children."

"That's Judd and Jason Webster," Cindy supplied, drawing daisies on the church bulletin. "They're in my Sunday school class. They're twins."

"He's married, then?" Reba's heart sank with the realization.

Jayne looked to her daughter.

Cindy shook her head. "Their mommy died in a car accident a long time ago. They don't even remember what she looks like."

"Do you know his name?"

Cindy nodded. Her grin spread from ear to ear; obviously she was pleased to be the center of attention, the one with all the answers. "That's Mr. Webster, their dad."

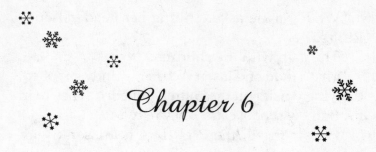

Chapter 6

Some marriages are made in heaven,
but they all have to be maintained on earth.

—Mrs. Miracle

S haron Palmer's marriage was dying. A long, slow, painful death. She sat on the edge of her mattress and brushed her fingers through the thick tangles in her dark, rich hair.

She'd slept far later than normal, but she didn't feel rested. A part of her longed to crawl back into bed, bury her head under a pillow, and weep. She wasn't sure why she should feel this way. Then again, she did know. Jerry.

Her gaze drifted to the rumpled half of the other side of the bed. She'd slept next to the same man for nearly forty years. That should account for something. It was a sad commentary that she could have lived with Jerry all this time and come to the sudden realization that she no longer loved him. No, that was too harsh. Of course she loved Jerry. She'd loved him from the moment she'd first seen him as a college freshman. So brash and handsome. Her heart had pounded like a ramrod against her youthful breast at the mere sight of him. In the last three decades together they'd borne, raised, and educated three children.

And buried one.

When did this unhappiness, this discontent, start? she wondered. Sharon tried to trace the path of her dissatisfaction, but no clear answer came to her.

After Pamela's death, she guessed. Sharon's entire world had been tossed upside-down with the loss of their only daughter. Then the twins had come to live with her and Jerry. Having the babies with them had helped ease the shock and pain. With two toddlers underfoot, Sharon hadn't had time to grieve or dwell on her loss. Her day had been absorbed with the care and feeding of her grandchildren. The twins had helped Jerry deal with Pamela's death as well.

When they'd first heard the horrible news, they'd wept in each other's arms. Clinging to one another had helped them through the terrible dark weeks that followed. Soon afterward, however,

Jerry had grown introspective and sullen; but then the children had come to live with them and that had all changed. With Judd and Jason around he was soon his old self again. Both patient and indulgent with the kids, Jerry had been wonderful. And not only with the twins, but with her as well. Then, as time progressed, all that had subtly changed.

Just recently her husband had retired. They'd talked about traveling, playing golf, developing other interests. It had all sounded so good. Sleeping in every morning, staying up late. Chasing each other around the house like newlyweds.

Only none of those things had come to pass. Jerry had retired, and once again their well-organized life had taken a sharp turn for the unexpected.

Sharon had believed that once the twins returned to their father everything would right itself again, but that hadn't been the case. Whatever was wrong between her and her husband had intensified in the months since Judd and Jason had gone back to live with Seth.

"It's about time you were awake." Her husband paused in the doorway leading to their bedroom. Looking at him, Sharon reflected that even now, in his early sixties, Jerry was a fine figure of a man. Although his hair had receded from his forehead, it was a thick mixture of white and gray.

He remained fit and routinely played eighteen holes of golf with his friends. Several of Sharon's friends envied her outright and told her she was fortunate to have such an attractive, active husband.

"I thought you might be tempted to stay in bed all morning." He didn't need to tell her he disapproved of her sleeping in: the message came across loud and clear. His gaze rested briefly on the clock next to the bed. "It's eight-thirty already. I made my own breakfast."

This too was a not-so-subtle accusation. For more years than she wanted to count, she'd cooked Jerry's breakfast. Even when she'd held down a forty-hour-a-week job of her own, she'd taken the time to see that he left the house with a warm meal in his stomach.

"You sick or something?" he pressed.

"No."

"How late did you stay up, anyway?"

"Around eleven or so. Not late." They rarely went to bed at the same time these days. She couldn't remember the last time they'd made love. Months ago, she realized sadly. But then they were both over sixty, and a decrease in sexual activity was to be expected. At least that was what she told herself.

"Did you look over those travel brochures?"

"Yes." She stood and walked toward her closet.

Jerry had suggested a cruise sometime after the first of the year. It had sounded good, in theory. She envisioned visiting exotic locations, shopping in the Far East. The Orient had always intrigued her. But Jerry wanted none of that. He'd decided early on that if they were going to cruise, it would be through the Panama Canal.

"Well," he said with a bite of impatience, "which cruise line did you decide on?"

She turned around and glared at her husband. This was the big compromise. He decided where they would tour and she was given the opportunity to choose which cruise line. "I don't care. They all look the same to me. You decide."

Jerry scowled at her.

Sharon could see that her answer didn't please him, but that didn't concern her, either. It didn't matter to her which cruise ship they booked. Not when she had no desire to spend thousands of dollars to visit a destination that had never appealed to her.

"You want me to decide?"

"Feel free." He did everything else, why not this?

"I'd appreciate it if you showed a little more enthusiasm. We've been planning this trip for years."

"We?" That was almost enough to make her laugh. "You were the one who wanted to see the Panama Canal, not me."

It was as though he hadn't heard her. "Why do you always leave everything to me?"

It amazed her that he didn't know. She wondered if her husband had always been obtuse.

"I'm trying to arrange the vacation of our lives," he muttered impatiently, "and you're fighting me every step of the way."

"I'm not fighting you."

"Then the least you can do is show a little enthusiasm," he snapped.

She pinched her lips together to keep from arguing. Jerry was right. This cruise meant a great deal to him. He'd talked of little else for weeks—no, months. Ever since it was decided the twins would move back with their father.

"I'd like to spend Christmas with Seth and the children." The best way to handle discord, Sharon had learned early on in their relationship, was to change the subject. And of late it was the only way they could remain civil with each other, bouncing like a Ping-Pong ball from one subject to the next.

"I don't think that's a good idea."

"Why not?" she demanded defiantly. He had selfishly insisted on the cruise he wanted. All she cared about was sharing the holidays with her two precious grandchildren. "Clay and Neal won't be home and—"

"The twins are only now adjusting to life with

Seth. I don't think it'd be a good idea for us to interfere."

"I'm not going to interfere!" She reached for the brush and jerked it through the long, thick tresses. Tugging at the tangles brought unexpected tears to her eyes. She'd been married to Jerry all these years. Had loved him, borne his children, kept his home. Yet the man she'd married, the man she'd spent the last forty years of her life loving, didn't know her. Not really.

It hadn't been easy for her to hand her grandchildren back to their father. Jerry didn't seem to realize or appreciate what it had cost her to send the twins home with Seth. The emptiness in her life had never been more pronounced.

"I just don't think it's a good idea," Jerry insisted.

The hot surge of anger that assaulted her came as a surprise. She fought down the urge to throw the brush and shout. Her fingers tightened around the handle until her hand ached. Sharon wasn't sure what would have happened if the phone hadn't rung at precisely that moment.

"I'll get it." Grateful for the intrusion, she walked over to the bedstand. "Hello," she greeted as if her world were in perfect order, when it felt as if the edges had crumpled beyond repair.

"Grandma, it's Jason."

"Jason." Sharon's heart gladdened instantly.

She routinely talked to the twins once a week. She worried about them. Worried that they missed her and would have a difficult time adjusting to their new lives in Seattle. "How are you, sweetheart?"

"I miss you."

She bit down on her lower lip at the swell of tenderness she experienced for her grandson. "I miss you, too. How's everything?"

"Okay. You know Mrs. Hampston quit, don't you?"

Jason asked this with glee, as if he were reporting a good grade on a school project. Sharon had heard that bit of unfortunate news a couple of weeks earlier. She realized the kids weren't thrilled with Mrs. Hampston, but Seth was fortunate to have found someone dependable. Especially in light of what had happened with the other housekeepers.

"Judd and I didn't like her."

"Has your father hired a replacement?" Sharon could hear background noise and suspected Judd was demanding the phone. It was his turn to talk.

The sounds of a scuffle ensued. "Jason! Judd!" It did her little good to shout into the mouthpiece. A couple of minutes passed before Seth came on the line.

"Sharon, are you still there?"

"What's going on?"

He apparently thought she was asking about the twins. "Sorry, the kids were squabbling—"

"I mean with the housekeeper."

"Not to worry, I've got someone new."

Sharon was relieved. "That's good."

"No need to concern yourself. Everything's coming along nicely. No more mishaps, this one fits right in."

"I'm glad to hear it, but do you need—" She stopped herself in time from asking if he needed her. She had decided that when the twins moved back to Seattle, she wouldn't rush to the rescue the minute something went awry.

"Everything's fine, you don't need to worry. Mrs. Miracle stepped in as if she'd been with me from the beginning."

"Mrs. Miracle?"

"Her name's actually Merkle, but the kids call her Mrs. Miracle."

"Does she know about Jason's—" Again she stopped herself from speaking. She wasn't the one responsible for the twins any longer. Matters were well in hand with Seth, and he'd see to it that the children's needs were met. Then she cast a glance toward Jerry and sat up a bit straighter. It irritated her that he would tell her she couldn't see the children over Christmas. "Have you made any plans for the holidays, Seth?"

"Not yet. If you're thinking of paying a visit, the kids and I would love it."

"You're sure?" The relief was evident in her voice. She noticed Jerry glancing her way, but she ignored him.

"Positive. Judd and Jason would be thrilled. They're involved in the church Christmas pageant and would love it if you and Jerry could be there to see them. I won't say anything to the kids, of course, not until your plans are definite, but we'd love to have you."

Even from where she was standing, Sharon could see her husband's shoulders tense.

Hearing Seth's enthusiasm, Sharon felt the faint stirring of her own. It wouldn't be Christmas without Judd and Jason. Despite Jerry's protests, she fully intended to spend the holidays with her grandchildren. Their sons, Clay and Neal, had both made other plans and wouldn't be home. Sharon could see no reason to spend the day alone. Christmas was an empty holiday without children; she and Jerry hadn't celebrated the season alone in years. Only when the boys or the grandchildren were with them had they bought each other presents or done much of anything. The thought of remaining in California when she could be with her precious grandchildren was intolerable.

"I'll make the arrangements, then, as soon as I can," she said into the phone.

"Wonderful."

They must have talked ten minutes more before she replaced the telephone receiver. She released a soft sigh of satisfaction, but not because she'd decided to ignore her husband's wishes. If the truth be known, she'd rather not defy Jerry. But it would take a lot more than her husband to stand between her and her grandchildren, no matter how many years they'd been married.

"I wish you hadn't said anything about Christmas," Jerry said, his words stiff and tight with anger.

"Why? It's time to make the flight arrangements. Past time, really."

"I told you that I didn't think it was a good idea to visit the kids."

"And I disagree. I miss them. They're as much a part of me as my own children." Surely he could understand that.

"I want you to call Seth back and tell him—"

"I most certainly will not!" Sharon cried, too outraged even to let him finish. With her housecoat flowing behind her like the train of a wedding dress, she swept out of the bedroom.

She stood in the kitchen and looked around her, eyes narrowing at the sight. Jerry had cooked his own breakfast all right, and he'd used every frying pan in the house to do it. Her spotlessly clean kitchen resembled a construction site. The travel brochures for the Panama cruise littered the round oak table.

Jerry followed her, his face red and his eyes hot. She rarely went against her husband, but she was standing her ground now. He walked toward the phone.

"Who are you phoning?"

"Seth." He lifted the receiver from the hook.

"If you call Seth, I'll refuse to take that ridiculous cruise with you."

Jerry's eyes widened with shock. "Ridiculous cruise?"

"It was never my idea to sail through the Panama Canal. I wanted to go to Hong Kong, remember?"

He cringed as though the very idea were repugnant to him. They glared at each other, each waiting for the other to capitulate. Slowly Jerry hung up the phone. "Maybe I should take that cruise by myself, then," he muttered.

She stiffened. "Maybe you should."

His gaze narrowed as he filled his coffee cup and stalked out of the kitchen. At first Sharon was tempted to call after him, explain how much it meant for her to visit the grandchildren; but she said nothing. Jerry didn't want to hear it. Didn't understand. Or care to.

She sagged onto a kitchen chair. It was difficult to know when their relationship had gone wrong. She loved her husband, but she couldn't imagine spending the rest of her life with him. Not with things the way they currently were. She couldn't believe this was happening. It would take a miracle to heal her marriage.

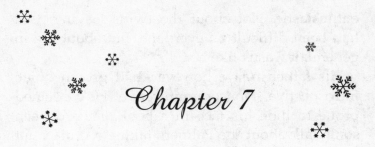

Chapter 7

Sorrow looks back, worry looks around,
and faith looks up.

—Mrs. Miracle

*S*eth's hand lingered on the telephone. Something was wrong with Sharon. He knew his mother-in-law, could sense her uneasiness, her unhappiness. He heard it in the telltale inflection in her voice, the hesitation, the weariness. He wished he knew what he could do to help, or if that were even possible. He felt close to his in-laws. Close and grateful, as well he should.

During his most recent visit to California, when he'd driven down to move the twins back with him, he'd noticed something then. Sharon had laughed a little too loudly, sounded a shade too enthusiastic. Not about the twins leaving; that had been difficult on everyone. But about life in general. It wasn't like her.

His father-in-law, however, had grown quiet, introspective. Noncommunicative. He'd seemed prone to hide his face in a book. There'd been some talk about the Palmers taking a cruise, but since then he hadn't heard anything more about this long-awaited vacation.

Seth had attributed their odd behavior to the stress of his taking the children. But whatever the reason, it didn't seem to have gone away. The tension was as thick as tar.

Not until he was puttering around inside the garage while the twins helped Mrs. Merkle with dinner did he realize that he hadn't spoken to Jerry, and neither had the twins. His father-in-law generally made a practice of speaking briefly with the twins each week. Seth understood that the kids' grandfather didn't like talking on a phone, but he got a kick out of chatting with his two grandchildren. Not so this Sunday.

Seth reached for the toaster. It had stopped working a month or so earlier, when Mrs. Hamilton had ruled the roost. He'd promised to take a look at it, but this was the first chance he'd had. Not that he held out much hope of repairing it. It would probably save a lot of time and effort if he were to pop into the car and buy a new one. And he might have, if fixing it hadn't afforded him the opportunity to piddle around the garage and enjoy the solitude.

In another hour the Seahawk football game would be televised, and the kids would be crawling all over him. The toaster offered him the perfect excuse to spend a few peaceful moments alone.

For a long time, Seth had avoided opportunities to think. Then, just when he'd felt it was no longer necessary to restrain his thoughts from dwelling on his dead wife, the children had returned. Every now and again one of the twins would glance up at him and it was like looking into Pamela's eyes, seeing his wife smile again. He might as well have been hit from behind. The pain was back, ever-present. Ever reminding him of all that he'd lost.

He sought his own company this afternoon for another reason, however. He'd seen her in church that morning.

Her.

He didn't know her name. A face. A friendly, pretty face, with wide, hauntingly beautiful eyes that seemed to reach out and touch him. She'd been sitting toward the back of the church, hidden behind a marble column, looking as fresh and lovely as a bouquet of springtime flowers.

He should have walked over and introduced himself then and there and been done with it.

Instead he'd steered the kids out of the church as fast as he could without being obvious. Later he'd wanted to kick himself. He'd acted like a school-boy, and all over a woman. One whose name he'd been too shy to ask.

She worked at the travel agency next to the Safeway store, that much he knew. He should, since he frequently invented excuses to stop off at the grocery on his way home from the office. Just on the off chance he might see her. Naturally he tried not to be obvious about it, but he couldn't help wondering if she'd noticed him.

He'd been out of the dating scene for so long, he wasn't sure how to go about meeting a woman. Not without someone introducing him. The last time he'd walked up to a woman cold turkey and struck up a conversation, he'd been in high school.

He hadn't minded making a fool of himself back then, but it bothered the hell out of him now. The fact he was interested said a lot. Perhaps he was ready to meet someone. All he had to figure out was how to go about it.

Following the near panic attack in church that morning, Seth was no longer sure of anything. He'd become so disgusted with himself that the only clear option was to drop the issue entirely. It encouraged him that he found himself attracted to another woman. It was progress, he supposed, but he wasn't in the place where he felt comfortable seeking her out.

She did intrigue him, however, Seth admitted as he dismantled the bottom of the toaster. Crumbs fell onto his workbench, and he brushed them aside. But there were plenty of attractive women around. If that was what appealed to him, all he had to do was look around the office. There were any number of eligible, good-looking women in search of a meaningful relationship there.

Why her? Why this travel agent?

Why now?

Seth didn't have the answers to those questions any more than he knew what was wrong with the toaster.

The look in her eyes, he decided. Yes, she was attractive, and even from a distance he could see that her eyes were a pretty shade of blue. Alpine blue, if he were to give the color a name. Deep, dark, intense. It was the intense part that spoke to him. In the fathomless depths he saw her pain. Naturally he could be seeing something that wasn't there, a reflection off the window, but he didn't think so. The pain was what he recognized because it was a reflection of his own. Whoever this woman was, whatever had happened in her life, she'd suffered. The same way he'd suffered. He felt her hurt, realized in those brief seconds when their eyes had held that her anguish lay just below the surface the way his did.

Then, too, he could be imagining it all. He wasn't a psychologist. Nor had he done any counseling. But he'd walked that same rut-filled pathway himself, and he recognized the pitfalls.

So they attended the same church. Great. It was a beginning. It made matters a bit easier. Now all he needed to do was develop a few more of the social graces, like learning to say his name without stuttering or stumbling over his own two feet.

Hey, introducing himself didn't sound like such a bad idea, if it didn't take him five years or more. But for now he was content to let matters be. He wasn't unhappy. His life had meaning. If he wanted to risk his heart again, it wouldn't be anytime soon.

"Daddy." Judd stepped inside the garage. "The football game's going to start."

"I'll be inside in just a minute."

"Okay." But Judd lingered. Not that it was unusual. His son enjoyed watching him work. Often Seth invented a project that required Judd's or Jason's help. Both had already proved themselves to be worthy nail pounders.

"You know what Mrs. Miracle said?"

Seth didn't have a clue. "What?"

"She said we should take a vacation."

Seth hesitated. "A vacation?"

"Yup. During spring break. When's that?"

"March or April." He'd need to check the school calendar. It was an odd comment for the housekeeper to make, although she'd made a habit of saying some pretty unusual things. Just the other night she'd gotten a chuckle out of him. She'd said something about a woodpecker owing his success to his head and not just his pecker. He chuckled anew.

"Are we going on vacation?"

He had plenty of vacation time due him, and it sounded like a fun thing to do. "I'll think about it." He brushed the bread crumbs from his hands and ruffled his son's hair affectionately. "First let's go see the Seahawks whop the Broncos."

"Yeah." Judd thrust his fist into the air.

Smiling to himself, Seth walked from the garage into the kitchen.

Mrs. Merkle was busy, Jason at her side, helping her prepare dinner—"helping" being the operative word. What he saw set his mouth to watering. The woman cooked like a dream.

"I'm making pie," Jason proclaimed proudly. "From scratch."

"Great." He beamed Mrs. Miracle an appreciative smile. Apple pie was his personal favorite.

The housekeeper skillfully ran the sharp edge of the knife around the Granny Smith apple. The peeling twisted and curled away from the blade like a tight ringlet. "I always said that a good cook starts from scratch and keeps on scratching."

Seth grinned, acknowledging her wit. "Judd and I are about to watch the football game."

"Are we going on vacation?" The same question, this time from Jason.

"I'm thinking about it."

"There's a travel agency," the housekeeper commented, her eye on the apple. "Right next to the Safeway store—you know the one I mean, don't you? There's that nice young lady who owns it. The same one who was in church this morning with Harriett Foster's niece. I'm sure she'd be more than happy to help you plan a trip with the children."

Seth stopped abruptly, and so did his heart. "How is it you know Harriett Foster?" To the best of his knowledge, this was Mrs. Merkle's first week at the church.

"Oh, my, anyone who attends Community Christian knows Harriett Foster."

It wasn't possible that the housekeeper knew that he held any tenderness for this nameless woman he'd spotted in church that very morning. Was it?

"You might stop after work in the next day or so. It isn't too early to book now for springtime," she continued, concentrating on peeling the apples.

"I'll need to think on it," he stated matter-of-factly, making sure no emotion bled into his voice.

"Don't wait too long. He who hesitates misses the worm."

"Excuse me?"

"Well, it doesn't matter what you miss, just that you're going to be missing. Right?"

"I suppose," Seth said, and moved into the family room, where Judd had already turned on the television. It was a relief to focus his attention on the sporting event rather than dwell on Mrs. Merkle's uncanny suggestions.

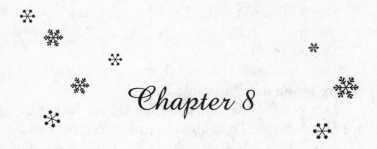

Chapter 8

Pick your friends, but not to pieces.

—Mrs. Miracle

"We did it," Jayne announced triumphantly when she walked into work bright and early Monday morning. Reba had been at the office since seven, going over the books, checking the finances. The profit margin on the travel agency was so narrow that she had to keep close tabs on expenses.

She glanced up from the computer screen. "Did what?"

"Escaped Aunt Harriett. She didn't corner me in church, thanks to you." Jayne's grin stretched from ear to ear. "Naturally I screened my calls all day, and yes, Aunt Harriett did try a number of times, but I thwarted her. We thwarted her," Jayne amended.

Reba chewed on the end of her pen. She hadn't been able to take her mind off Seth Webster from the moment she'd seen him in church. A little investigative work had helped dig up a few cherished facts. First and foremost was his first name and the fact he'd remained single following his wife's death.

He had two children. Six-year-old twins. Apparently there was a housekeeper, too, one the children referred to as Mrs. Miracle. The one who'd made a point of making eye contact with her. The woman seemed a bit unusual. She looked perfectly normal, an older version of Mary Poppins. Twinkling eyes, a mischievous smile, a look about her that said she knew far more than she let on. Reba suspected she was reading too much into that pointed look the Websters' housekeeper had sent her, but it had given her an uncanny feeling.

"What's with you and Mr. Webster?" Jayne shocked her by asking. It was almost as if her employee had read her mind.

"What's with me and . . . Nothing! How could there be? I don't even know the man." Reba attempted to hide how flustered the question made her, but it was obvious by the way her hands fluttered over the keyboard.

"But you'd like to know him."

It would do no good to pretend otherwise. Reba lifted one delicate shoulder. "I suppose . . ."

"I wish you could have seen the way your eyes lit up when you first saw him. Even Cindy noticed."

Reba's face colored.

Jayne hung up her coat and sat down at the desk across from her. "You know what I've been thinking?"

Reba hadn't a clue, and furthermore she wasn't entirely sure she wanted to know. "You intend to tell me whether I want to know or not, right?"

Jayne chuckled. "You guessed it."

Reba waited. Jayne glanced at her almost as if she were afraid to speak. "The church needs an adult, someone who's good with children, to step in and oversee the Christmas pageant."

"Yes, and your wonderfully generous aunt Harriett volunteered you. Remember?"

"I'm not the right person." Jayne's objection was adamant. "But I know someone well suited to the task. A woman who's familiar with overseeing large projects. Someone with infinite patience, flexible hours, and a love of children. Someone who sings like a dream."

Reba shook her head before Jayne got around to making the suggestion. She raised both hands to stop her friend from continuing. "Don't even say it."

"You, Reba Maxwell. You're the perfect choice."

This was all a bad joke. Limitless patience, her? Besides, Reba knew next to nothing about children, zilch about the Christmas program and what it entailed, and although she liked children, her experience with them was limited to her teenage baby-sitting years. She'd be an idiot to step into the coordinator's role with less than a month before Christmas.

"You're wrong, Jayne. I'm flattered you think so highly of my talents, but in this case it'd never work."

"You want to meet Mr. Webster, don't you?"

She hesitated.

"What better way than to involve yourself with his children?"

It was too cold, too calculated. Too ridiculous. Reba dismissed the idea immediately.

She walked over to the coffee machine and refilled her mug. To hear her employee, this might well be her one and only chance of having a relationship. While it was true that eligible men weren't beating a path to her door, she didn't think of herself as desperate, either. She was attracted to Seth Webster, but that didn't mean she was willing to take on the impossible task of directing the Christmas pageant.

Jayne followed her. "You do want to meet him, don't you?" she stressed once more.

"It seems to me," Reba said, exhaling softly, "that you inherited more from your aunt Harriett than you realize."

"Ouch." Jayne grimaced.

"You deserved that for even suggesting such a thing. Me directing a Christmas program? Why, that's the most outrageous thing I've ever heard."

"You're missing something here."

Reba gazed pointedly at her watch and removed the CLOSED sign from the front window. "It's starting time."

"We've got a couple of minutes yet. First I want to know if you heard what I said."

"Yes, but I don't have a response."

"The Christmas pageant takes place Christmas Eve." Her voice escalated softly, as if this fact were of some importance.

"So?" Reba was growing tired of this conversation. She returned to her desk, intent on refocusing her attention on the ledgers.

"Wasn't it Christmas Eve your parents wanted you to attend some big family shindig?"

"Yes," Reba answered tiredly.

"And doesn't the Christmas program offer you the perfect excuse not to be stuck with relatives you don't want to see?"

Reba hesitated. Her mother couldn't very well take issue with her if she was involved with the church Christmas program. Still, she wasn't convinced a ready excuse would be worth all the time and effort it would take to direct thirty or more grade-school children in some play revolving around the Nativity. There were limits to how far she was willing to go to keep the peace with her family.

Her parents had taken Vicki's side in the issue. That much had been painfully obvious from the first. But she didn't want to drag her aunt Gerty and uncle Bill into this mess. If she failed to attend the family dinner, they were sure to feel hurt, especially since they were her godparents.

There was something else, too. The thought of everyone gathered around the festive holiday table, talking about her when she wasn't there to defend herself . . . It was grossly unfair.

"As an extra benefit you'd have the perfect opportunity to meet Judd and Jason Webster." Jayne's piercing eyes held hers. "And their father," she added with meaning.

"Jayne Preston, you're shameless."

"True. Are you going to do it?"

Reba hesitated, unsure. "I don't know yet. The church might already have someone."

"They don't," Jayne said, sounding utterly confident.

"And I know why." She was a fool for even considering taking on the responsibility. But Jayne made a strong point on a number of issues. It did offer her a ready excuse to avoid the family get-together. It wasn't as if her mother could argue when she learned Reba was involved in a church activity.

Jayne made a good case regarding Reba's organizational skills. Her hours were flexible, and she could leave the office on short notice. Her staff of two full-time and one part-time employee were well trained and able to carry on their duties without her standing over them with a whip and chair.

She was a natural with children, although she hadn't had much opportunity of late to get involved with them. Working with the younger generation didn't intimidate her, not the way it would others. The truth was, she was desperately lonely. The holidays were always difficult for her. Others had family, friends, obligations. At no other time of the year did it bother her more that she wasn't married. The Christmas project would help take her mind off all that she'd missed.

But the most convincing argument, the one that carried the most weight, was what her employee had said about meeting Seth Webster. He didn't know her. Had no reason to make her acquaintance. Weeks, months, could pass before she had an opportunity to invent an excuse to meet him. Yet here was the golden opportunity to not only meet him, but work with his children, get to know him and his sons. Talk about having something handed to her on a silver platter.

"No one knows me," she said several minutes later, picking up the conversation where they'd left off.

Jayne looked at her and blinked. "You mean at church? Sure they do. Maybe not by name, but certainly they know your face."

"It'd be like asking a stranger to step in."

"There'll be other adults there as well. It isn't unusual for a number of parents to pitch in."

"It isn't?" This gave her hope.

"Mrs. Darling has been teaching the children the music ever since September. I think you'll find that it isn't nearly as demanding as everyone's made it seem. All that's really required is the right person."

"And you think that's me?" She remained skeptical, but Jayne was right: this was a golden opportunity.

"Beyond a doubt. You're perfect."

"Hardly," Reba said. She was a long way from that.

"As an added bonus you get to meet Mr. Webster."

"Seth," she supplied without thinking.

"*Seth*, is it? And just how did you find that out?"

The corners of Reba's mouth tickled with the effort to repress a smile. "I have my ways."

"I'm sure you do."

The morning passed quickly. With the holidays fast approaching, the foot traffic was higher than usual. It amazed Reba that people actually expected to walk into a travel agency and book an extensive trip for the holidays. November and December were two of the most popular vacation months of the entire year.

"You'll thank me for this later, you know," Jayne commented after Reba called and talked to Pastor Lovelace. He seemed genuinely pleased to hear from her and ecstatic when she told him the reason for her phone call.

"Don't be so sure. Depending on how this turns out, I might be forced to hire a hit man."

"Just you wait, you're going to thank me for this," Jayne said with utter confidence. Lights from the Christmas tree stand on the other side of the parking lot blinked on in the descending daylight. "Who knows how long it would have taken you to meet Seth Webster if it weren't for me?"

Reba pinched her lips together to keep from retorting. Yes, meeting Seth was one of the reasons she'd agreed to take over the coordinator's job, but it wasn't the only one.

The bell over the door jingled as the latest customer entered the shop.

Reba glanced up and smiled automatically. "Can I help you?" It wasn't until the words had slipped past her lips that she realized it was Seth Webster who stood in front of her desk.

The air between them sizzled. Reba wondered if anyone else noticed. She did, and she knew he did, too.

"Hello again," he said, and smiled.

It took a great deal to unnerve her, but he'd succeeded.

"How can I help you?" she asked in what she hoped was a nonchalant manner, gesturing toward the empty chair in front of her desk. Now all she had to do was figure out a way to carry on an intelligent conversation.

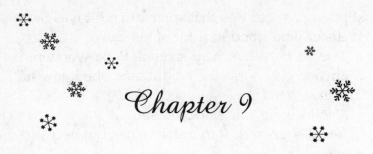

Chapter 9

*Standing in the middle of the road is very
dangerous: you get knocked down by the
traffic from both sides.*

—Margaret Thatcher, as told to Mrs. Miracle

Emily Merkle hummed softly to herself as she
went about preparing dinner for Mr. Webster and the children. It was these short-term as-
signments that she enjoyed the most. Timing was
everything.

She never doubted that broken hearts could be
mended, but all the pieces had to be gathered together first. She'd see to that, of course, and in fact
had already begun going about the task.

Mr. Webster wasn't a fool. It wouldn't take him
long to discover her talents stretched beyond the

job description listed for housekeeper. Her smile brightened with all she had to accomplish and the sheer entertainment she derived from doing it.

Seth Webster was a prime example, grieving for his young wife the way he did. Pamela wouldn't like that one bit; she was a generous, warm-hearted soul who didn't begrudge her husband happiness.

Emily dumped a glob of hamburger into the palm of her wet hand and skillfully formed a meatball. The recipe, her grandmother's, from the old country, was sure to please.

The door leading from the garage to the kitchen opened and Mr. Webster moseyed inside the house like someone in a daze.

"Good evening," Emily greeted him cheerfully, looking past him to be sure he'd remembered to close the garage door. He had.

She rinsed her hands off under the faucet. "How was your day?" she asked in the same up-beat mode, hoping it would snap him out of his spell.

Mr. Webster glanced at her as if he hadn't heard her speak.

"Mr. Webster?" She noticed the hint of red at the top of his ears. "You stopped off at the travel agency, didn't you?"

He blinked and then frowned. "How'd you know that?"

It was fairly obvious by the flustered look about him. She didn't comment on that but instead offered a convenient excuse. "You're a bit later this evening."

"Yes . . . yes, I suppose I am."

"Did Ms. Maxwell have any suggestions for you?"

"Ah . . . yes." He cleared his throat, and his ears brightened to a deeper shade of red. "She's putting together several packages and prices for me and the kids to review."

"She's rather nice, isn't she?" Emily strived to sound nonchalant, but she could see that his visit had achieved the desired results. She was delighted. This was all going so smoothly, better than she'd hoped.

"You know Reba Maxwell?" her employer asked, sounding surprised.

"Only from church." Emily quickly occupied herself with dinner preparations, methodically adding the perfectly shaped meatballs to the simmering marinara sauce.

"From church," Seth repeated.

"She's taking over as coordinator of the Christmas program. She made a wise choice. Those who bury their talents make a grave mistake." The decision had been a difficult one for Reba, and Emily was proud of her. Having the travel agent work with the children was all part of the big picture.

The rewards would far outweigh any inconveniences, but Reba didn't know that yet. Such wonders awaited her. Emily was impatient to see it come to pass.

Everything was coming together nicely. Very nicely indeed.

The best was yet to be.

Emily had outdone herself, which was saying something, Seth mused following the evening meal. As time passed he'd come to realize that the children's name for her fit her to a tee. Mrs. Miracle had worked wonders in all their lives.

As promised, Emily read to the children following their bath, while he washed the dishes.

He'd followed his housekeeper's suggestion and stopped off at the travel agency. He'd be finished with the Firecracker Project in a couple of months and could use the time away. Although Judd and Jason had been to Disneyland a number of times, they'd never been to Florida. Reba had suggested a number of cruise ideas as well, with prices that fell easily within his budget. But it wasn't the vacation plans that had brought him into the travel agency. It was the idea of meeting the owner, of talking to her one on one, getting to know her. Letting her know him.

Even now his heart raced like an Indy 500 engine. He bent forward and rested his elbows against the desktop and rubbed his hand down his face. He'd never experienced anything like this. Had never felt this strongly attracted to a woman—not since Pamela. He barely knew her name, and already he couldn't wait to see her again.

"Reba." He said her name aloud, thinking that the mere sound of it was musical. Magical.

Seth was convinced that he'd made a first-class idiot of himself, staring at her the way he had. He'd hardly seemed able to connect one coherent thought to another.

Some self-preservation had kicked into place when he'd realized he'd been standing in front of her desk staring at her the way a boy does a puppy in a pet shop window. When he'd finally had the presence of mind to ask about vacations for him and the twins, Reba had seemed as flustered as he. She'd promised to put together several ideas and get back to him.

He'd walked out of the agency, taking small backward steps until he'd backed into the door. It wasn't until he'd raced across the parking lot and was sitting inside his vehicle that he'd realized he hadn't given her his name or phone number. He'd started back to leave the necessary information when she'd met him in the parking lot.

"I need—"

"Could you . . . Dinner. Friday night?"

His heart returned to his throat at the awkward way in which he'd asked her to dinner. He was certain she hadn't understood a word he'd said until she'd laughed and nodded. They'd set a time to meet and he'd hurried back to his car, his heart jumping rope inside his chest.

He had a date, his first in longer than he could remember. All he had to do now was behave like a human instead of an alien from outer space. Excitement swelled like a water-soaked sponge inside him.

Seth started for his study with a fresh cup of coffee, then hesitated. He needed to ask Mrs. Merkle if she would be available to baby-sit the twins Friday evening. There weren't provisions in her contract for weekend baby-sitting. Naturally he'd pay her overtime, whatever she wanted. The woman was worth ten Mrs. Hampstons.

With his coffee in his hand he walked into the living room, to find the children snuggled one on each side of the housekeeper. Her reading glasses were balanced halfway down her nose, a book open. The children were enraptured. The only time Seth had ever seen them this still was when they were sound asleep.

Jason braced his head against the housekeeper's pudgy arm. Judd's arms were tucked about his bent knees, and his chin rested there.

It took Seth a couple of moments to recognize

the story: it was C. S. Lewis's *The Lion, the Witch and the Wardrobe,* Pamela's favorite childhood story. The one she'd longed to read to her children one day, only to be cheated out of the long awaited joy.

Mrs. Merkle glanced up and smiled.

"Hi, Daddy." Jason covered his mouth and yawned loudly. "Mrs. Miracle is reading us a new story."

"So I see." Some of his tension leaked into his voice. Of all the books in the world, he wondered how it was that she'd chosen that particular one.

"It's good, too," Judd added. "None of that mushy girl stuff."

Seth's gaze fell to the book itself. Moments earlier his heart had raced with thoughts of Reba and the impromptu dinner date he'd arranged. Now it skidded to a sudden, grinding halt. His chest tightened painfully.

"Where'd you get that book?" he demanded, not bothering to disguise his distress.

"The book." Mrs. Merkle closed the volume and stared at the front cover. "It's mine. I brought it with me."

"It's Pamela's," he countered sharply. The woman had been in his den and had searched through his desk drawers. He didn't care how good a cook she was, he wouldn't have her sneaking around in his office.

"Mr. Webster, let me assure you—"

"I'll prove it," he said, his voice rough with shock and anger. Without another word he marched back into his office and sat down at the desk he'd recently vacated. The children raced into the room after him, and Mrs. Merkle followed, looking flustered and red in the face.

"I put it here myself just recently," he said, jerking open the bottom drawer. He'd held that very book in his hands. Seen for himself how the corners had frayed and worn down so that the filler showed through, just the way the one she had did. The gold lettering had faded on the title, the same as with the book Mrs. Merkle held.

"See," he said, leveling his gaze toward the drawer.

The book was there. Seth's mouth dropped, and he glanced up at the housekeeper, dumbfounded. Slowly, almost as if he were afraid Pam's volume would vanish if he touched it, he lifted it from its resting place.

His round, shock-filled eyes returned to Mrs. Merkle.

"Did she take Mommy's book?" Judd asked.

Seth shook his head. "I'm afraid I owe you an apology," he said, nearly choking on the words. Not because he wasn't sorry, for he was. But he'd been so sure. Not only had the woman chosen to read the one book his wife had loved, but she'd read from a copy that was identical to Pam's in every way.

How was that possible? Had he walked into an episode of *The Twilight Zone?* If he looked at himself in the mirror, would he see Rod Serling's reflection? Seth was almost afraid to find out.

"Come on, you two," Mrs. Merkle said, ushering the kids back into the room. "Let's find out what happens to the children next."

"They shouldn't go in the wardrobe, should they?" Judd asked.

"That, my fine young man, is a matter of opinion." His housekeeper looked over her shoulder at Seth. "Everyone needs to take a risk now and again, don't you agree, Mr. Webster?"

Red Sauce

    3 tablespoons olive oil
    2 cloves crushed garlic
    1 onion, chopped
    1 28-ounce can ready crushed tomatoes
    1 28-ounce can of tomato puree
    1 can tomato paste, plus 1 can water
    2 teaspoons basil
    2 teaspoons oregano
    2 tablespoons Parmesan cheese
Simmer all ingredients together for 1½ hours. Add meatballs.

Italian Meatballs

    1 pound lean ground beef
    ½ pound Italian sausage
    ½ cup fresh parsley, chopped
    ⅔ cup Italian-flavored bread crumbs
    2 eggs
    1 or 2 clovers fresh garlic
    A little milk to moisten mixture
Mix all ingredients well, roll into golf-size balls, and add to simmering spaghetti sauce. Cook 10 to 15 minutes on low heat.

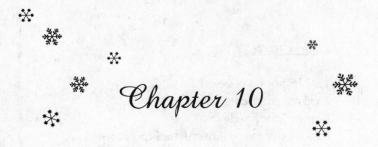

Chapter 10

A closed mouth gathers no foot.

—Mrs. Miracle

*S*haron Palmer quietly put dinner on the table. Her husband sat reading the newspaper in front of the television, doing his best to ignore her. She knew what he was up to. He'd barely said a civil word to her all week, but then she hadn't behaved any better.

"Dinner's ready," she told him without enthusiasm, sitting down at the round oak table in the alcove off the kitchen. She didn't wait for Jerry to join her before unfolding and placing the napkin on her lap.

Leaving the television on, Jerry claimed his seat at the table and kept his eyes on the screen. For years it had been customary to turn the set off completely. Dinnertime was sacred, a time set aside to share the happenings of their day. No longer. Her husband didn't so much as look at the meal she'd spent the better part of the afternoon preparing. His gaze left the sportscaster only long enough to reach for the serving spoon.

Not until he'd finished heaping his plate did he bother to ask, "What is it?" A frown dominated his still-handsome face.

"A casserole," Sharon assured him, not meeting his eyes.

"What's in it?" he demanded.

Jerry had never been a picky eater.

"Eggplant."

His gaze hardened. "You know I don't like eggplant."

"It's cleverly disguised with cheese. Taste it. Who knows, you might surprise yourself." The recipe came from Maggie, her best friend, who was an excellent cook.

"I don't like eggplant," he insisted.

"And I do. Why is it if you don't like something, I can never have it myself? Eggplant happens to be my favorite vegetable."

"Then order it in a restaurant, don't serve it to me."

"If you don't like it, don't eat it."

Jerry slammed his fork against the table. "Fine,

I won't." The chair nearly toppled as he shoved himself away from the table. He stalked across the kitchen to the refrigerator, took out a loaf of bread, and promptly made himself a peanut-butter-and-jelly sandwich. Sharon figured she was supposed to feel sorry for him, but she didn't.

Instead she poured herself a small glass of red wine and turned on the radio so that the classical music played softly in the background. Jerry did his best to counteract the soothing music by slamming around the room. Sharon ignored him the same way he'd been ignoring her all week.

Finally Jerry took his seat again and wolfed down his sandwich like a man eating his last meal.

The eggplant Parmesan was heavenly. She hadn't made the dish in years and wondered now why she'd deprived herself of her favorite dish. Jerry didn't appreciate her sacrifice. She wasn't fond of salmon but served it at least once a month because it was her husband's favorite. It was time he learned to give as well as take in this partnership. He expected her to pander to his every whim. Well, those days were over. Jerry had retired, but she hadn't been given any such reprieve. She still washed, cleaned, and cooked while he played golf with his cronies. If she showed any signs of doing something for herself, her husband invariably disapproved. The eggplant dinner was a good example. Visiting Seth and the children was another.

When he finished his sandwich Jerry sat for a moment and stared at her. "What's wrong?"

"Why does something have to be wrong?" she asked. She took pride in pretending nothing was amiss.

"You haven't been yourself lately. You don't seem to have as much energy. You hardly laugh, and frankly you've gotten to be something of a drag. If you're sick, see a doctor, but do something."

"In other words you're suggesting I snap out of it?" Her husband had never been known for his sensitivity.

He hesitated, then nodded. "Yes. You're the one with the problem."

"Me?" She noticed the way he assumed the "problem" lay entirely with her.

"You sleep in every morning."

"We're retired, remember?"

"And when you do come to bed, you toss and turn half the night."

"I've been having a bit of a problem sleeping, is all. The doctor said this sometimes happens as people age."

"You're only sixty-two."

How kind of him to remind her of her age.

"You're only as old as you feel."

At the moment, Sharon felt a hundred and ten. "I called the travel agent this afternoon," she announced, falling into the familiar habit of changing subjects rather than dealing with the unpleasantness between them.

The change in Jerry was immediate. His face muscles relaxed and softened, as if the words had pleased him. "You called about the cruise. I knew you'd eventually have a change of heart." He leaned forward and affectionately brushed his mouth against her cheek, then reached for the bottle of wine and poured himself a glass. "Burgundy and peanut butter don't necessarily go together, but this is reason to celebrate." He clinked his glass against hers and raised it to his lips.

Sharon lowered her gaze, feeling guilty when she had no reason to. He'd find out sooner or later that her call had had nothing to do with the cruise, which had been put on hold. To mislead him would be cruel, but she couldn't see any reason they couldn't compromise.

"It wasn't about the cruise," she admitted with a certain reluctance.

The light in her husband's eyes dimmed. "It wasn't?"

Sharon nervously dabbed the napkin at the corner of her mouth. "I . . . I booked a flight to Seattle to spend Christmas with Seth and the twins.

There were only a few seats left on the flight, so I booked one for you, too. I thought—"

"You did what?" Jerry bolted upright like a jack-in-the-box escaping his confines. His face reddened and his jaw tightened with indignation and outrage. "I told you before that I didn't want you disrupting the twins their first Christmas with their father."

"Clay and Neal aren't going to be home, and—"

"What's wrong with spending the holiday here, just the two of us? It used to be you enjoyed my company."

"So we can spend the holidays fighting?" she asked, slapping her napkin down against the table. She'd lost her appetite.

Jerry folded his arms in a defensive gesture and glared at her, challenging her to deny his role as head of the family. "You're not going."

For nearly forty years she'd lived with his dictatorial ways, put up with his arbitrary decisions, swallowed her pride; but she would do so no longer. "I've already bought our tickets."

"Then you'll return them," he said, leaving no room for argument.

"Feel free to return your ticket if that's what you wish, but I'm spending Christmas with my grandchildren. I don't know why you're being so stubborn about this, Jerry. I miss the twins and they miss me."

"You're darn right I'm taking back that ticket."

Sharon recognized that tone of voice only too well. She hadn't lived with Jerry all these years not to know when his mind was made up. Nothing she said or did beyond this point would do one whit of good.

"We'll miss you," she said quietly. It would be the first Christmas she'd spent apart from her husband since they'd met in college. Her heart ached knowing they'd be apart because that was the way he wanted it.

"You'll miss me," he repeated, sounding more than a little stunned. "That's all you have to say?"

"Do you want me to add anything more?" She wasn't being flippant, only inquisitive.

He didn't answer her. Instead he moved back to his recliner and pointed the remote control at the TV, turning up the volume until it was so loud she couldn't think without the grating sound of the newscast echoing in her ear. She turned off the classical music, saddened that her marriage had dissolved to this childish display of temper on both their parts.

Jerry didn't speak to her while she cleared the table and washed the dishes herself. Applying lotion to her hands, she joined him in front of the television to watch their favorite game show, *Jeopardy*. It used to be that they'd call out the answers and keep a friendly score between them. Jerry didn't seem to want to continue the tradition that night, so she reached for her knitting.

He left her soon after final jeopardy and disappeared inside the garage, where he was tinkering with some project. The moment he was gone the tension evaporated as if someone had sucked it away with a powerful vacuum. Left in its wake was a fragile contentment as Sharon worked the worsted yarn, weaving together a sweater.

Her fingers worked the metal needles. They made soft clashing sounds as they clanked against each other. The tentative contentment began to fade as the regrets took turns lining up in her mind. She didn't like what was happening between her and her husband but felt powerless to stop it. Jerry was harsh, unreasonable, and dictatorial. She wasn't willing to let him control her life any longer. She'd made her stand, defied him, but she experienced no sense of exhilaration, no rush of triumph. Her heart felt heavy and burdened with sadness. The dull ache reminded her of those first months following Pamela's funeral.

In many ways she was dealing with another death, only this time it was the death of her marriage.

Jerry finished in the garage and without a word headed toward their bedroom. He showered and reappeared in his robe and slippers. Sharon concentrated on the television screen as if the murder mystery movie of the week were tossing out fat-free recipes. He walked over to his chair and reached for the novel he'd recently been reading, then headed back to the bedroom. He didn't tell her he was going to bed or wish her good night. She didn't say anything to him, either.

By the time the movie was over and she'd watched the eleven o'clock news and listened for the weather forecast, Jerry was sound asleep. He lay on his back, sprawled with his arms outstretched.

Irritated that he'd taken more than his share of the bed, Sharon frowned and jerked her pajamas out of the top dresser drawer. If he was so keen to spend the holidays alone, then maybe she should let him sleep by himself and see how he liked that as well.

With a sense of purpose she moved into the guest bedroom. This would show him how miserable he'd be without her and without family during the holidays. He'd soon learn that she was her own woman, with her own mind and her own will. She didn't need someone to stand guard over her twenty-four hours a day. She was intelligent and articulate. It was time Jerry appreciated her.

Those were all the things she said to herself as she readied for bed. The things she repeated as she tossed and turned until all hours of the night. The room was dark and cold, the bed uncomfortable. Pride was what kept her there. Pride and pure stubbornness. She wanted Jerry to wake and find her gone and worry, just a little, when he realized she hadn't been to bed. She wanted him to regret the way he'd treated her.

If he did, he didn't show it. When she wandered into the kitchen early the next morning, her husband was dressed and ready for a golf match with his friends. The coffee was brewed and he was humming softly to himself. Apparently he'd slept better than he had in months, as well he should since he'd taken his half of the bed out of the middle.

"Mornin'," he greeted her, sounding as bright and chipper as she could remember.

Sharon reached for a mug. "Mornin'."

"Did you sleep well?" her husband asked, leaning against the counter. He wore his favorite golf sweater, the one she'd knitted for him several years back. His lucky one. The very sweater he'd been wearing when he scored his hole in one.

"Like a log," she answered, stretching the truth. No need for Jerry to know how restless the night had been, how she'd yearned for morning, waited to hear him stir before venturing into the kitchen herself.

"Me too." He smiled as if auditioning for a toothpaste advertisement.

She sipped her coffee and stared at him over the edge of the cup.

He stared back, his gaze unwavering. "With all the trouble you've been having sleeping lately, maybe you'd rest more comfortably in the guest bedroom."

This wasn't what Sharon expected. He was supposed to have missed her. Supposed to have awakened and felt lost and lonely without her beside him. There'd been a time when neither one of them slept well when the other was away. It had happened so rarely that they'd talked about it for days afterward, cuddled each other each night, grateful for the warm feel of one another.

"Are you suggesting," she said, not allowing the hurt to show, "that you want me to move into the guest bedroom?"

The question appeared to take Jerry by surprise. He froze and then quietly set aside his mug. "You said yourself you slept better without me."

That wasn't true in the least. She'd grossly exaggerated her comfort. "I'm asking you if you want me to move out of our bedroom, Jerry. Quit avoiding the issue."

His shoulders rose and fell sharply. "All I'm saying is that you seem to sleep better there than with me."

"Do you want me to move out of the bedroom or don't you?"

He hesitated, then shrugged. "Do as you like."

She swallowed tightly and stiffened her spine. "I'll move, then."

"Suit yourself. You seem to anyway. Why should this be any different?"

Having said that, he headed for the garage.

Sharon stood frozen as she heard the garage door whirl open and then a few moments later close again. The painful tightening in her chest ached as she battled back the need to cry.

So that was the way it was to be. After dumping the rest of her coffee into the sink, she rushed to the master bedroom, threw open the closet, and scooped up as many clothes as she could carry. With her arms loaded, dresses dangling, metal hangers cutting into her fingers, she all but stumbled into the guest bedroom and dumped everything on top of the mattress.

The room that at one time had belonged to Pamela. Her dead daughter. It seemed fitting that this was where Sharon would live out the last days of her marriage. Forty years and sinking fast.

Forty years and dying.

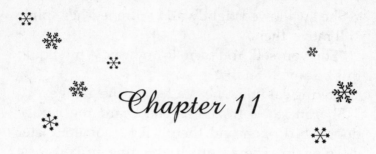

Chapter 11

Words are windows to the heart.

—Mrs. Miracle

The blue dress. No, the red one. Reba couldn't decide. Both were festive, one in silk, the other in a lightweight wool. She'd tried on the two outfits at least a dozen times, those dresses and everything else inside her closet, including a couple of items left over from her college days.

This wasn't an ordinary dinner date. This was an evening to be spent with Seth Webster. She closed her eyes and cradled her arms around her middle, breathing in deeply as she contemplated what was in store for her.

Disillusionment, no doubt, Reba decided. She'd

set herself up for a major disappointment and knew it. Brad Pitt himself couldn't live up to the fantasy she'd created in her mind with Seth. He was her dream man. Why she'd picked him out of all the men she saw in the strip mall parking lot, she couldn't even begin to guess. Theories had bounced around her mind all week, and she'd dissected and examined them until she couldn't think straight any longer. She'd worried and stewed over this one date more than she had over her high school prom.

She wanted everything to be perfect: her dress, her hair, her . . . attitude. For one night, one short period of time, she longed to place the hurts of the past behind her, forget that the two people she'd loved most in the world had betrayed her. Forget that this one act had colored the way she'd looked at all relationships since.

For this one night she wanted to pretend her heart hadn't been stricken. That she was footloose, carefree. That she was capable of dreaming again and having those dreams come true.

The doorbell chimed. Panic set in, and Reba glanced at her watch as her heart bounded to her throat like a bouncing basketball. It had to be Seth. Not so soon. Not already.

She calmed herself, then opened the front door and let him inside her home. If she'd gone to trouble to look her best—and she had—then Seth had, too. His hair was freshly cut, she noticed, and he'd donned a crisp-looking business suit.

"You didn't say where we were dining," she commented as he helped her on with her coat.

"I didn't know," he admitted, and chuckled. "I ended up getting a couple of suggestions from my housekeeper. She made the reservations. I hope you like Thai food. If not . . ."

"It's my favorite." It'd been months since she'd eaten at a Thai restaurant, and it sounded perfect. Perfect.

Although they were both a bit nervous at first, the uneasiness soon disappeared, and as Seth drove to the restaurant they chatted like longtime friends. Rarely had Reba felt more at ease with a man, especially one she barely knew.

"I understand you met the twins," he commented. "My twins, Judd and Jason."

"Wednesday night." Her first night working with the children for the Christmas pageant.

"Jason's actually glad to play the role of an angel." The two boys struggled to be different from each other, seek their own identity.

Reba grinned. The six-year-old's animated face had sprung to life with delight. "Judd wasn't nearly as keen on the idea," she said, hiding a smile. It'd been easy to read the first-grader's thoughts. He'd wanted to play a Roman soldier and carry a spear and shield. Instead he'd be flapping a pair of aluminum wings and a tinsel-wrapped halo. To be fair, she didn't blame the lad, but the older boys had dibs on the more masculine roles.

"He's adjusting," Seth assured her. He looked away from the road long enough to smile at her. "That's quite a project you've taken on."

She was only beginning to understand how large the task was going to be. "Practice went well, and several adults volunteered to lend a hand."

"I'll help too if you find you need it."

"Thanks, I just might take you up on that." The inside of the car was warm and cozy. Warm and intimate. Comfortable in a way that was foreign to her. Since breaking her engagement with John, Reba had felt uneasy with men. Oh, she'd dated, but she'd never allowed a relationship to grow serious. Generally, after a few times out, she found a convenient excuse to call it quits. Counseling probably would have helped her face her fears, but in seeking professional assistance, she'd have to confront far more than her reluctance to enter into another relationship. A trained professional would soon root out the heart of the matter, and she'd be forced to peel back the wound of betrayal and talk about what had happened with John and Vicki.

Reba couldn't bear it. Not with a stranger. Not

with anyone. She wanted to think it would be different with Seth, but it was too soon to know.

The restaurant was perfect. Romantic, exotic. Fun. They removed their shoes and were seated at a low-lying table, the seats padded with large satin pillows propped against the wall. The waitress, a beautiful, unbelievably small Asian woman, filled the gold-edged china cups with fragrant tea and left them to read over the menu.

"Everything looks wonderful."

"I'm partial to anything with peanut sauce," Seth said.

"Me too."

Their eyes met and held, and some unfathomable emotion flickered between them, as though this one small detail were crammed with incredible meaning.

Reba discovered her appreciation of Thai food wasn't the only thing they had in common. With every subject introduced they uncovered a link in one form or another. For years she had been a Seahawks fan. Seth loved football, too.

She adored Steve Martini courtroom dramas. Seth had devoured every one of his books and considered him as fine a writer as Grisham.

She collected stamps and had from the time she was in high school. Seth's collection dated back to his grandfather.

Reba barely noticed when their food arrived.

Although every bite was delicious, she found it to be something of a distraction. She could have talked to him all night.

"This is almost spooky," she said as she piled steaming rice onto her plate. "The next thing I know you're going to tell me that you play the piano as well." She'd taken lessons for six years and loved to sit down even now and pound out her favorite songs.

"I do." His eyes crinkled with silent laughter; then abruptly it faded. "Or I did at one time . . . years ago. I haven't touched a piano in quite some time." This last bit was mumbled almost as if he didn't want her to hear.

"It's easy to get out of practice."

"I haven't played since Pam died." He watched her as he spoke, as if he expected her to tell him it was pointless to deny himself that one small pleasure. She didn't.

"People don't understand why. Most people," he amended.

"You don't need to explain it to me."

"I want to," he said, his eyes solemn. "I suspect I need to." His shoulders tightened as he leaned against the pillows, and he paused as though needing time to formulate his thoughts. "The piano was something we shared. Pamela loved to hear me play. She loved music. She'd lie down and close her eyes and . . . I can't explain it, not with words. It sounds humdrum, almost silly. After I buried her, I couldn't look at the piano any longer. Playing it again was intolerable, and soon after the funeral I sold it. Having it out of the house was a relief. Over time a lot of people have tried to convince me to play again. But I have no desire to do so." His gaze held hers. "I suspect it sounds theatrical, perhaps a bit hysterical."

"It doesn't," Reba rushed to tell him, wanting to assure him that his actions made sense, at least to her. She leaned forward and pressed her hand over his. "I understand, Seth." And she did, more than he realized. More than he'd ever know. He'd given up his music because that part of himself, this one fiber of his life, was interwoven with his memories of his young wife. To sit down and run his fingers over those ivory keys again would be reliving those times he'd treasured with Pamela. The joy he'd once experienced with music would now produce only pain.

"Thank you," he whispered after an awkward moment. "For not lecturing me, for not attempting to reason with me. It's been four years. . . ."

Four years. The rest of his words faded away. Another coincidence. Another irony. It'd been four years since she'd broken off her engagement with John, since she'd last talked to or had anything to do with her sister. Four long years.

The evening took a turn toward the somber following the discussion about music, but even that didn't dim the sense of discovery she experienced.

Seth drove her home, and while they didn't speak, the silence was warm and friendly. It was as though each one needed to absorb what had happened, absorb this second chance they'd been unexpectedly handed. Afraid to consider anything more than this one dinner together.

"I'll see you Sunday at church, won't I?" Seth asked as he walked her toward her front door.

"Of course. I'm going to sit in with the children during Sunday school. I'm a stranger to most of them, and my chances of a successful Christmas program will increase the sooner they're more familiar with me."

"Afterward . . . how about dinner with me and the boys? Mrs. Miracle is a fabulous cook."

Reba was amused by the children's pet name for the housekeeper. Mrs. Miracle. It felt as though a miracle had happened in her life already, just meeting Seth. She wondered if he'd kiss her and was amazed by how much she wanted him to.

The house was dark, the porch light dim, encouraging, and she longed for the feel of Seth's arms. Hungered for the comfort she instinctively recognized she'd find in his embrace. When he did take her gently in his arms, she experienced that and much more.

Seth's kiss was sweet and undemanding.

Slowly, as though he wasn't sure he was doing the right thing, his lips found hers. His touch was tentative, light yet tender and fierce all at once, as if he too were dealing with an abundance of frightening emotions. Exploring them, she suspected, was as scary for him as it was for her. Perhaps more so, since he'd been married.

When he lifted his head from hers, she sighed softly, then wrapped her arms around his middle and braced her forehead against his shoulder.

"I wasn't sure if kissing you was the thing to do."

"I'm glad you did," she whispered.

"Me too." He stroked her hair, his fingers tangling with the short curls. "You'll come to the house after church? For dinner with me and the kids?"

"Yes." Her voice was barely audible.

"Good." He tilted her head upward to meet his descending mouth and kissed her again. Hunger mingled with gentleness, and this time they ended the contact with heady reluctance. Once more Reba hid her face in his shoulder and inhaled deeply, seeking to find her equilibrium.

"I'd better get back."

She nodded. "Dinner was wonderful."

"I thought so, too." He retreated two steps.

She raised her hand and wiggled her fingertips. "Good night," she said as though everything were normal when in fact it wasn't. She wasn't. Many years earlier, while visiting her grandmother in

California, a six-year-old Reba had been awakened by a violent earthquake. The experience had been traumatic. She'd clung to her grandmother, shaken both emotionally and physically. One date with Seth and Reba felt six years old all over again.

All because of Seth's kisses. She felt renewed. Reawakened. Alive. And frightened. Terribly frightened. So much so that she was trembling almost uncontrollably by the time she walked inside her home.

Not turning on the light, she moved into her living room and sank onto the sofa. The darkness closed in around her, hiding her, letting her hide. From what, she wasn't sure. Herself. Her feelings. The future.

The future?

She wondered if she dared trust another man again. Expose herself to another bout of pain.

Gradually a smile came into place. Seth wouldn't hurt her, not when he'd been so deeply hurt himself. Her heart was safe with Seth Webster. Of that she was confident. Safe and secure.

Chapter 12

A skeptic is a person who when he sees the handwriting on the wall claims it's a forgery.

—Morris Bender, as told to Mrs. Miracle

"Daddy, wake up!" Judd bounced onto Seth's bed with all the energy of a Saint Bernard puppy.

Seth longed to bury his head beneath his pillow and possibly would have if Jason hadn't hurled himself into the bed after his brother. Whatever chance he had of returning to sleep was forever lost. This was what he got for letting the kids crawl in bed with him on weekends.

"Is Miss Maxwell going to be our new mommy?"

"Ah . . ." Seth groaned. He needed coffee and a

shower before facing an inquisition from his two children. The word "mommy" implied marriage, and he wasn't anywhere close to considering a step that drastic. Sure, he'd enjoyed Reba's company, but that was a hell of a long way from taking the proverbial plunge into matrimony. The mere word put the fear of God into him.

"Mrs. Miracle showed us Mommy's picture last night," Jason announced.

Seth's head reared back with shocked surprise. He didn't keep out any pictures of Pamela. Like the piano, they'd all been removed and stored carefully in the attic. It'd been a rash thing to do, perhaps even unreasonable, but at the time it had seemed necessary.

One evening, several weeks after he'd sent the boys to live with their grandparents, Seth had gone on a rampage through the house, collecting every snapshot, every photograph, he could lay his hands on. His shoulders had shaken with emotion as he'd gathered them together. Sometime later he'd tucked them away in the storage space in the attic.

No longer would he be blindsided by the pain. It wasn't until much later that Seth realized that out of sight didn't mean out of mind. Pamela's picture didn't rest on the piano any longer, but she was with him. Every time he walked in the house she was there to greet him. To welcome him. To tell him she was pleased he was home. Not with words, naturally. But with memories.

After time, when the pain of losing her wasn't as sharp, he found comfort in those small remembrances. At his loneliest moments, he sat in the living room and wrapped them around himself the way one did a winter coat in the dead of a snowstorm. He closed his eyes and pretended.

Imagination was a powerful thing, and it didn't take more than a small dose to conjure what his life would have been like had Pamela lived. Even with the solace he'd received from those visions, he'd never crawled back into the attic and retrieved the pictures.

"I'd almost forgotten what Mommy looked like," Jason said, "until Mrs. Miracle gave me the photograph."

"Which photograph?" Seth demanded, and Jason flinched with surprise. He didn't mean to shout. His anger certainly wasn't directed at them. The incident with *The Lion, the Witch and the Wardrobe* was one thing, but Pamela's picture was another in a long list of the unexplainable.

"The one in my room," Jason answered. "I'll get it."

He was gone in an instant, flying off the bed with an agility and speed reserved for children. Before Seth could think to call him back, he returned, holding an eight-by-ten-inch frame against his chest.

"This one," he announced breathlessly.

The photograph was of Pamela soon after the birth of the twins, the very one he'd loved the most. Pamela radiantly happy, a newborn infant on each arm, smiling at him, smiling at the camera.

Seth was furious, so angry that he couldn't speak.

"What's wrong, Daddy?" Judd asked, cocking his head to get a better look at his father.

"I need to talk to Mrs. Merkle."

"She's in the kitchen."

Seth climbed out of bed and reached for his robe. As he walked past Jason he took the picture frame out of his hands.

"Where'd you get this?" he demanded before he was all the way into the kitchen.

Mrs. Merkle was standing at the kitchen counter, stirring eggs. She looked up at him, her eyes wide. "I beg your pardon?"

"This photograph of my wife. Where'd you get it?"

"Oh, Mr. Webster, I do hope you don't mind. The children were filled with questions about their mother. I assume it had something to do with you going out with Miss Maxwell and all."

"Where did you get this picture?" he repeated between gritted teeth.

"Yes, well . . ." She hesitated and dried her hands on her apron. "I found it in the bookcase when I dusted the other morning. Someone had stuck it in between two volumes. Apparently it's been there for some time. Of course I wasn't sure it was your wife, but with the babies in her arms, I felt it must have been. Judd has her eyes."

Seth's gaze traveled to his son, and he recognized that what the older woman said was true. Judd's dark brown eyes were the precise shape and color Pamela's had been. Funny he'd never noticed that before.

"In the bookcase, you say?"

"I apologize if I did something I shouldn't have." She certainly looked contrite. "I bought the frame the other day. It seems to go rather nicely, don't you think?"

Seth sighed. He hadn't meant to make a federal case out of a silly thing like a photograph. Although he'd been in the bookcase himself more times than he could count, he could easily have overlooked the picture. Who was to know how it came to be there in the first place? Perhaps Pamela stuck it there herself. Perhaps he'd been the one to do it. Not that it mattered.

"Mommy had brown eyes like me, too, didn't she?" Jason asked, looking at him expectantly.

"Yes, partner."

"Will my new mommy?"

It was all Seth could do to keep from groaning aloud. He looked to Mrs. Merkle to rescue him, but she was back stirring eggs, humming softly to herself.

"Dad?" Judd pulled at his sleeve. "Will she?"

He squatted down so that his gaze was level with that of his children. "There isn't going to be another mommy, kids."

They both looked stunned. He might as well have announced there was no such thing as Santa Claus from the shock he read in their expressive faces.

"But—"

"Mrs. Miracle said there would be."

Irritated, Seth shot a glance toward his housekeeper, but she was busy with breakfast and either didn't hear or was pretending not to. He wasn't about to have the woman telling the children something like that. When he had a private moment, he'd mention it to her.

"I even drew my new mommy's picture," Judd told him. The lad raced out of the kitchen and was back a few moments later with a crayon drawing. Seth barely glanced at it and wouldn't have given it a second's notice if it wasn't for two small matters. The woman Judd pictured had short curly hair and was wearing a shiny red dress.

Reba's hair was short and curly and she'd been wearing a bright red dress. Coincidence. Pure coincidence.

"She's real pretty, isn't she?" Judd asked, proud of his efforts.

"She sure is," Seth muttered with no real enthusiasm.

"You like Miss Maxwell, don't you?" This came from Jason.

"Yes," he admitted, "but that doesn't mean I'm going to marry her."

Both of his children had that same woebegone look of bitter disappointment. "You'll look for a new mommy, won't you?"

"Look for someone with brown eyes and curly hair and a red dress," Judd advised, and waved the picture under his nose once more.

Seth was saved from having to answer when the housekeeper called them to the table.

He bided his time and waited until after breakfast before he confronted Mrs. Merkle. It didn't take a genius to figure out where the children were getting the notion that he was about to remarry, and he wouldn't have it.

"Do you have a moment?" he asked her as he carried the dirty dishes from the table to the sink.

"Of course."

Ill at ease, and disliking confrontation, he hesitated. "I was wondering if you'd said anything to the children about me remarrying."

She didn't answer him right away, which was an answer in itself. "I don't mean to complain," he continued. "The kids call you Mrs. Miracle, and frankly, I've come to think of you that way. I don't know what we would have done without you, but I'd prefer it if you didn't fill the children's heads with this talk about another mother."

"So you don't plan to remarry?" She looked as disappointed as the children.

"No," he returned emphatically.

If his words discouraged her, it didn't last long. Her eyes rounded with a hint of mischief. "Not ever, Mr. Webster? Forever is a long, long time."

"Not ever," he assured her, raising his voice slightly.

She laughed once, shortly, as if his answer had amused her and she wasn't able to contain it. "Time will tell, won't it?"

"Time most certainly will." He turned and stalked out of the kitchen and into the garage. He opened his car door before he realized he still had on his pajamas and robe. Not to mention that this was Saturday morning.

Mrs. Merkle left the house an hour later, and Seth was alone with the children. Although he was grateful to have a housekeeper, he couldn't help being curious about Emily Merkle. She certainly had a way about her. She'd taken his restless, spirited children under her wing and within a matter of days had made a marked difference in their behavior and attitude. Not once since her arrival had he received a call from the school or a note from their teacher.

He found it curious, however, the way she'd arrived, without notice. It was almost as if she'd descended from the clouds, using an umbrella as a parachute. Not that she resembled Mary Poppins. No, he definitely viewed her as a Mother Goose.

Once he'd showered and shaved, Seth moved into his den. It certainly wouldn't hurt to contact the employment agency and make a few inquiries about her. It wouldn't hurt to check on her references, either.

Luckily the agency was staffed on Saturdays.

"Hello, this is Seth Webster," he said when Mrs. Ackerman, the agency owner, answered herself.

"Oh, Mr. Webster, I'm so very sorry. I can't imagine what you must think of me."

"Mrs. Ackerman?" Seth couldn't fathom why she should apologize.

"Yes, yes, I realize that you've been waiting several weeks to hear back from me. I can't imagine how you've managed all this time."

"I don't believe I understand."

"A housekeeper. You do still need one, don't you?"

"Ah . . ." Seth was too stunned to respond.

"I want you to know that I've made inquiries each and every day, but a full-time housekeeper, willing to live in and care for two small children, why, they're few and far between these days."

"But—"

"Not to mention the fact that you've gone through every domestic I have in short order."

"What about Emily Merkle?" he asked. "Didn't you send her?"

"Emily Merkle."

He could hear the rustle of papers in the background. "We don't have anyone by that name listed here. Let me check the computer data file."

He waited a moment. The sound of fingers typing against the computer keys echoed over the telephone line.

"I'm afraid we don't have anyone by that name listed with the agency. Are you sure her name is Merkle?"

"Yes." All of a sudden Seth was sure of nothing.

Exactly who was this woman who'd insinuated herself into his and the children's lives?

Chapter 13

*It isn't difficult to make a mountain
out of a molehill. Just add a little dirt.*

—Mrs. Miracle

*O*t was her responsibility as a Christian, Harriett Foster determined. As an upstanding member of the church, it was her duty to talk with Pastor Lovelace about what was happening between Ruth Darling and Lyle Fawcett.

Even though Harriett played the organ for the eleven o'clock worship service, she had eyes in her head. She could see what was happening. Ruth Darling was flirting with sin, and the worst part of it was that she did so right inside the house of God. Why, a blind man could see that Ruth was making eyes at Lyle Fawcett.

Harriett was worried about Ruth. That was it. Worried. She'd start off by telling Pastor Lovelace how very concerned she was over her dear, dear friend's recent behavior. Her words couldn't be misconstrued as gossip in that case. This had been a matter of prayer for a good while, and she'd felt the need to share her burden.

Harriett checked her reflection in the car window to be sure her hat was fastened securely to her head before she approached the church. She had a perfect excuse for being there on a Saturday. Not that she ever really needed a reason.

Not only was she playing the piano for the Christmas program—the children were due to arrive in another hour—but it took an hour or more at the organ to familiarize herself with the music for the Sunday morning worship service.

It did feel as though the church took advantage of her musical talents. When Harriett talked to Pastor Lovelace, she'd be sure to mention how much of her valuable time she sacrificed for the church's benefit. Subtly, of course. She didn't want him to think she was overly burdened or that she didn't enjoy being a slave for God's work.

Walking in from the parking lot, she clenched her purse against her side and strolled purposely past the pastor's office. The door was closed, and she sighed with disappointment. She'd hoped that the office door would be open and she could stick her head inside and say hello. She hesitated, wondering if she should knock, then decided against it. She'd much rather that their discussion appeared spontaneous and nothing that she'd planned beforehand. As it was, she'd carefully gone over exactly what she would say, after which she'd leave the touchy matter in his capable hands. Surely Pastor Lovelace would recognize what was happening and take decisive action. No man of God could allow this kind of behavior to continue within his own church.

Lyle Fawcett was a gentleman, a recent widower himself. He needed gentle concern, someone who could appreciate his grief, a woman who would take it upon herself to see to his comfort.

He needed someone like her, Harriett reasoned.

She'd lost her life's mate and could well appreciate Lyle's grief. What he didn't need was Ruth Darling hovering over him, making a nuisance of herself. As the Bible leader for the Martha and Mary Circle, Ruth had other responsibilities. More important, Ruth had a husband!

Apparently Fred Darling didn't even see what was going on right under his nose; he would never put up with his wife's blatant behavior if he did. Harriett would have thought better of the man, but then, as was so often the case, the spouse was the last to know. Men in particular were blind when it suited their purposes. To Harriett's way of thinking, Fred was acting like an ostrich with his head buried in the sand. She almost felt sorry for the poor soul.

Feeling thwarted and more than a little disappointed, Harriett headed for the sanctuary. She'd play the organ, and if luck was with her, Pastor Lovelace would hear the soothing sounds of her music and make himself available. It wasn't uncommon for him to enter the sanctuary when she played or to make last minute changes in the music.

Harriett was just inside the vestibule when she heard Pastor Lovelace's door open.

She whirled around, delighted. "Pastor," she greeted him warmly, excitedly. "How are you this fine day?" He was a young man in his early thirties, and wise for his years. Kind-hearted and generous, Pastor Lovelace made himself available to the people of his congregation. A good shepherd.

"Mrs. Foster." He smiled, looking a bit uncomfortable. "I thought I heard someone."

"You did," she said, speaking the obvious. "Me. I'm here to play the piano for practice with the children. The Christmas program is coming along nicely, even if I say so myself." She was about to remind him that she'd been the one responsible for finding a replacement for Milly Waters. Actually, she'd volunteered Jayne, but her niece had suggested Reba Maxwell, and that had worked out beautifully.

It went without saying that if Harriett hadn't stepped in when she had, the entire Christmas program might have been canceled. More and more it was becoming clear to her that she was not appreciated the way she should be. If it wasn't for her efforts, there was no telling what would happen to the church.

Pastor Lovelace glanced at his watch. "I didn't think practice with the children was for another hour."

"It isn't. I'm here to rehearse for the worship service." She looked pointedly at her hands. "With my arthritis as bad as it is, it's a wonder I can still play at all."

"We do appreciate your efforts, Mrs. Foster, but if ever you feel that you can't continue, then—"

"No, no, I'm fine. Of course there's a bit of pain, but then I'm accustomed to that." She smiled bravely, and Pastor Lovelace patted her shoulder in that caring, gentle way of his.

He started to retreat back into his office.

"Pastor," she said quickly, "it's fortuitous that we should meet like this, since there's a matter, a rather delicate one, I feel needs discussing. It has to do with one of the women of the church . . . a married woman," she added pointedly.

"I'm afraid I have an appointment, Mrs. Foster."

"This should only take a few moments, and its importance can't be underrated. I feel terrible to be the one to bring this unfortunate situation to your notice, but someone must."

"Perhaps we could talk later."

"If I don't say this now, I might never have the courage again." Harriett planted her hand over her heart, as if speaking the words pained her. "It has to do with—"

Ruth Darling's name never left her lips. Just then, with impeccable timing, the church door opened and the very woman herself strolled inside.

Harriett almost swallowed her tongue.

Ruth hesitated, then smiled and nodded. "Hello, Harriett."

"Ruth." The name fell stiffly from her lips.

"Perhaps we could talk another time," Pastor Lovelace suggested, directing the comment to Harriett.

"Of course," she murmured, and turned away, but not before she saw Ruth enter Pastor Lovelace's study. Whatever the other woman had come to discuss required an appointment. The subject was plainly serious.

Harriett had seen it coming. The Darling marriage, after forty years or longer, was in deep trouble. Rightly so, with Ruth making goo-goo eyes at Lyle Fawcett.

Chapter 14

A successful marriage isn't finding the right person,
it's being the right person.

—Mrs. Miracle

Humming to herself, Sharon Palmer read over the recipe and assembled the necessary ingredients. She was tired of tossing and turning the night away in the guest bedroom, tired of pretending she enjoyed sleeping apart from her husband.

The chocolate-chip cookies, his favorite, were a peace offering, a subtle one. A means of telling him she was sorry. That she regretted this whole business and wanted it to end.

Jerry had left earlier that morning to play a round of golf with his friends, other retirees. The way Sharon figured, the cookies would be warm from the oven by the time he returned. Warm and gooey, just the way he liked them best.

Then perhaps they could sit down and talk. Really talk. They hadn't communicated in months. Not the way they should for a couple married close to forty years.

As she added the chocolate chips and walnuts to the dough, she smiled, pleased with this recent decision to work out the bumps in her marriage. They were both strong-willed and stubborn. Both old fools.

Jerry wanted to take a trip through the Panama Canal. There would be other cruises, other vacations, and next time she could choose when and where. It was silly for them both to be so unreasonable with one another.

Perhaps if she gave in on this, Jerry would see his way clear to flying to Seattle with her to visit the grandkids over Christmas. If she showed her willingness to compromise, he would, too. Jerry was a fair man. She hadn't been married to him all these years without knowing that.

The first sheet of cookies were cooling when her husband walked in the door. If he noticed the scent of freshly baked cookies, he said nothing. It'd been a good long while since she'd last baked. This was a rare treat.

He ignored her and opened the refrigerator

door, glaring inside as if seeking buried treasure.

"Do you want a cookie?" she asked, playing it cool.

The last few days the tension between them had been as thick as glue.

"Did you put nuts in them?" he asked.

She nodded. "Walnuts." His favorite.

"I don't like walnuts," he said, bringing out a bowl of leftover spaghetti.

"Since when?" she demanded. He'd been eating her chocolate-chip cookies with walnuts for years and never said a word before now.

"Since I was a kid." He set the spaghetti on the counter and reached for a plate.

"You always ate walnuts before."

"Yeah, and I didn't like it."

Sharon planted her mitt-covered hand on her hip. "Do you mean to tell me that it took you forty years to tell me you don't like walnuts?" She didn't believe it, not for a moment. He was being deliberately argumentative, deliberately unappreciative.

"It took me forty years longer than it should have," he snapped. He slapped a glob of spaghetti on the plate and stuck it inside the microwave. He punched a few buttons and glared back at her.

The sound of the microwave in process whirled through the kitchen as it warmed his lunch. Sharon had purposely waited to eat so that she could sit down and join him, but her appetite had vanished, replaced by a sick feeling in the pit of her stomach.

"Is there anything else you don't like that you haven't mentioned?" she asked without emotion.

"Plenty. I prefer spaghetti with meatballs instead of the meat all crumbled in with the sauce."

Sharon had made her spaghetti from the same recipe all these years, and not once had he said one word about preferring meatballs.

He must have seen the stricken look on her face because he added, "You asked, didn't you?"

The oven timer beeped.

Sharon had no defense, and rather than answer him, she removed the last cookie sheet from the oven. She stared at the perfectly shaped cookies, with the chocolate chips bright and melting. After only a moment's hesitation she dumped them straight into the garbage.

"What'd you do that for?" Jerry demanded, irritation raising his voice half an octave.

"You don't like walnuts," she reminded him, doing her best to keep the hurt out of her voice. "I'd hate to force you to eat something not to your liking."

The microwave beeped, and Jerry grabbed the plate before she had a chance to take that away from him as well.

"What's wrong with you?" he demanded. His

gaze narrowed as he studied her intently. "Did you take your hormones this morning?"

"Forty years, and not once did you tell me you don't like walnuts." The words were an accusation of all that was wrong with their marriage.

"I don't hate them," he argued. He walked over to the kitchen cabinet where she kept her medication, removed the bottle, and shook it before putting it back. "Maybe that's what the problem is."

"The only problem I have is you, Jerry Palmer."

His eyes rounded as he slapped his hand over his heart. "You think I'm your problem? Sweetheart, you'd better take a look in the mirror. If there's problems in this family, I'm not the one—"

"If you don't like the way I cook, maybe you should do your own cooking," she challenged.

"Maybe I should," Jerry countered. "I've cooked my own breakfast all week."

"Great, now you can try your hand at lunch and dinner as well."

"No problem."

Sharon slammed the mitt down on the counter. "I'm sure it won't be." She stalked past him and made her way into the guest bedroom. Sitting at the end of the twin mattress, she intertwined her fingers in an attempt to still the trembling in her hands.

She wasn't a woman who often succumbed to

tears, but they blurred her eyes now. Tilting her head back, she blinked furiously, refusing to let them fall, refusing to allow her pain to roll free.

She was the emotionally strong one in the family. Not until Pamela's death did she realize how strong. When they'd heard the terrible news, Jerry had withdrawn behind a brick wall of pain, unwilling and perhaps afraid to reveal his anguish. Seth had been in shock, blinded by grief and fear of what would happen to him and the children without Pamela.

So everyone had turned to her. She was the one who had made the funeral arrangements. She was the one others had turned to for comfort and help. She was emotionally strong. Calm. A pillar on which others could lean.

The base of that pillar was crumbling now, Sharon realized, and threatening to collapse.

The knot blocking her throat felt as big as a watermelon. She'd started out her day with such good intentions, hoping to bridge the gap between her and Jerry, but he wanted none of it.

She lay down on the bed, pulled a blanket over her shoulders, and stared at the wall.

Forty years and she never knew Jerry didn't like walnuts.

Forty years was a long time to live with a man and never know he liked his spaghetti with meatballs.

Some time later Sharon heard a sound, but she didn't move her gaze away from the wall to investigate.

"Darn it, Sharon, say something."

She could picture Jerry framed in the doorway, but she hadn't the strength or the will to pull her attention away from the blank wall.

"I'm talking to you," he said again.

She'd heard all she wanted to from him. More than she'd needed to know.

"The hell with you, then," Jerry muttered, and stalked away.

Forty years she'd invested in this marriage, in this man. She'd kept his home, borne him children, molded her life to fit his. Forty years and they could barely tolerate one another.

Seth had never intended to stay for the Christmas program practice. He'd thought to drop the boys off at the church and head home to catch up on some job-related reading. Besides, he wanted to be there when Mrs. Merkle returned. They had several matters to discuss.

His head had been spinning ever since his conversation with Mrs. Ackerman. If the employment agency hadn't sent Mrs. Merkle, who had? He proposed to find out at the earliest opportunity.

The twins were excited about their part in the Christmas pageant and had chatted like magpies

during the short drive to the church. When he'd
arrived, Seth had impulsively decided to park and
go inside. He'd stay just long enough to say hello
to Reba, thank her for their dinner date, and be on
his way.

That's what he'd told himself he'd do, but the
minute he'd entered the room, he'd felt compelled
to sit back and watch Reba manage the children.
For a single woman with limited experience
working with kids, she did a masterful job. Two
or three other women were there to lend a hand,
but it was Reba who was in charge.

The practice started out with all the children
grouped together. Mrs. Foster was there as well,
tight-lipped and looking miserable as she banged
away on the piano keys without much finesse. He
grimaced a couple of times at her basic lack of
talent.

To the best of his memory, Seth had never seen
the older woman smile. Half the time she looked
as if she'd been sucking on something bitter.

The children, while familiar with the songs,
gave it a halfhearted effort. Their voices blended
nicely, but from the back of the room, Seth couldn't
understand the words. Reba's shoulders sagged,
and she said something that made everyone laugh.
The next attempt was much better.

A few minutes later she broke the group into
three sections to rehearse their individual roles.

Seth decided to wait until Judd and Jason came on the scene. Judd may have been assigned the role of an angel, but he burst onto the stage with the shepherds watching over their sheep like Rambo intent on revenge. All he needed was a submachine gun for a prop. Jason followed and growled like a lion.

Reba handled the situation well, reminding his six-year-old sons that they weren't there to frighten anyone. Their mission, if they chose to accept it, was to tell the shepherds wonderful, exciting news. Judd and Jason smiled and nodded.

The boys second attempt was much better. Judd's voice bellowed out loud and clear as he shared the wondrous news.

Before Seth realized it, the hour was gone. The twins raced to his side the minute they'd finished. Seth waited until most of the other kids were gone before he approached Reba. He felt a bit awkward, hiding in the back of the room that way, but had derived a good deal of pleasure just watching her.

He was afraid that he'd built up their date in his mind, made more of it than he should have. But as he moved toward her, he realized if anything, he'd discounted his attraction for her. Reba was patient and kind. Her rapport with the kids had been instantaneous, and he hadn't been able to take his eyes off her for the entire hour. He wasn't succeeding now, either.

"It looks like everything's going great," he commented, understating what should have been obvious.

She sank onto a chair and rubbed her hand along the back of her neck. "You think so?"

"You've got the entire program organized."

"I can't take the credit for that. Milly Waters worked with me. I'm just following her example."

Judd sank onto the floor next to her, staring up at her as if memorizing her features. "She looks like the lady in my picture," he announced with childlike enthusiasm.

"Judd," Seth warned in a whisper. If his son embarrassed him by suggesting he marry Reba, he didn't know what he'd do.

"Not exactly like the lady, but real close," Jason said before Seth had a chance to quiet him.

"It's time to go," he stated with an eagerness that bordered on panic.

The twins and Reba looked saddened and surprised by his abrupt announcement.

"Not so soon, Dad."

"What picture?" Reba asked, looking from Judd to Jason.

"It's nothing," Seth said, wanting to be on his way before the twins embarrassed him further.

"Judd drew a picture of a woman with short hair and a red dress," Jason explained when it became obvious his father wasn't going to explain.

"The woman in my drawing looks a lot like you," Judd said, his eyes bright and eager.

Seth urged both his children toward the door. "I'll see you tomorrow, then," he said, hoping against hope to make a clean getaway.

"Tomorrow?" Jason perked up instantly.

"Ms. Maxwell is coming to the house for dinner," he explained, and remembered that he hadn't said anything to Mrs. Merkle about inviting company.

"Good-bye, Ms. Maxwell."

"Good-bye, everyone."

Seth heaved a sigh of relief as they headed toward the door. "She does look like the lady in Judd's picture," Jason said, and slipped his small hand into his. He seemed to be waiting for Seth to respond.

"A little," he admitted reluctantly.

Jason looked over his shoulder and sighed expressively before calling out in a loud voice, "I hope you do marry my dad."

"I beg your pardon?" Reba said.

"My dad," Judd shouted. "We hope you marry him."

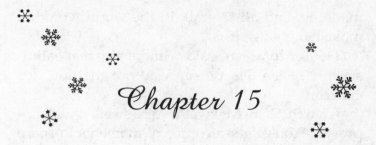

Chapter 15

Scatter sunshine.

—Mrs. Miracle

𝒯he phone pealed just as Reba started out the door Sunday morning for church. She was tempted not to answer, afraid it would be her mother. She hesitated, then quickly crossed the room and reached for the receiver. It might be important. It might be Seth.

"Hello."

"Reba, sweetheart, I wondered if you'd be up and about."

Her mother. Reba gritted her teeth. She knew it would be more of this Christmas business, and she didn't want to discuss it again. Her mind was made up, and all the talk in the world wouldn't make her change it.

"Hello, Mom," she said without any real enthusiasm. "Listen, I'm on my way out the door for church."

"Church." Joan Maxwell's voice swelled with approval. "You've got a couple of moments to spare for your mother, don't you?"

Reba wasn't given the chance to say no.

"You remember Betty Gleason, don't you?"

Reba didn't; impatiently she glanced at her watch. She was meeting Seth and didn't want to be late. "No, Mom, I'm afraid I don't."

"I attended the early church service and met up with Betty. She and Ernie were in this fancy Thai restaurant in Federal Way and she thought she saw you with a nice-looking young man."

Reba swore her mother had informants who routinely reported her activities. "That was Seth Webster," she said, making sure none of her feelings for the aeronautical engineer bled into her voice. It would be just like her mother to make more of this dinner date than there was.

"Seth Webster . . ." Joan Maxwell repeated the name slowly, as if saying it aloud magically released the information she craved. "Have you known him long?"

"Mother, I'm going to be late for church."

"Are you meeting Seth there?"

The woman was a mind-reader. "Yes, and—"

"I think it's a wonderful thing you're doing, taking over the Christmas program at the last minute like this. You always were good with children. You don't know how I've prayed that you'd get involved in the church again. I couldn't be more pleased."

"Did I mention that I was on my way to church?" she asked pointedly, not that it would do much good. Reba knew her mother all too well. She was on a fact-finding mission and wouldn't let up until she'd ferreted out the information she sought.

"Tell me about Seth. Where'd you meet him? How long have you been dating?" All this came in one giant breath. "Betty claimed the two of you only had eyes for each other. She seemed to think the fire alarm could have gone off and neither of you would have noticed."

"Mother—"

"Betty claims it's clear that the two of you are serious. I do wish you'd said something to us before, sweetheart. It's a bit disconcerting, not to say embarrassing, to have a family friend know more about what's going on in my own daughter's life than her own mother."

"Mom. Church."

"I know, I know, but the worship leaders generally start the service a few minutes past eleven. It won't hurt to be a couple of minutes late. We've barely had a chance to talk. You so rarely phone me." Her voice contained just the right amount of injury for Reba to experience a twinge of guilt. She did avoid calling her mother and for this very reason.

"Why don't we meet for lunch one day next week?" Reba suggested. She was as susceptible to guilt as the next person, and her mother knew all the right buttons to punch.

"Tomorrow," Joan Maxwell suggested. "I can't wait to hear all about Seth. I'll meet you at the agency at eleven-thirty. Don't plan to be back in the office for an hour, either, okay?" Having said that, she hung up.

Reba held the phone away from her ear and looked at it. No one on earth could drive her crazier faster than her own mother. Joan sounded like a little girl, all excited, eager to hear the details of Reba's romance.

She exhaled slowly. It was too soon to be telling her mother anything about her and Seth. They'd only gone on one official date, and her mother made it sound as though they should meet as soon as possible to discuss the details of her upcoming wedding.

A wedding.

Four years earlier Reba had worked with her mother to plan a large, formal wedding ceremony. She'd taken time and effort with every detail, choosing the invitations and bridesmaid dresses and everything else that went with the special occasion. The thought of going through all that needless hassle again left a sour taste in her mouth.

It had been humiliating to call her family and friends and announce that she wouldn't be marrying John after all. She'd escaped shortly afterward, putting herself up at the beach alone for several days, thinking matters through.

Returning the gifts had taken weeks. Although she'd sent out notices that the wedding had been canceled, gifts staggered in for thirty days or longer, and she had to deal with their timely return. Reba wanted no part of a large, conventional affair.

If she ever married, it would be a small, casual gathering. As she had with so much else in life, Vicki had robbed her of the beautiful wedding she'd always dreamed of.

Not wanting thoughts of her sister to ruin her day, Reba hurried out the door for church. She smiled as she thought ahead to spending the afternoon with Seth and his family. An image of Judd in the Christmas pageant came to mind, and she chuckled. He might have resigned himself to playing the role of an angel, but he wanted to make sure everyone knew he was a man angel and not some blue-eyed blond sissy. Seth's children were so easy to love.

What her mother had said about her being good with children was true. After the broken engagement, she'd shoved the thought of being a mother to the back of her mind. It hurt too much to dwell on all the might-have-beens.

Vicki had a child, Reba mused, and at the thought a strong stab of resentment shot through her. Again she mentally released her anger. Nevertheless, she couldn't help thinking how unfair it was that Vicki could have a home with a husband and a child when she had neither. The sister who'd betrayed her, the sister who'd stolen away everything Reba treasured, was happy while she, Reba, wallowed in the injustice of it all.

The church parking lot was almost full. Reba hurried into the sanctuary just as the congregation stood to sing the opening song, "Oh Come, All Ye Faithful." Organ music swelled and filled the room. She found a seat and set her purse on the pew and reached for the hymnal.

Out of the corner of her eye, she noticed Seth with his two children, and the resentment and sadness that had settled over her like a dark cloud lifted unexpectedly. Sunlight filtered into her soul. For whatever reason, she'd been given this second chance at finding happiness. She intended to take hold of the opportunity with both hands and let it take her where it would. Through-out the remainder of the service, her gaze con-tinually strayed to Seth and the children. Every time she glanced in his direction, the warmth returned.

During the closing hymn, Reba felt Seth's eyes on her. She held his look and smiled, surprised by how shy and uncertain she felt. It was a little thing, this dinner with him and his children. But she'd rarely looked forward to any time more.

They met on the concrete steps outside the church. "There's been a small change in plans," Seth announced.

"Oh?" She could see by his look that the revi-sion had unsettled him.

"Unbeknownst to me, Mrs. Merkle promised the twins she'd take them to the movies this after-noon. She said she could make us soup and sand-wiches before she left if you wanted. I'd thought . . . I'd hoped . . . What I'm trying to say is that we can make it another time if you'd like."

So both the housekeeper and the twins would be gone. "Would you rather I came another time?" she asked, preferring he make the decision.

His eyes scooted past her. "No. I was looking forward to seeing you again."

"I don't want to wait, either."

This appeared to surprise him, but a smile soon formed and he reached for her hand, his fingers tightening around hers. "Actually I make a mean toasted cheese sandwich."

"Does this mean you'll be doing the cooking?"

"Don't let him," Judd advised, glancing up at his father. "We eat a lot better since Mrs. Miracle came."

Mrs. Miracle. Reba's gaze went to the plump older woman. The children gathered about her like chicks seeking the protection of a mother's wing.

"I do hope my taking the children won't be too much of an inconvenience," the housekeeper said, looking to Reba. A smile courted her lips, causing the edges to quiver. "I would stay and fix dinner, but I'd hate to disappoint the twins. They've been extra good all week, and this is their reward."

"It's no problem," Seth assured her.

Reba drove to Seth's house. Mrs. Merkle had the children change their clothes while she set sandwich makings on the kitchen counter.

"There's plenty of leftovers," she called out.

"Don't worry, we'll see to everything ourselves," Seth told her.

The housekeeper's gaze slipped from her employer to Reba. She looked well pleased with herself. Reba glanced around, suddenly uneasy with the thought of being alone with Seth. The attraction she felt toward him was strong and was sure to grow more so once they were alone. Perhaps it was the conversation with her mother earlier in the day, the coming inquisition lunch on Monday would bring. She couldn't very well play down their relationship when meeting Seth was the best thing that had happened to her in four long years.

"All things are possible with God," Mrs. Merkle said out of the blue, looking intently at them both. "But no one said they'd be easy."

Reba glanced at Seth, wondering if he could explain the comment. He looked as puzzled as she.

In a matter of minutes the housekeeper had disappeared with both children. The silence that followed engulfed both her and Seth.

"I can't shake the feeling that she somehow arranged this in advance," Seth mumbled as he carried two cups of coffee into the living room. She wasn't in the mood for lunch yet, and neither was he.

Hoping to give a relaxed impression, Reba removed her shoes and tucked her feet up against the side of the chair. This was the first time she'd been inside Seth's house. She liked it. The style was homey and comfortable, the furniture large and bulky. Sturdy, like the man himself.

Seth handed Reba the coffee and sat across from her. He seemed deeply wrapped up in his thoughts.

"Do you get the feeling we're being purposely thrown together?" she asked.

He nodded. "It seems that way, but Emily didn't know that I'd invited you to dinner. I forgot to mention it," he added sheepishly.

"She's an unusual woman."

Seth shook his head and relaxed against the cushion. "You're telling me! I can't help but wonder . . ." He let whatever he was going to say fade.

"Wonder?" she prodded. Although she'd met Mrs. Merkle only once, Reba had the same feeling about her. She found the older woman to be something of a puzzle. Perhaps it had something to do with the way Seth's housekeeper regarded her. It was as though she had looked straight through her and read her soul. The feeling prompted the oddest sensation.

"She showed up out of the blue one night, like a . . . miracle. I hate to say it, but it's true. The former housekeeper had been gone for some time, and the house was a disaster. Because of all the uncertainty, the kids were in an uproar and I was at my wits' end. All at once Mrs. Miracle was there. I didn't even think to check her references or contact the agency until . . ." He hesitated again, as if caught in some warped memory.

"Seth?"

"The agency hadn't sent her."

"What?" He certainly had her attention now.

"When I asked Mrs. Merkle about it, she had a perfectly logical explanation. The Ackerman

Agency, the one I'd been working with, contacted another agency, Heath, Health, Heaven . . . something like that. And they're the ones who'd sent her. I checked her references, and she was given the highest recommendation. I certainly can't find fault with her. What she's done for the children is nothing short of miraculous." He tossed her a chagrined look, then chuckled. "There's that word again."

"You're reassured, then?" He regarded her blankly, and Reba added, "With her explanation about the agency?"

"Yes. She was adamant that she'd told me the name of the agency earlier, but I don't seem to remember her saying anything. There's been a few other things—minor things, really—that leave me to wondering. And the things she says . . ."

"Says?"

He chuckled. "This morning when the offering was taken in church, she leaned close and murmured something about not being able to take our money with us, but we can send it on ahead."

Reba laughed. "You're not worried about her, are you?"

"Heavens, no. She's wonderful, and as I said, I did check out her references." He raised the coffee cup to his mouth and hesitated with the mug halfway to his lips. His gaze stretched to the far side of the room.

Reba glanced over her shoulder and discovered a twig of mistletoe dangling from the doorway leading into the kitchen. The twins or possibly Mrs. Merkle had placed it there before they'd left for the movie.

The air in the room seemed to grow warm as the awareness between them became stronger. Reba moistened her lips, remembering their exchange the night of their first date. The kisses had been wonderful. A renewal. A discovery. Reba was confident that Seth had experienced the power of their attraction as strongly as she.

"Mrs. Merkle, no doubt," he offered, clearing his throat. "I don't want you to think . . . you know, that I brought you over here on the pretext of . . . well, seducing you."

"With mistletoe?"

"Yes." He stood and walked over to the fireplace, which was the farthest point he could be from her and still remain in the same room. "I invited you to dinner, and the next thing you know we're here in the house, alone, and there's all these not-so-subtle hints that I'd like to pick up where we left off Friday night."

"Would you?" she asked, lowering her gaze.

"Yes." His response was sharp and immediate. "Maybe I should lie about it, but I don't see much sense in that. It's been a lot of years since I was in the dating scene, and I don't know how to play those games any longer."

"I don't, either."

"You were married?" His eyes held hers, his look intense.

"No," she whispered, and then amended, "Almost . . . the engagement was broken." She didn't offer any other information; didn't see the point. He couldn't possibly understand, and she wouldn't ask it of him.

"It does seem a shame to waste that mistletoe, don't you think?" He moved toward the kitchen doorway and stood under the Christmas decoration.

Smiling, Reba set aside her coffee and walked toward him. They stood facing each other, and for a long moment neither spoke. Then, as if this were what they'd been waiting for, what they'd both anticipated from the moment Mrs. Merkle had left with the twins, they moved into each other's arms.

Reba's eyes fluttered closed as Seth gathered her close. She wanted this, needed this, and sighed audibly when his lips met hers. His kiss left her breathless and clinging. It had been like this the first time, too. Her head had been spinning ever since. He gave her hope, helped her to believe that there could be a future for them.

"Do you think this is what she was talking about?" Reba asked.

Seth spread small kisses on the underside of her neck. "Who?"

"Mrs. Miracle." She'd said all things were possible with God. Only this felt easy, much too easy.

"Maybe so." Seth assured her once more with another deep, soul-stirring kiss.

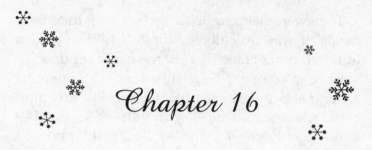

Chapter 16

If you're waiting for a sign from God, this is it.

—Mrs. Miracle

"You left the milk out again," Sharon reminded her husband pointedly.

Without comment, Jerry scooted his chair away from the table, removed the milk carton from the counter, and placed it back inside the refrigerator.

Her husband looked at her as if he had something on his mind, but whatever it was, he let it go. They seemed to be at an impasse. Once they would have joked and laughed at how silly they were being, but that time was gone, and they both knew it. What had started out as a minor disagreement over a cruise and Christmas had evolved into something much more serious.

They were sleeping apart and cooking their own meals. It was ridiculous. Stupid. Childish, and a hundred other adjectives Sharon could think of.

Jerry cooking! She cringed as she glanced around at her once orderly kitchen. How any man could make such a mess scrambling eggs was beyond her. Eggshells and spilled milk puddled across the countertop, and runny egg had dried on her once spotless stovetop. The peanut butter had been left out, along with the bread and just about everything else Jerry had touched in the last several days.

Regretfully Sharon realized she had no one to blame but herself. She was the one who'd insisted her husband cook his own meals. The words had been spoken in anger, but she'd regretted them almost immediately. Surely Jerry knew that, yet he chose to carry out this ridiculous charade. Even then she didn't completely blame him. She wasn't any better, opting to sleep in the guest bedroom when it was apparent they were both miserable.

If she hadn't had Maggie to talk to, she didn't know what she would have done. Her best friend had tried to help, but all she could do was listen. If ever Sharon needed a sympathetic ear, it was now. They'd gone shopping, and Maggie had taken her to lunch afterward. When she'd heard about Jerry and the cookie incident, she'd been furious with him.

As soon as he finished his breakfast, Jerry left the house. Sharon watched him leave. The problems within their marriage were compounding instead of simplifying. Maggie had listened, and although she hadn't said it, the subject was there. Divorce. It had happened to some of their friends. Sharon just had never expected it would happen to Jerry and her.

For the first time since she'd spoken her vows, Sharon seriously considered contacting an attorney. With a heavy heart, she sat down, opened the local phone directory, and ran her fingers down the long list of lawyers' names, shocked by how many claimed to specialize in divorce cases.

Divorce. What an ugly word it was, even uglier with a forty-year investment in what had once been a satisfying marriage. But something had to be done, Sharon realized. They couldn't continue the way they were, constantly at odds, working against one another. Their home had become a battlefield.

She stared at the door. Jerry had walked out without telling her where he was going or what time he'd return. Sharon had a general idea of how he kept himself occupied. He golfed a couple of days a week, played pinochle with his cronies, and coached basketball for a group of junior high kids.

She had her own life, her own interests, her own friends. It would be difficult, but she could learn to live without Jerry. She might as well be alone now—what they shared wasn't worthy of the word "marriage." Their love had become a contest of wills and frequent battles.

Depressed and unsure if she was doing the right thing, she closed the phone book. As strained as their relationship was, she loved her husband and was convinced that in his own way he loved her.

The house was empty and silent. In an effort to lift her mood, she put on a Christmas album, turning up the volume as she finished with the housework. The cheerful, happy music was infectious, and she had the sudden desire to go shopping. With Christmas less than two weeks away, she still had several things she wanted to buy for the twins. Generally Jerry went Christmas shopping with her, but she would go without him this year. Just as she was visiting Seth and the grandkids for the holidays alone.

The rest of the morning proved to be productive, and her spirits lifted considerably. She wished Maggie could join her, but her best friend had made other plans. Her arms loaded down with packages, Sharon headed for the restaurant in Nordstrom. Their Chinese chicken salad was one of her favorites.

A line had formed outside the restaurant, and as she stood awaiting her turn, Sharon's eyes wandered over the crowded room. By chance, she caught a glimpse of long red hair. Maggie. This was a pleasant surprise. She was just about to raise her hand and call out to her friend when she noticed Maggie wasn't dining alone. She was with Jerry.

Jerry.

The two were deeply involved in conversation, their heads close together.

Sharon felt as if someone had kicked her in the stomach. The classic scenario: her husband and her best friend. Blindly she whirled around, nearly colliding with a young mother pushing a stroller.

"I'm sorry," she murmured. "So sorry." Escaping before Maggie and Jerry saw her was of the utmost importance. She all but stumbled out of the store.

Inside the mall, she stood still and silent as her mind processed what her eyes had seen. People flowed past her like rushing water scooting around a large rock. All at once everything that had happened between her and her husband made sense.

Everything added up.

Jerry and Maggie.

Seth was busy tabulating a long list of numbers when the phone on his desk pealed loudly, breaking his concentration. He frowned and absently

reached for the receiver, irritated with the inter-
ruption. He wanted to get away from the office on
time that evening, and it had nothing to do with
meeting Reba. All right, so it had everything to do
with Reba.

"Hello," he muttered.

"Seth? I hope it's all right that I called you at the
office."

"Sharon?" The last person he expected to hear
from was his mother-in-law. "Is something
wrong?"

"No . . . everything's just wonderful, as always."

It didn't sound that way. Her thin voice sounded
fragile and unsure, which wasn't like her.

"I apologize for interrupting you at work, but I
needed . . ." She hesitated, and he could hear her
taking in a deep breath as though she needed to
calm herself before continuing. "It's about me
coming up for Christmas."

Christmas? She was calling him at work to con-
firm Christmas? Something was definitely up.

"I was wondering if you had any objection to
my coming a few days early."

"Sharon, you know you and Jerry are welcome
any time."

"Jerry won't be coming."

Seth couldn't believe his ears. Sharon was planning to visit on her own? That made no sense

whatsoever. It took him a moment to recover enough to respond. "What's happened to Jerry?"

"He's decided not to. I realize I'm arriving a few days earlier than what I mentioned and that . . . that you weren't anticipating my arrival until next week, but if it wouldn't be too much of a problem, I'd appreciate . . ." She paused when her voice wobbled to the point that he could barely understand her.

"Sharon? Are you all right?"

"Yes, of course. . . . What could possibly be wrong?"

"You tell me." Seth couldn't recall a time when his mother-in-law had been anything but the Rock of Gibraltar. After Pamela's accident she'd been the voice of reason in a world that had suddenly turned chaotic. Seth didn't know how he would have coped without her.

"I'm fine," she insisted, her words pleading with him to believe her.

Seth knew a lie when he heard one. "What time does your flight land?" he asked, reaching for a pad. "I'll pick you up at the airport."

"Pick me up . . . Yes, please, I'll need someone there." She gave him the flight number and the time.

Seth glanced at his watch. "But that's less than an hour from now."

"Yes . . . I know, I'm calling from the plane."

"The plane?" His echo revealed his shock.

"If I couldn't have stayed with you, I'd have found a hotel room. You'll be there, won't you, Seth?"

"Yes, of course. Don't worry about a thing. This will be a wonderful surprise for the twins." It would play havoc with his schedule, but that couldn't be helped. Something was drastically wrong, and after the way his mother-in-law had stepped in and helped him, he could hardly refuse her now.

Seth sat with his hand on the telephone receiver, uncertain whom to contact first, Reba or his housekeeper. Mrs. Merkle, he decided. She'd need to make up the guest bedroom. After he'd talked to her, he'd call Reba and tell her that he wouldn't be able to stop in after work the way he'd planned.

The vacation packages Reba had assembled for his review were only an excuse to see her again, Seth acknowledged freely. He was scheduled to meet with her after work before she went to church for Christmas practice with the kids. He'd seen her every night that week.

On Monday she'd gone Christmas shopping with him, and on Tuesday she'd been to the house for dinner. Mrs. Merkle had done herself proud with a fried chicken succulent enough to tempt the Colonel.

Jason answered when he rang the house. "Hi, Daddy."

"Hello, sweetheart, is Mrs. Merkle there?"

"Yup." He heard Jason drop the phone, the sound of the receiver clanging in his ear. He returned breathless a moment later. "Mrs. Miracle's real busy getting the extra bedroom all cleaned up," his son told him. "Who's coming?"

"Ask Mrs. Miracle," he suggested, frowning.

"Mr. Webster, I'm sorry to keep you waiting." The housekeeper came on the line, breathing hard.

"I'm calling to let you know I'll be picking up the children's grandmother at the airport this afternoon." He waited, half expecting his housekeeper to explain why Sharon was arriving a full week early and without Jerry. If anyone knew, it would be Mrs. Merkle. The woman apparently possessed some form of telepathy.

"Ah, I wondered."

"Sharon phoned the house?"

"No."

"Then how'd you know she was coming?"

"I didn't," she answered cheerfully. "It never hurts to have the spare room freshened up now and again. I had a few extra minutes this afternoon and decided to give it the once-over. How fortuitous in light of Mrs. Palmer's unexpected arrival."

"I don't know if it'd be a good idea to say anything to the twins just yet," Seth cautioned, wondering how much he should say. "My mother-in-law seems to be feeling a bit under the weather."

A short pause followed his announcement. "Do you need me to drop the kids off at practice at the church, then?"

Seth had forgotten all about that. "Yes, please, if it isn't too much of a problem."

"None at all. I'll stay and visit with the women's group as well and leave the house to you and Mrs. Palmer."

"I appreciate it," Seth murmured, trying to think if there was anything else he'd forgotten.

"I'll put two dinners to warm in the oven. Don't you worry, Mr. Webster, everything is going to work out just fine."

She spoke as if she knew more about the situation than Seth did himself. "Good," he muttered, hoping she was right. He didn't know what was wrong between Sharon and Jerry or if he was reading more into the matter than he should. Perhaps Jerry was ill. . . . No, that couldn't be it. Sharon would be the first one to stand at his side through any health problems. She'd sounded shaken to the core, rattled and shocked. Seth certainly hoped he knew what to say in order to help.

A glance at the wall clock told him he barely

had time to call Reba. He dialed and, while he waited for someone to answer, stood and slipped into his suit jacket.

"Reba, please," he said when her assistant answered.

"Seth?" She was on the line a moment later.

"I'm afraid I won't be able to see you tonight." As he said the words he realized he was more disappointed than he'd thought. Perhaps a bit of a break was for the best with them. It wouldn't take much to become accustomed to spending time with Reba each and every day. She was fast becoming addictive. A good kind of addictive. She made him feel again, dream again, hope again.

"Is something wrong?"

He explained the situation with Sharon, hoping Reba might have some insights to give him. "Mrs. Merkle is driving the kids to practice. I hope all Sharon needs is some time away."

"I'm sure you're right. And don't worry, I can give you the price quotes any time."

He wasn't worried, but he'd been looking forward to seeing her all day. Every now and again he found himself staring at the time, mentally tabulating how long it'd be before he'd be with her. He wanted to suggest she stop off at the house after church, but he couldn't. Not knowing what was happening between his in-laws was one thing, but Reba was sure to be physically and emotionally exhausted after her time with the kids. From what he understood she'd already received her share of bad news.

The baby Jesus had come down with a bad cold, and one of the shepherds had broken his leg. This was terrific news as far as Judd was concerned, since he preferred that role over being an angel.

"I've got to scoot," Seth told her with regret, and then, because this brief conversation wouldn't be enough to see him through until he could be with her again, he added, "Can I call you later?"

"Yes, please do. I hope everything's all right with your mother-in-law."

"I hope so, too."

The words echoed in his mind some forty minutes later as he was at Sea-Tac, waiting for Sharon to step out of the jetway. He knew the instant he saw her that something was drastically wrong. She looked straight past him, as pale as death, stricken and shell-shocked.

"Sharon." He stepped forward and took the carry-on bag out of her hand.

She looked at him as if seeing a stranger. "Seth. Thank you for coming. I can't tell you how much I appreciate it." She hugged him briefly, and he could tell she was struggling not to weep.

"It's good to see you." He studied her, wondering what had happened and how much he should urge her to tell him. "How much luggage do you have with you?" he asked, leading the way to the baggage claim area.

"Luggage . . . Oh, my, I don't think I brought any. I have my carry-on, but I don't seem to remember packing. . . . I suppose I should have. No, I did have a suitcase, but I left it at the house. Oh, dear."

"Don't worry, you can buy whatever you need."

Seth carried the conversation as they walked toward the parking garage. She answered him, but only when he asked a direct question, only when absolutely necessary.

Seth helped her into the car and stuck her carry-on bag on the backseat. As he set it on the cushion, the bag fell open, exposing one slipper and a novel. She'd come for the holidays, arriving ten days before Christmas, with one shoe? He closed his eyes, wishing he were better at handling this sort of situation. He wanted to help but feared he was grossly inadequate.

Once they were home, he placed Sharon's bag in the spare bedroom and took the two heaping dinner plates out of the oven. He set them on the table and sat across from her. He might as well have served Sharon mowed lawn for all the interest she showed in it.

"How's Jerry?" he ventured.

Her gaze narrowed, and tears moistened her eyes. "Fine, I suspect, just fine."

"He's in California?" No telling where Jerry was, with Sharon here.

"Yes." She looked away.

"Is there a problem with you two?" he asked next, gently exploring with questions the way a physician carefully examines a painful wound.

Sharon was saved from answering when the phone rang loudly and unexpectedly. Seth answered it with a certain reluctance.

"Hello."

"Is Sharon there?" his father-in-law asked without any preliminaries.

"Jerry?"

Sharon's eyes rounded. "Don't tell him I'm here."

"I want to talk to my wife," Jerry demanded, loudly enough to be heard on the other side of the room.

Seth's mother-in-law squared her shoulders and glared across the room, her pain-filled eyes as sharp as the polished edge of a sword. "You can tell Jerry Palmer that as of twelve-thirty this afternoon, I ceased being his wife."

Seth didn't want to be trapped as a go-between in this situation. "Perhaps it would be better if you talked to him yourself."

"No," she said with conviction. "I don't ever

plan to talk to that man again. Maggie's welcome to him."

"Maggie!" Jerry exploded on the other end of the line. "What is she talking about?"

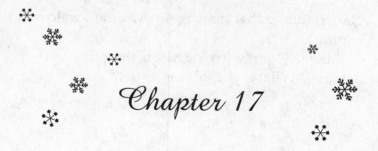

Chapter 17

*People don't care how much you know
until they know how much you care.*

—Mrs. Miracle

Reba lay on the carpet next to the fireplace, her head propped against a decorator pillow, her legs bent and crossed and the phone cradled against her ear. Christmas music played softly in the background.

"I wish I'd been able to see you tonight," Seth said, his voice low and seductive.

"I wish you could have, too." She knew he was worried about his mother-in-law. "How's Sharon?"

"Not good." The unexpected arrival appeared to mystify him. "Jerry phoned, and the two got into a shouting match with me holding the phone.

As best I can make out, Sharon saw him with another woman."

Reba bit into her lower lip, remembering the time she'd walked in and discovered her fiancé and her sister together. The shock, the horror, and the pain of betrayal by two people she loved had overwhelmed her until it was all she could do to remember to breathe.

"Jerry would never cheat on Sharon," Seth said confidently. "I'd bet my life on it. He's just not the type."

"Is Sharon the kind of woman who'd jump to conclusions?"

"No," Seth admitted, and she heard the reluctance in his voice. "There's got to be an explanation, but all she does is blast out at Jerry. The poor guy can barely get a word in edgewise."

"She has a right to be angry." Reba was all too familiar with the anger that followed the shock of such a discovery. She'd carried hers around with her for four long years. It burned as brightly now as it had the day she'd stumbled upon John and Vicki in bed together.

At first, when she'd been numb with shock, John had tried to reason with her, explain it all away with the sweetest of lies. Vicki's eyes had said it all. They'd been filled with horror and regret, but it was too late. Much too late for apologies or forgiveness.

"Of course she has a right to be angry, but she isn't even giving Jerry a chance to explain himself. It's like she wants to believe he'd purposely hurt her."

"Perhaps he already has." Reba's hand tightened around the telephone receiver. Eventually she'd need to tell Seth about her strained relationship with her family. In the years since her broken engagement she hadn't related the story often, but she felt Seth had a right to know this painful part of her past. She cared about him, wanted with all of her heart for this relationship to work. Wanted it enough to bare her soul. The irony of it was that she could tell him only over the phone. She needed the separation, the protection of distance, in order to relate the details of what had shaped the last few years of her life.

"Do you remember what I said about me avoiding my family?"

He hesitated, as if he instinctively knew the importance of what she was about to tell him. "I remember," he said.

She drew in a deep breath, anticipating the pain the story was sure to bring. "Four years ago . . . the same year Pamela died, I was engaged to an architectural student by the name of John Goddard. We'd met in college and fallen deeply in love. We planned our wedding; every detail was of the utmost importance. My older sister, Vicki, was to be my maid of honor. I've never spent a more wonderful summer. I'd graduated from college with a business degree, and was in love and about to be married. Then . . ." The sudden knot that tightened her throat made it impossible to continue.

"Reba?"

The gentle concern in his voice nearly undid her, and she struggled to hold back the emotion. "Vicki was jealous . . . I knew it, saw it. We'd always been competitive, but for the first time in our lives I had something she wanted. You see, she was always the one who blazed new territory. Grades, sports, and just about everything else. It was important to her to outdo me, to be first. Yet I was the one who was engaged, I was to be the first one married.

"She didn't love John, but she flirted with him, teased him, and asked him if he was sure he was marrying the right sister. I laughed it off. What else could I do but laugh?"

"What happened?" Seth asked with tender concern.

She braced herself and between gritted teeth said the words. Each one fell from her lips as hard as concrete. As hard and as unbending. "A week before the wedding I found my sister in bed with my fiancé. I'm convinced she planned it that way, that she wanted me to find them. She wanted to show me that she could have anything that was mine. Anything, including my soon-to-be husband." There couldn't be any other explanation. But Vicki's victory had turned out to be a shallow one. Reba recognized that the moment she saw her sister and the sick regret in her eyes. The remorse and honest grief.

"You broke off the engagement?" Seth asked, again with cautious tenderness, recognizing what it had cost her to peel back the wounds of the past.

"I canceled the wedding that very day, and I haven't spoken to my sister since." She tensed, waiting for him to tell her how foolish she was being, that by refusing to forgive her sister, she was only hurting herself. Well-meaning friends had said it before, and it was a theme her mother sang at every opportunity. No one understood that what Vicki had done was unforgivable.

"The ironic part of it is that my sister's married now to another man and has a child. The adored, lone grandchild." Hiding her bitterness was an impossible task. That her sister should find happiness while she lived alone rankled every time she allowed her mind to dwell on it.

"In other words, your sister came away from all this smelling like a rose."

Her eyes flew open. Seth knew. Seth understood. "Yes," she whispered, grateful that he appreciated the irony of her situation.

"Meanwhile you broke off the wedding at the

last minute and everyone was left to speculate what had happened. That speculation made it seem that the fault was with you. You were fickle, didn't know what you wanted, were afraid of commitment, that sort of thing. You were the one who bore the shame."

"Yes." She had to restrain herself to keep from shouting. The days and weeks following the canceled wedding were a nightmarish blur in her mind. In order to save himself from embarrassment, John had told their friends a story that didn't vaguely resemble the truth.

In an effort to escape the probing questions and the curious stares, Reba had escaped to the beach, telling no one where she was. When she'd returned she'd invested her time and energy in establishing her travel agency. Some claimed that her success in the highly competitive travel industry was phenomenal. She wouldn't discount her efforts or the long hours she'd invested, but the drive, the urge to succeed, could be credited to John and Vicki's treachery and her need to escape the memory of their betrayal.

"Aren't you going to tell me how foolish I am to leave this matter between my sister and me unresolved?" Reba challenged. Eventually Seth would comment on it, and she'd rather have it out in the open. "People say leaving the matter this way is like not treating an open, festering wound."

"Have you ever had a boil?" he asked, baffling her by changing the subject.

"No."

"I did as a kid, twice. They're ugly things, painful and full of pus. Eventually they come to a head. My mother put hot compresses on the one on my arm, but the other . . . well, it was in an area I didn't want my mother looking at." He chuckled softly. "I imagine this matter with your sister is something like an emotional boil. Eventually it'll come to a head, and it'll hurt like crazy, but once the poison's out of your system, you'll heal, but not until you're ready."

"I don't ever plan on speaking to her again."

"I didn't want to deal with the boil, either. You can delay it, ignore it as long as you want, but it isn't going to go away. If you want to live with it, well, that's your decision. When the time's right to set matters straight with your sister, you'll know it."

How wise Seth was, and understanding.

"I wish I was with you right now," he murmured.

She did, too, although she'd opted to explain the situation over the phone. She needed him, and for a woman who'd insulated her life against needing anyone, this was a moment of truth. She did need Seth. Needed him in ways she was only beginning to understand.

"You've been badly hurt. Betrayed by your own flesh and blood, and by the man you were ready to commit your life to. You have a right to your anger, a right to your pain."

"No one understood that." She had to whisper the words because she feared if she spoke normally, her voice wouldn't hold. "My family seemed to think I was better off without John."

"But you loved him."

"Yes. I knew what they said was true, but that didn't make me hurt any less." Her voice shook, but she managed to keep the tears at bay.

"Of course it didn't."

"What happened afterward is beyond comprehension," she said. "That's what I find so crazy. No one faulted Vicki. My parents completely absolved her from any wrongdoing. Because she was sorry, I was supposed to look the other way and pretend this was nothing out of the ordinary. She kept telling me she never meant for it to happen. She sobbed and cried and pleaded with me to forgive her, and I couldn't. The irony is I felt nothing. Not hate, not right away. That came later. I just looked at her, unable to believe that she was capable of anything that ugly, that deceitful."

"I wish I could put my arms around you and take away the hurt," Seth said with such tenderness that she had to fight back the emotion.

"I wish you could, too."

"Close your eyes and pretend I am. Pretend your head's on my shoulder and my arms are wrapped around you."

She shut her eyes and did as he instructed. Caught in the fantasy, she could almost feel his fragrant breath close to her ear. Feel the comfort of his hands as he ran them up and down her spine. Feel the sweet pressure of his lips molding against hers, the taste of his tongue as he claimed her mouth and drove away the demons of the past.

"I think I could love you, Seth Webster." Reba didn't realize what she'd said until she heard the husky words leave her lips. She cringed at revealing her own vulnerability and tilted her head toward the ceiling.

"I'm beginning to think the same thing about you, Reba Maxwell. It's as if we're two of a kind, a matched set."

The line hummed with awareness. Reba would have given anything to actually be in his arms just then. "Thank you for not lecturing me about my relationship with my sister."

"You understood why I gave up playing the piano," Seth reminded her. "Plenty of people have given me grief over that."

"We've both been hurt," she said, realizing that it was this knowledge of pain that had drawn them to each other. They had come together like magnets, two of the world's walking wounded.

They talked for an hour longer, the barriers down, freely and without reserve, laughing and crying together. They shared secrets and dreams, and when she hung up, Reba had rarely felt closer to anyone, male or female.

A half hour later she crawled into bed. The sheets felt cool and crisp against her heated skin. She stretched out her arm and ran it along the wide-open space beside her. She'd found him. The man who would return to her everything that she'd lost. Her sanity, her pride, her dreams. Utterly content for the first time since her canceled wedding, she closed her eyes.

Beyond a doubt she realized that one day she would sleep with Seth, would share her bed and her life with this man who understood her pain.

Jerry Palmer paced the house like a caged gorilla, walking from one empty room to the next. He wasn't sure what he sought, but whatever it was repeatedly escaped him.

Movement seemed only to agitate him further, but sitting and doing nothing was intolerable.

He'd been married to Sharon for forty years and overnight she had become a stranger to him. Without rhyme or reason his loving wife had turned into a hotheaded feminist. It was enough to drive a man to drink.

At first he'd assumed the brusque personality changes in his wife were due to a hormonal imbalance. A few years back she'd had every window in the house open and was fanning herself like crazy because of one of her hot flashes. He'd been forced to don his coat in the middle of his own house while she sweated until her clothes were damp enough to wring out.

She'd visited her doctor soon afterward, and there hadn't been any more repeats of that. Unfortunately whatever the doctor had given her hadn't done anything to improve her waspish nature. Jerry had gotten into the habit of checking her prescription. She appeared to be taking the tablets regularly, not that it'd done much good.

For years Jerry had looked forward to retirement. He'd worked all his life for a chance to golf every day if he wanted. At first he'd thought that was exactly what he'd do, but to his surprise he'd soon grown tired of traipsing over the greens. Oh, it was good sport, and he enjoyed a couple of rounds a week, but more than that and the sport lost its appeal.

Playing cards was a good pastime, as was working with thirteen- and fourteen-year-olds on the basketball court, but all in all, retirement wasn't what it was touted to be. He found himself restless and antsy and fighting with his wife to the point where she'd walked out on him and left her suitcase behind. She must have been upset to have taken off without it.

He sat and rubbed a hand across his eyes. Maggie claimed he'd been harsh and unreasonable with Sharon about visiting the grandkids over the holidays. His jaw tensed as he recalled the way she'd gone against his wishes and ordered the airline tickets. It used to be that Sharon valued his opinion and readily accepted his decisions. No more. If she didn't like what he had to say, she did as she pleased. Exactly what kind of wife ignored her husband's decisions? *But then,* a small voice nagged at the back of his mind, *how often have you ignored hers?*

Fine, Sharon could believe what she wanted about him and Maggie, he decided.

Unable to sit with his thoughts, he reached for the television controller and turned on the television, then just as abruptly turned it off again. He was in no mood to be entertained. Before he knew it, he was on his feet again.

Holding the refrigerator door open, he stared inside at the contents. This wouldn't be the first night he'd cooked his own dinner. He reached for the bread and pulled a jar of peanut butter from the shelf. He'd never thought he'd see the day that he'd be married and responsible for cooking his own meals. But then he'd never expected to be married and sleeping alone, either. It wasn't right. It just wasn't right.

He slapped the two pieces of bread together and was about to take the first bite when he noticed Sharon's prescription bottle on the windowsill. In addition to her suitcase, she'd apparently forgotten to take her pills with her to Seattle.

He scratched the side of his head. There was only one thing to do.

He'd deliver them himself.

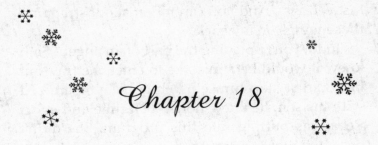

Chapter 18

The mighty oak tree was once a little nut that held its ground.

—Mrs. Miracle

"I'm not wearing any dress," Judd insisted, crossing his arms and tilting his chin at a stubborn angle. Seth recognized that look all too well and was pleased his mother-in-law was the one dealing with his son's bullheadedness.

"It's not a dress," Sharon returned calmly. "It's your costume for the Christmas pageant." After a good night's sleep, she was almost herself once again. She hadn't offered any explanations as to what had happened between her and Jerry, and Seth hadn't pressured her.

"It's a dress." Judd left no room for doubt as to

his feelings. "And you can forget about strapping those wings on my back."

"Judd, you're playing the part of an angel." Seth knew it would be a mistake to enter the fray, but he couldn't stop himself. While he sympathized with his son, he knew how much time and effort Reba was putting into this program. She didn't need any more problems.

"I want to be a soldier," Judd announced, and raised his arms the way he'd seen the older boys do when carrying the painted cardboard shields. "They won't let me because I'm only in the first grade."

"You'll get your turn at being a soldier," Seth assured him.

"Perhaps we could make the angel costume something other than white," Sharon suggested, stepping back from the chair. Judd and Jason stood on the seats, both wearing old white sheets that had been fashioned into—Seth hated to admit it—dresses.

"The shepherds get to wear bathrobes," Jason muttered, his head drooping. "Am I too young to be a shepherd, too?"

"Maybe next year," Seth said.

"Aaron Greenburg broke his leg, and I thought that Miss Maxwell might give me the part and everything, seeing that you like to look at her in church and kiss her under the mistletoe."

Seth noticed the way his mother-in-law diverted her attention to him. He swallowed uncomfortably and ignored the comment, hoping that Sharon would as well. He planned to tell the kids' grandmother about Reba, but he'd wanted to do it in his own time.

"Miss Maxwell's got short curly hair," Judd added for his grandmother's benefit. This fact seemed to have some significance to the first-grader.

Seth wasn't sure how Sharon would feel about him dating someone else. She'd encouraged him to do so, but saying it was one thing and introducing her to the woman who might one day assume her daughter's role in his and the children's lives was another.

"Miss Maxwell?" Sharon's question was directed at Seth.

"A friend," he said, making light of the relationship. He couldn't very well admit that she occupied every waking thought and had from the moment he'd walked into the travel agency.

"She's our teacher at church," Jason explained, then frowned. "Sort of teacher."

"Reba's directing the Christmas pageant," Seth explained, wishing now that he'd remained in the living room. He should have known that the conversation would soon work its way to Reba. The kids talked about her constantly.

"What's this business about her having short hair?" Sharon asked.

Again it was Jason who took it upon himself to explain. "Dad and Reba went out to dinner, and Mrs. Miracle was watching us."

"She's better than any baby-sitter we ever had 'cause she lets us do fun things," Judd added.

Jason glared at his brother. "I was the one telling this."

"All right, all right." His twin looked greatly put-upon. It was one thing to have to wear a white dress and another to let his brother do his talking for him.

"That was when Mrs. Miracle asked us what we thought about having a new mother. She said Daddy might marry again and wondered what Judd and I thought."

"I think it'd be great. I want a mother who lives on earth and not just in heaven," Judd added, and dared his brother to fault him for interrupting.

"I don't remember Mommy very well," Jason said sadly. "Judd says he does, but I don't."

"She used to sing to us," Judd insisted.

Seth doubted that either child could possibly remember Pamela. They'd both been so young.

"She used to come and sing to us at night when everything was dark and quiet."

"I don't remember, I don't remember," Jason repeated wistfully. "I want to remember, but I don't."

Seth noticed how Sharon averted her eyes as the children talked about their mother. This was hard for her, he knew, because it was difficult for him to hear his twins talk about their dead mother.

"I got to thinking about what a new mommy would look like," Judd added, picking up the tale. "So I drew her picture."

"And Judd's picture looks like Miss Maxwell," Jason finished triumphantly.

"That's wonderful," Sharon said, but Seth noticed that her voice trembled slightly. She walked over to the other side of the kitchen and picked up the aluminum-covered wings. A silver garland-wrapped halo was attached, rising from the back side of the wings and held into place with a bent hanger. Seth had to give Sharon credit, she'd done a good job.

"Dad." Jason looked to his father for support, his eyes large and imploring. "You aren't going to make me wear wings and a halo, are you?"

"Son, the show couldn't go on without you. Being an angel is an important role."

"The guys are going to make stupid jokes." Judd tucked his chin against his chest and pouted. "It's bad enough that I've got to wear a dress." He spread out the material at the hips, making sure Seth recognized the sacrifice he was already making. "But wings and a halo?"

Seth had to admit that the twins weren't the ones he would have chosen for the parts, given their bent toward the mischievous, but it was too late to quibble now. The pageant was only a little more than a week away.

"Mrs. Miracle said that not all angels have wings," Judd added on a near frantic note.

"Really?" Seth didn't appreciate the housekeeper taking his son's side in this issue.

"It's true," Jason added. "Mrs. Miracle said that some angels look like ordinary people, with regular jobs and everything. Some even come disguised as regular people. God sends them down to earth when He has a special task that needs careful handling."

"Complicated circum ... circumstances and such," Judd said, sounding very adult for his tender years.

"It seems to me that Mrs. Miracle is a wise woman," Sharon murmured.

"She cooks real good, too," Jason said, and then whispered just loudly enough for Seth to hear, "Lots better than Dad. I was worried about what was going to happen to us before Mrs. Miracle arrived. We might have starved."

As if hearing her name, the housekeeper strolled into the kitchen with a fresh batch of folded towels.

"Isn't that right, Mrs. Miracle?" Judd asked, all

but leaping down from the chair and grabbing hold of the portly woman.

"What?" the housekeeper asked, taken aback by the frontal attack.

"What you said about some angels not wearing wings. My dad says I have to put them on for the Christmas pageant."

"Well," she murmured thoughtfully, "while it's true enough some angels don't need wings, I wonder how the church audience would know exactly what you were without them. It's an unfortunate truth that some narrow-minded people wouldn't recognize an angel without something to flap behind them."

"They make me look like a girl," Judd insisted.

"Don't let the Archangel Michael hear you talk like that," Mrs. Merkle said with great dignity. "Why, he's one of the mightiest warriors of heaven."

"You mean angels can be soldiers, too?"

"The fiercest kind of all."

"It's true," Seth added, wishing he'd thought of that himself.

"Michael carries a sword of truth with him at all times. And from what I understand, he isn't afraid of using it, either."

"Then so will I," Judd said, satisfied. "I'll be a warrior angel. And if anyone calls me a sissy, they better watch out, 'cause I'll knock them down with the sword of truth." He thrust his imaginary weapon forward, leaping down from the chair, prepared to wage battle. Jason's actions pantomimed his brother's.

"As I recall the Christmas story, the shepherds guarding their sheep were afraid of the angels," Sharon reminded him.

" 'Fear not,' " Jason shouted his memorized line, " 'for we come with news of great joy.' "

" 'For unto you this night is born a Savior,' " Judd added, and for good measure growled.

"This is what I love about Christmas," Sharon said, laughing for the first time since her arrival. "The season of love and goodwill toward all mankind."

"I'm not going to hurt anyone," Judd promised, "I just want to scare people. No one told us angels could be soldiers." He straightened and stood a little taller. "How come I didn't know about this Michael dude before now?"

"We just weren't thinking, son."

Judd yanked the costume over his head and handed it to his grandmother. "I'll wear the wings and the halo, as long as I can carry a sword, too."

Seth grinned. "I'm sure that can be arranged." He shared a smile with his mother-in-law.

"It seems to me it's time for you two to head toward bed," Mrs. Merkle said, tapping the face of her watch.

"Already?"

"Already." She had a no-nonsense manner about her that his children rarely questioned.

It seemed to take forever to get the kids down, although the mission was accomplished in less than a half hour. Judd talked nonstop about being a warrior angel, and Jason kept repeating his lines for the program, saying them with greater and greater conviction.

Once the two were asleep, Seth poured himself a cup of coffee. This was the first time he'd had a chance to speak to Sharon without interruptions. He knew she was eager to hear about Reba, and he had a few questions of his own. Clearly things had gone drastically wrong between her and Jerry.

"Want some?" he asked, automatically filling a mug for her. He carried both to the table and took the seat across from his mother-in-law.

"You're dating?"

Sharon never had been one to hedge when she wanted to know something.

"We haven't known each other long," he said, wanting to make light of his involvement with Reba.

"It's this woman the children mentioned?"

"Reba," he said. "She owns a travel agency, and stepped in at the last minute and took over coordinating the Christmas program."

"The children certainly seem to like her."

"They do." He didn't add that his own feelings for Reba grew stronger by the day.

"I was the one who used to sing to the children at night," Sharon whispered, a faraway look in her eye. "It was a song I once sang to Pamela, an old German lullaby my mother taught me. When the twins first came to live with Jerry and me I'd sit in their room at night with the lights off." She paused and nibbled on her lower lip. "Singing that familiar song helped me accept that my daughter was forever gone. Having the children with me gave me purpose again. Judd remembers. He was so young, but he remembers."

Seth knew this was difficult for Sharon. He reached across the table and squeezed her hand. "Pamela will always be their mother."

"I know," she said bravely. "I don't begrudge you happiness, Seth."

"I didn't think for a moment that you did."

Her gaze wandered down the hallway toward the bedrooms. "Judd and Jason appear to have adjusted well."

"We've had our moments." He didn't elaborate, but more than once he'd been tempted to reach for the phone and call Sharon. It had taken every bit of restraint he possessed not to plead with her to take over, to admit that he couldn't handle the kids on his own. His lowest point had been just before Mrs. Miracle arrived. Mrs. Miracle, the kids had him doing it now. Mrs. Merkle.

"Mrs. Merkle's a wonder."

Seth couldn't agree with her more. "It's good to see you again, Sharon."

She looked away. "But you're wondering what I'm doing here now. I wasn't scheduled to arrive until next week."

"The thought had crossed my mind," he admitted, thinking of last night's angry phone call.

"Jerry and I—"

The doorbell interrupted her, and she glanced over her shoulder.

"I'm not expecting anyone." It was after nine, and he doubted that the paperboy would be collecting this late.

While he answered the door, Sharon stood and walked over to the refrigerator to take out the milk.

"Sorry," he said on his way to the door. "I forgot you like your coffee with cream."

"No problem." She looked much better today, he mused. Her color was back, and some of the weariness had left her eyes.

He checked the peephole and then, astonished, hurriedly opened the door for his father-in-law. "Jerry," he said, trying to hide his shock, "this is a pleasant surprise."

He heard the crash behind him and whirled around to find the coffee mug shattered across the kitchen floor and Sharon looking at her husband as if viewing a ghost.

Chapter 19

Too many people offer God prayers
with claw marks all over them.

—Mrs. Miracle

S haron couldn't have been more surprised if Elvis himself had showed up at the front door. Certainly the last person she'd expected to see was her own husband. She'd have thought he'd rather pluck chickens than chase after her. Not that he was exactly chasing her.

They stood a room apart, staring at one another, each waiting for the other to speak first. Neither seemed willing to be the first to breach the gap.

"I came to talk to my wife," Jerry announced stiffly to Seth.

"Talk . . . fine. I'm sure you two would like some privacy."

"That won't be necessary," Sharon said, preferring that her son-in-law stay in the room. If Jerry assumed they could neatly sweep everything under the carpet, he'd made a wasted trip.

"I didn't come all this way to be left standing on the porch twiddling my thumbs," Jerry argued.

To Sharon's way of thinking, that was exactly where he deserved to be. The man had put her through hell. By the time she'd arrived in Seattle she could barely function emotionally. Her husband and her best friend!

"Why don't you two sit down here in the living room and sort matters out," Seth suggested, and gestured toward the sofa. "I'll clean up the spilled coffee and give you some space—I mean, peace."

Jerry didn't wait for Sharon to agree, but moved from the entry into the living room, hauling two suitcases with him. She was grateful to see him, if for no other reason than to have the clothes he'd brought along.

"Sharon?" Jerry waited for her.

It was either cause a scene or accept the only civil option available to her. Reluctantly she walked into the other room, sitting as far away from Jerry as possible.

The silence was thick and uncomfortable. She'd

be damned before she'd speak first. An eternity passed, and the only sound came from Seth in the kitchen; soon that faded and disappeared.

"You forgot your medication," Jerry said, and removed the brown drugstore bottle from his jacket pocket.

She supposed she should be grateful that he didn't mention her luggage.

"I thought you might need your hormones."

She didn't know what it was that concerned Jerry about her pills. It was almost as though he feared she'd wake up with a beard one morning if she forgot to take them.

"Thank you," she said, attempting to remain courteous without revealing how absolutely delighted she was to see him. She didn't want to be, but she couldn't keep her heart from banging against her chest. For forty years she'd loved this man, and despite their many differences she couldn't stop.

That made her decision to divorce him all the more difficult, all the more painful. They'd grown apart and weren't the same people any longer.

"About me and Maggie," Jerry said, the words falling awkwardly from his lips. "It's not what you . . . it's not the way it looked."

Sharon bided her time. She'd figured that out for herself. It'd taken her the better part of two days, but she knew in the deepest part of her soul that Jerry wouldn't cheat on her. Furthermore, she trusted Maggie, who was happily married.

"We'd been having so many problems lately," Jerry said, and cleared his throat. "I asked Maggie's opinion."

"About what?"

His face reddened slightly. "I thought you might need the dosage on your hormones upped or something."

"You think what?"

"She understands you better than I do," he shouted, his eyes boring into her accusingly. "I can't ever talk to you anymore. I have to go to your friends to find out what you're thinking. For all intents and purposes we're living separate lives, and doing it in the same house. Something's got to change."

"I couldn't agree with you more." Six months ago she would never have believed she and Jerry would consider such a drastic measure as divorce, but it appeared to be the only feasible solution to their troubles.

Jerry lowered his head and seemed to find it necessary to clean beneath his fingernails. He leveled his gaze at her and asked, "You believe me about Maggie, don't you?"

Once her head had cleared, she'd suspected it was innocent. Perhaps because she so desperately wanted to believe her husband and her best friend wouldn't betray her.

Jerry's eyes bored holes into her, silently pleading with her to believe him. Fool that she was, she did. "I know."

"If you knew that, then why'd you run off without so much as leaving me a note? I didn't know what happened to you." His words were full of anger and accusation. "Edna was the one who said she saw you get in a taxi."

Edna, the neighborhood busybody. Her tongue must really be wagging now.

How it must have hurt Jerry's pride to seek out their nosy neighbor for information. To her credit, Sharon hadn't purposely gone without leaving him a note. She regretted that, but a note wasn't the only thing she'd forgotten.

"It was a taxi driver who told me he'd taken you to the airport," Jerry added. "From there it wasn't difficult to figure out where you'd gone. What was I to think? I come home to an empty house with no note, only to discover from the neighbor that you'd left me."

"I want a divorce." Some might fault her timing, but it needed to be said, and the sooner the better.

Jerry looked as if she'd pulled out a handgun, aimed, and fired. He opened his mouth and closed it twice. "A divorce?" he echoed, exhaling sharply. "You want a divorce."

"Don't try to tell me this is a surprise. What did you think? That I enjoy living with this constant tension, with this continual battle of wills? We're both miserable, and I can see no reason to continue with this farce of a marriage."

He blinked as if he couldn't believe what he was hearing.

Sharon realized her words had been abrupt and harsh. "You don't know how much this saddens me, Jerry," she whispered, lowering her gaze to her clenched hands. "It isn't that I blame you or even myself, but we aren't the same people we used to be. Things change. People change."

"If this has to do with my having lunch with Maggie . . ."

"It doesn't," she assured him, realizing he was looking for something to pinpoint.

"That's not it?" He furrowed his brow. "But I thought, I mean, I realize it must have been a shock . . ."

"We haven't made love in months." She laughed shortly, a bit hysterically. "We don't even sleep together any longer. You cook your meals, I cook mine." As far as she could see, it was only a matter of time before he reached the same conclusion. "We seem to be constantly at odds. It isn't that you've done anything wrong, or that I haven't been a good wife."

"You want this, Sharon?"

She didn't. Had never dreamed that this calamity would befall them. She'd assumed their marriage was safe. They'd lived, loved, and grieved together, but somewhere along the way they'd stopped trying, stopped communicating. He had an entire life that had nothing to do with her, and the same applied to her.

That this would happen to them now was one of life's cruel jokes; only she wasn't laughing, and neither was Jerry. She hadn't reached the decision lightly. This was quite possibly the most difficult thing she'd ever done, with the exception of burying her daughter.

"I know you've tried to make this work," she said, avoiding his question. "So have I."

"Is a divorce what you want?" he asked again, a bit louder.

She remembered the way her heart had leapt when she saw that he'd come for her, and she buried that small shred of joy in the deepest part of her soul.

"Do you?" he pressed, his gaze holding hers.

"Yes," she whispered brokenly.

Jerry sagged against the back of the chair. "I never thought this would happen to us."

"Me either," she admitted sadly.

"Do you have an attorney yet?"

She shook her head. "I want this to be as amicable as possible."

He nodded. "It'll take work on both our parts."

It hurt that he was so damned agreeable. While
it was true she was the one who'd asked for the
divorce, she'd hoped he'd fight to save their marriage. Her pride would have preferred for him to
put up some resistance, even if it was only token.
After a forty-year investment one would think
he'd want to try harder.

At first she'd prayed he wouldn't. It would be
easier on both of them if he accepted her decision
calmly. The reality of that was quite different. Sharon was grateful she was seated. His fine-if-this-is-
what-you-want attitude left her feeling as if the
rug had been pulled out from under her. Her emotions spiraled downward, crashing, taking what
remained of her pride.

"We had some good years." If he wouldn't mention those, she would.

"Some great years and some not so great."

She wondered if he was remembering the year
Pamela had died, or if his mind was dwelling on
the last twelve months, when they didn't seem to
have anything in common any longer.

"Do you want to break the news to the kids
now?" Jerry asked.

He made it sound as though they should run to the phone and call their sons and announce it with great ceremony. Sharon dreaded telling her sons more than she did Jerry. They were both responsible adults, but it would hit them hard, rock their foundation, and she'd have liked to spare them that.

"I'd prefer to wait until after Christmas," she said, hoping he was agreeable to that. She could see no reason to ruin everyone else's holiday.

He nodded. "All right, if that's what you want."

After weeks of not having a civil word to say to her, he'd become amicable overnight. She bit her tongue to keep from saying so.

"It's going to come as something of a shock to Clay and Neal," her husband murmured, saying what she'd been thinking moments earlier.

Although she'd been the one to request the divorce, it came as a shock to her as well.

A terrible sadness settled over her. The last time she'd experienced anything this heavy, this debilitating, had been shortly after the news of Pamela's car accident. As it had then, it felt now as if her heart would never heal.

"Would you mind terribly if I stayed and spent Christmas with Seth and the twins?" Before she could answer, he rushed to add as if he needed to convince her, "Seeing that I'm already here and all."

The tightness in her throat made it difficult to answer with words, so she nodded.

"We can get along that long, can't we?"

"I'm sure we can," Sharon managed. "If we're both on our best behavior."

The silence was back, less strained this time. Having reached an agreement, even one that set the terms of the dissolution of their marriage, produced a certain accord. The irony of it didn't escape Sharon.

With some hesitation Seth stepped into the room and glanced from one to the other. "Is everything okay between you two, or do you need more time?"

"Everything's fine," Jerry lied, answering for them both. Sharon was grateful he did; she wasn't sure she could have sounded nearly as convincing.

"You'll be staying on for the holidays, then?" Seth directed the question to Jerry.

"If it's not a problem?"

"None. It'll be good to have you."

Unable to deal with the small talk, Sharon stood abruptly. "I've had a full day. I hope you'll both excuse me." She faked a yawn. "I can't believe how tired I am."

"Sure, honey," Jerry said, sounding as if there weren't a thing wrong with the world.

"By all means, Sharon," Seth added. "Thanks for all your help with the twins' costumes."

"It was a pleasure."

"Sit down," Jerry invited his son-in-law, "and tell me how everything's going with you and the kids."

Sharon managed a smile as she slipped past her son-in-law and down the hallway to the guest bedroom. The voices of the two men faded as she closed the bedroom door.

Jerry was by far the better actor. It helped that Seth and her husband were such good friends. The two could easily talk the night away.

Sharon slumped onto the side of the mattress. Her lower lip trembled and she bit into it hard, until she sampled the sweet taste and knew she'd drawn blood. With her eyes closed she rocked gently, her arms cradling her stomach. She felt alone and afraid. The future without Jerry frightened her almost as much as the future with him.

A divorce was what she wanted, what she'd asked for. She should be pleased that Jerry had been so willing, so agreeable. He could have made it difficult, but he too seemed to want out of a marriage that had suddenly turned sour.

Sharon couldn't blame him. Even when they tried to make the marriage work, they were both miserable. He had his own ideas of what their lives should be like now that he'd retired, and she had hers. How sad that their visions no longer matched.

How sad indeed.

Brushing the hair from her face, she gathered a reserved measure of energy and undressed. The nightdress Mrs. Merkle had loaned her was three sizes too large. The flannel gown hung on her like an empty potato sack. It was by far the most unflattering piece of apparel she'd ever worn.

With her thoughts tangled and dark, she removed her makeup and cleaned her teeth, then sat up in bed, reading. When someone knocked politely, her gaze flew to the door.

"Yes?"

Jerry stood in the doorway, a suitcase in each hand. "Seth has to be in the office early tomorrow morning," he said, walking into the room. He closed the door, and the latch clicked softly as it connected.

Sharon's reading glasses slid down the bridge of her nose. Surely Jerry didn't intend to sleep with her. She opened her mouth to say as much when she realized that he had no choice. Consequently neither did she.

Jerry must have read the look in her eyes because he said, "We slept together for nearly forty years. I imagine we can do so for a couple more weeks, don't you?"

"I'm sure we can," she answered crisply.

"In fact, I think we should make the most of this time."

She didn't like the implication and tugged the blankets more closely around her breasts. "How do you mean?"

He grinned as if he found her actions amusing. "With Judd and Jason. It'll probably be the last time we'll spend time with them together."

"You're right." That too was a sad realization. The twins were the glue that had held them together for the last four years. Neither of them had realized it at the time, but the truth couldn't be ignored in light of what had happened since the children had gone back to live with their father.

Jerry sat on the edge of the bed, his weight causing the mattress to dip. His back was to her. "I want you to know that I'll make everything as financially comfortable for you as I can."

"I know you will," she whispered.

"You've been a good wife to me, Sharon. I can't tell you how sorry I am that it has to end like this."

If this was the time for confessions, she had a few of her own. "I apologize for the childish way I behaved the last few weeks."

"Yeah, well, you weren't the only one." He unbuttoned his shirt. "With effort we should be able to make it through the holidays without embarrassing ourselves."

"We should," she agreed. She closed her novel and set it aside, removed her glasses, and lay down, her hands clenching the blanket. Her eyes focused on the ceiling while Jerry undressed and pulled back the covers. She held her breath as he slipped between the sheets. A moment later the room went dark.

"Good night, Sharon."

"Good night."

Jerry rolled onto his side. Sharon lay, her head cradled by the thick feather pillow, and stared sightlessly into the darkness.

This was quite possibly the most tragic moment of her life.

Within moments her husband snored softly at her side.

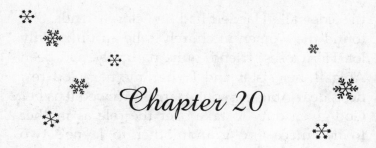

Chapter 20

The tongue must be heavy indeed,
for so few people can hold it.

—Mrs. Miracle

*H*arriett Foster decided she didn't see near enough of her niece. Jayne did try, but between work and children, the young mother simply didn't have time for extended family. The only way to visit with Jayne and her household was to stop off unexpectedly and unannounced. With anyone else, she would have considered such behavior the height of bad manners, but this was family. One had a responsibility to family, however burdensome.

Early Saturday afternoon, Harriett parked her car outside Jayne's house and made her way up the sidewalk. Harriett had few close friends. She found the women in church to be an unfriendly lot. Her closest friend, quite naturally, had been Abigail, her sister and Jayne's mother. God rest dear, dear Abigail's soul. Harriett viewed it as her God-given duty to take over the role as mother to her niece and grandmother to Jayne's two children. It was the way Abigail would have wanted it.

She pressed the doorbell, and when there wasn't an immediate response she tried again, and then a third time. Finally she walked over to the window. Jayne's car was in the driveway—she had to be in the house somewhere.

Harriet placed her hand against the glass to kill the glare and peered inside. She could see nothing.

Just when she was prepared to leave, the front door opened.

"Hello, Aunt Harriett."

"Jayne, my dear, I was about to give up on you. I'm so pleased I didn't."

"I . . . I was in the laundry room."

"You probably didn't hear the doorbell over the dryer," Harriett said, which explained why her niece hadn't answered the door right away. "We haven't had much of a chance to talk lately, and I thought I'd stop in for tea."

"Tea," Jayne repeated slowly. "Well, actually the

girls haven't been feeling well. A touch of the flu. They're both napping. It's unusual to get them both down at the same time, and I was hoping—"

"Then I couldn't have come at a more opportune time." She stepped past Jayne and moved directly into the house.

If she sensed any hesitation in her niece, the condition of the house explained everything. The living room carpet was littered with toys. The Christmas tree leaned to one side, and the decorations looked to be mostly handmade, ones the children had crafted in school, which made the scrawny tree even more unattractive. Her own Christmas tree was a showpiece. The decorations had been carefully collected over the years and were of the finest quality.

Harriett's home had never been this untidy. Poor Jayne was embarrassed, as well she should be. There was no excuse for such a mess. A clean home was akin to godliness. Although she couldn't recall the precise Bible verse, she was sure that was scriptural.

"I'll make the tea," Harriett announced when Jayne hesitated. By all that was right, she should say something to her niece about the condition of her home; but Jayne had mentioned the girls weren't feeling well. With a job outside the home, the poor woman should be given a bit of slack.

Harriett wasn't often indulgent, but she was sure

God would be equally charitable with her niece. If she weren't already so involved with her many efforts at the church, she would offer to come help Jayne with the household chores. But one could take on only so much.

"I imagine you'll want me over for Christmas dinner again this year," Harriett said as she filled the teapot with hot water.

"Actually, Steve's family asked us to dinner."

"Oh." That left Harriett with several choices.

"You'd be welcome to join us," Jayne offered.

Harriett squared her shoulders. "Thank you, no. I'd be uncomfortable with a group of strangers on Christmas. I suppose I can change my plans and spend Christmas Eve with you and the children. We can open gifts then. Yes, that's what we'll do. Following the program Christmas Eve, we'll return to the house and the girls can open their gifts."

Jayne cleared the breakfast dishes from the table. "Ah . . . I'll need to check with Steve, but I think it should be all right."

"Of course it'll be all right. I'm your aunt." She carried the steeping tea to the table. Jayne brought down two delicate cups and pulled out a chair.

Harriett sighed as she settled across from her niece. Frankly it felt good to sit down. She'd been on her feet most of the day and was scheduled to meet with Reba Maxwell later in the afternoon to practice for the Christmas program.

"Well," Harriett said with a belabored sigh, "I have a number of concerns on my mind that I've made a matter of prayer."

"You mean about the holidays?"

"Some," Harriett answered, and stirred sugar into her tea. This issue with Ruth Darling and the new man at church was a delicate one, and she'd decided to test the waters with her niece. "You realize I'm playing the piano for the Christmas program."

"Yes, it's very generous of you."

"It is, but then I don't see that I had much choice," Harriett muttered, pinching her lips closed. "No one else seemed willing to step forward. It was the least I could do. No one seems to appreciate that if it wasn't for me, the program would have been canceled this year."

"You?"

"Why, yes," Harriett said, holding Jayne's gaze. "I was the only one of the women in the Martha and Mary Circle with the gumption to come up with someone who could take over the project. While it's true, I suggested you as the leader, a natural choice, you being related to me and all. You've got your mother's and my blood in your veins . . . it's only natural for you to step in wherever you're needed."

"Reba Maxwell took over as the pageant director."

"I know that," Harriett snapped, "but you were the one who convinced her to do so."

"But, if you're concerned about the Christmas program . . ."

"It isn't the pageant that concerns me."

"It isn't?"

Harriett took a tentative sip of her tea, eyeing her niece above the rim of the china cup. "I have a . . . delicate . . . prayer concern I want to share with you," she said, lowering her voice. This wasn't a conversation she wanted the children to overhear. "One that's been burdening my heart for several weeks now."

"Of course, Aunt Harriett. Who is it you'd like me to pray for?"

"It has to do with . . . one of the women at the church." Harriett averted her gaze. "You might know her. Ruth Darling."

"Mrs. Darling . . . oh, of course." Jayne perked up instantly and sounded positively delighted for the opportunity to pray for the older woman. "I know Mrs. Darling. She's such a dear heart. A month or so after I brought Suzie home from the hospital, Mrs. Darling spent an entire afternoon watching the baby so I could rest. It meant the world to have those few hours to myself. She's always been so kind and generous. She isn't ill, is she?"

To hear her niece, the woman was a candidate

for sainthood. "As far as I can tell, Ruth's in the best of health."

"Is everything all right with her husband? I think Fred is one of the nicest men I know."

This was the avenue that Harriett had been waiting to open. "I fear there are problems brewing with Fred and Ruth," she said. "It's for the two of them that I'm seeking prayers."

"Oh dear, what's the problem?"

"I'm afraid it's Ruth," Harriett said, hoping her words would show her niece exactly the kind of woman Ruth was. She squared her shoulders at the pure distastefulness of her disclosure. "Ruth has a roving eye."

"A roving eye?" Jayne repeated as if it were a medical condition. "What do you mean?"

"Have you met Mr. Fawcett yet? He's a widower who recently moved to Seattle and started attending church. He's been visiting for several months now. Tall, good-looking man."

"I'm sorry, Aunt Harriett, I can't place him."

"He sits on the right-hand side of the church, about halfway up in the middle of the pew." One would think her niece would notice such a strikingly handsome man. "Ruth's eyes have been roving in his direction, if you catch my drift." That was all she would say. Jayne would soon see for herself that Harriett had cause to be worried for her friend.

Jayne frowned. "Are you saying that Mrs. Darling is romantically interested in Mr. Fawcett?"

Harriett stiffened her spine. "That's exactly what I'm saying. I'm here to tell you that this woman you regard so highly is flirting with sin. I can see it plain as day. Just watch her, Jayne, and you'll know exactly what I mean."

"I'm sure you're mistaken, Aunt Harriett."

It didn't help that her own flesh and blood sided with the other woman. "I know what I see, and Ruth Darling has her eye on Lyle Fawcett. Trouble's brewing. Mark my words, Jayne. Mark my words."

"Aunt Harriett—"

"The only reason I'm sharing this deep spiritual burden God has placed on my heart," she continued, cutting Jayne off, "is so that you'll take it upon yourself to pray for the dear, weak woman."

"You want me to pray about Mrs. Darling's roving eye."

"Exactly."

"Have you shared this prayer request with anyone else?"

Harriett wasn't sure she liked her niece's tone of voice, but she gave her the benefit of the doubt. "A few carefully selected . . . friends."

"Aunt Harriett!"

"You will pray, won't you?" Harriett set the tea-cup in the saucer, glad now that she'd said her piece.

"Oh yes," Jayne murmured, "and while I'm at it, I'll say a few prayers for you!"

Chapter 21

*To forgive is to set the prisoner free and
then discover the prisoner was you.*

—Mrs. Miracle

"Your Aunt Gerty and Uncle Bill arrive late
on the twenty-third," Joan Maxwell said,
stabbing a large pink shrimp atop a seafood Cae-
sar salad. "Then they're leaving the morning of
the twenty-sixth for Hawaii. I can't tell you how
excited those two are. To hear your aunt talk, one
would think they were newlyweds. Gerty says
this is the honeymoon trip World War Two cheated
them out of." Reba's mother's delight overflowed
at the prospect of her aunt and uncle's arrival.

"It'll be good to see them again," Reba said. Her
aunt and uncle were favorites of hers. They lived

in the Midwest and now because of her uncle's poor eyesight didn't travel much. It had been three years or longer since Reba had last visited with them.

"Aunt Gerty is anxious to see you."

"I'm looking forward to seeing her, too." Her aunt had always made her feel special. It was her godmother who'd stood staunchly by Reba's decision not to marry John, at the same time recognizing her hurt and pain. Her reaction had been a blessed contrast to those of the other members of her family. Her parents had offered platitudes that it was all for the best. The best for whom? Reba had wanted to know. For her? It hadn't felt that way, not then.

She could remember her aunt saying how very sorry she was, when everyone else seemed to want to celebrate, wedding or no wedding. The food had been ordered, they pointed out, the cake baked, the hall rented, so why not get together? It had been her aunt who had wrapped her arms around her and comforted her. Her aunt who'd taken into consideration her anguish and humiliation. Aunt Gerty had helped her escape it all by finding her that cabin at the beach.

"You'll be there for dinner Christmas Eve, won't you?" her mother asked, her gaze sobering as she studied Reba.

So this was the reason for the unexpected

invitation to dinner out, Reba reflected. It all boiled down to this one question. One more chance to pull the rug out from under her.

Reba waited for the words to filter through her mind and emerge as a carefully measured response. Her mother already knew the answer: she'd been told perhaps a dozen times that Christmas Eve dinner was impossible. She'd even been given a reason that couldn't be argued with.

But apparently she wasn't ready to give up yet. Reba sighed, watching her mother as she waited for an answer. "Mom, I've told you and told you—I can't be there Christmas Eve."

"But I thought. I hoped—"

"I'm responsible for the church program, remember?"

"Yes, but I hoped that you might see your way clear to join us. It's just that Aunt Gerty and Uncle Bill—"

"There simply won't be time. There's too much to do. It's going to be hectic pulling everything together."

"You're sure you can't arrange something? This is your father's oldest brother, and he's getting on in years. Who knows if we'll get an opportunity to spend the holidays with them again?" The pleading quality was back in her mother's voice, the soft, almost whiny tone she used whenever Vicki was involved. Reba didn't doubt for a moment that her sister had something to do with this. It was all too convenient, this dinner too contrived.

"You've known for weeks that I can't make the dinner. Why are you bringing it up now?"

Joan shredded her dinner roll into tiny bits. One would think she was about to feed a flock of pigeons.

"Mother?"

"It's nothing. I'm sure everything will work out for the best, don't worry. Okay?"

Reba's agitation rose. "For whatever reason, this has to do with Vicki, doesn't it?" Her mother couldn't meet her eyes, a sure indication that something was amiss, which almost certainly meant the discussion ultimately involved her older sister.

"Just tell me." Reba wasn't up to playing guessing games.

Joan made a weak, frustrated motion with her hands, as if to say this was beyond her control. "You said to let Vicki choose which day she'd come and you'd take the other." Suddenly she pushed aside her salad plate as if the sight of food disgusted her. "Oh, dear, this isn't going to work at all."

"What isn't?"

"Vicki and Doug can't come for Christmas Eve, either. Doug's family is having a large gathering with his grandmother. She's almost eighty and in poor health, and Vicki doesn't seem to think she'll last much longer."

"Oh great, just great," Reba muttered. She bent over backward to accommodate everyone but herself, and as always happened, everything blew up in her face.

"Vicki, Doug, and Ellen are planning on spending Christmas Day with us."

Reba should have seen it coming. In other words, unless she changed her plans she wouldn't be able to spend time with her aunt and uncle. As it was, their stay in Seattle would be brief. Reba had assumed Vicki would opt to attend the family dinner her mother had planned, freeing her to be there Christmas Day.

"I see," she murmured.

"Vicki doesn't really have a choice." Once again her mother rushed to take her sister's side. "It's Doug's grandmother."

"Of course she has a choice, the same choice as me." The words echoed with her frustration.

"We could have an early dinner and then all come to the church program," Joan suggested.

Reba could see that her mother desperately wanted to correct matters as best she could, but it was impossible.

"It won't work," Reba insisted. "There won't be time. I'll have my hands full seeing to everything. I can't very well take time off to run to your house for dinner and leave my volunteers. The program's at seven."

"Afterward, then," her mother offered.

"I won't get out of here any time before nine-thirty. That's a bit late for dinner." She recalled that her aunt and uncle were early risers and were usually ready for bed by nine or ten. She couldn't very well drop in and expect to visit then.

"Oh, dear," Joan mumbled.

"Don't worry about it," Reba said stiffly, "I'll call Aunt Gerty and Uncle Bill on Christmas Day." At least she'd get a chance to talk to her favorite relatives over the phone.

"But that's ridiculous! They're your godparents, surely you should put aside this silliness with your sister and—"

Reba's jaw tightened. "Silliness? You call what Vicki did silliness?"

"No," her mother snapped, "that's what I call your behavior ever since. How many times does Vicki have to tell you she's sorry? How many times does she have to plead with you to forgive her?"

Reba deliberately pulled the white linen napkin from her lap and slammed it against the table. "Why is it you always take Vicki's side? I'm sick of it. Work it out with her, she's far more reasonable than I am. I'm the silly one, remember? Vicki's always been your little darling, the one who could do no wrong. The perfect daughter."

"I don't take her side. I've tried to stay out of this from the first, but you make it impossible."

Their voices were raised and angry. Reba was the first to notice how much attention they'd attracted. This dinner was supposed to have been fun for them both. A chance to get away, shop together, and chat. Reba had agreed with a certain amount of reluctance, fearing her mother would use the time as an excuse to wave her relationship with Vicki in her face. Until now the evening had been enjoyable, but she should have known better than to lower her guard.

"Tell me, Mother, what did you think when I told you I couldn't make it to dinner Christmas Eve?"

"You never said any such thing. You told me you were taking over the church program. How was I supposed to know that meant you wouldn't be able to make dinner?"

"It should have been obvious!" Reba argued.

"You might have explained."

"I think it's time I left," Reba said tightly, and reached for her purse.

"Don't run away," Joan pleaded, her voice much lower.

"Run away?" Reba challenged. "What makes you think I'm doing that?"

"You've been doing it for years."

"Mother, please, don't start on me."

"I can't help it," she cried. "You've been running away from your sister for four years. It's past time the two of you sat down and settled this."

"Why should I talk to a woman with the morals of an alley cat?"

"Reba!"

"There you go defending her again." She removed a ten-dollar bill from her wallet and set it on the table next to her half-eaten meal. "I love you, Mom, but I think it'd be better if we didn't have these little get-togethers any longer. We get along better when we don't see so much of each other." Having said that, she whirled around and quickly wove her way through the dining room and out of the restaurant.

By the time she arrived home, Reba was trembling. She sat in her car in the driveway, her hands clenching and unclenching on the steering wheel as she battled to keep her head above water in the flash flood of emotions that followed.

It sounded juvenile to claim her mother loved her sister best, but that was the way Reba felt. All her life she'd been forced to accommodate Vicki. Her sister's plans had always taken priority. And now, once more because of Vicki, she was about to be swindled—this time out of a visit with her favorite aunt and uncle.

Perhaps this was her mother's less-than-subtle attempt to trick her into mending fences with her sister; it wouldn't be the first time she'd tried to manipulate events. After four long years, she still refused to accept that Reba wanted nothing more to do with her sister.

She felt lost, alone. Friendless. The temptation to talk to Seth was strong, even though she hated to subject him to the emotional baggage she carried around with her; he deserved a woman whose life was not complicated with family problems. Still . . .

Before she could change her mind, she backed the car out of her driveway and drove to Seth's house. She'd told him that he wouldn't be hearing from her that evening, and why, but she needed to see him, needed the comfort of his reassurances, of his arms.

The woman she assumed was his mother-in-law answered the door and smiled a warm greeting. "Ah . . . is Seth available?" Reba asked.

Sharon ushered her inside. "You must be Reba."

Feeling self-conscious, Reba nodded. "Seth isn't expecting me. . . ."

"He'll be glad for the break. He's been busy inside his study all evening. I'll get him for you."

"Hi, Reba." Judd raced into the living room at full speed.

"Hi, Reba," Jason cried, following on the wave of excitement. "Our grandma and grandpa are visiting."

"I told Grandma all about you and how I drew your picture and that you might be our new mom, and—"

"Judd!" Seth's stern voice cut into his son's enthusiastic tirade, but his gaze softened as it met hers. "Hello, Reba."

"Seth." Her eyes pleaded with him, for what she wasn't sure. Support, she suspected. Comfort.

He walked across the room and took her hands, gripping them firmly with his own. "What's happened?"

The gentle concern in his voice produced tears. They filled her eyes and threatened to slip down her cheeks.

"Mom," he said, glancing over his shoulder at Sharon, "would you be kind enough to bring us some coffee in the den?"

"Right away. Come on, kids, you can help me make up the tray."

Judd and Jason willingly followed their grandmother.

"I shouldn't be here," Reba whispered. She was sorry now that she'd come, sorry to be involving Seth in her problems. She was a big girl, and this wasn't the first time her plans had clashed with those of her sister. Nor was it uncommon for her mother to take her sister's side.

He led her into the study and sat her down on the high-backed leather chair. Sitting on the ottoman directly in front of her, he reached forward and tenderly brushed the short curls away from her temple. His gentle touch sent shivers of awareness shooting down her spine.

"I thought you were having dinner with your mother."

"I did, but we got into a terrible argument." She bit down on her lower lip to keep from spilling out all the sorry details.

Seth leaned forward and wrapped his arms around her waist, scooting her forward enough to bring her into his arms.

"What happened?"

"It doesn't matter."

"You're shaking like a leaf," he countered.

She didn't want him to know that part of that was due to the thrill of being in his arms. They'd known each other such a short while, and they hadn't been able to see much of each other, what with his work schedule and hers, visiting relatives, the church Christmas program, and the busyness of the season. Still, they talked every day, often two and three times. . . .

"Would you mind kissing me?" she asked suddenly. It was a dangerous request with his mother-in-law due to walk in at any moment, but she didn't want to wait.

In response, he captured her face between his hands and smiled softly as his eyes met hers.

"What do you think?" He leaned forward and tenderly placed his mouth over hers.

The kiss was long and sweet. Involved. One kiss wasn't enough for either of them, and soon the kisses deepened.

His touch was like a healing balm, a soothing astringent after the pain her mother's words and actions had inflicted. With Seth she was safe. With Seth she was cherished. With Seth she was wanted.

He groaned, and she opened her mouth to the probing tip of his tongue. By the time Sharon knocked and proceeded into the room, carrying the tray of coffee, Reba was clinging mindlessly to Seth.

"I'll put this down right here," his mother-in-law announced cheerfully.

"Is Dad kissing Miss Maxwell again?" Reba heard one of the kids ask in a loud whisper.

"There's not any mistletoe in Dad's study, is there?" the other twin demanded. "I didn't think he'd do it without the mistletoe, did you?" The question was apparently directed at his brother. "Right on the lips, too." The comment was followed by a sound of disgust.

"Come along, children."

Reba hid her face in Seth's shoulder rather than meet the inquisitive stares of the children. "Seth, I'm sorry," she murmured.

"I'm not. Not in the least."

Reba remained embarrassed by how needy she'd been. She'd hurried to Seth, knowing he would lend her the comfort she needed without lengthy explanations.

"This worries me," Seth whispered on the tail end of a husky sigh.

"What does?"

"Touching you like this." But his hands stayed exactly where they were.

"Oh, Seth, I want it, too."

"That's what I was afraid you'd say." With what seemed to demand a colossal effort, he pulled his hands away and braced his forehead against hers, his breathing as deep and shaky as her own. "Tell me what happened with your mother."

"No," she said, and shook her head. "I'm better now, thanks to you. Much better."

"It has to do with your sister, doesn't it?"

"Seth, please. I don't want to talk about Vicki." She kissed him, using her tongue to outline the shape of his mouth, teasing him with short, nibbling kisses.

"If you're trying to distract me, it's working."

"Good." She smiled softly to herself. "Now pour me some coffee and tell me what's going on between your in-laws."

Her words appeared to sober him. He took a moment to straighten, then did as she requested.

After he'd brought her a cup of coffee, he sat on the leather chair next to hers.

"Something's happened between those two."

"Good or bad?"

He frowned. "I don't know, but I suspect it's bad. Jerry arrived, and the two talked privately for a while. I assumed they'd cleared up whatever was wrong between them, but my feeling is that it hasn't gone away."

"Are they fighting?"

"No," he said, holding the coffee mug with both hands. He leaned forward and braced his elbows against his knees. "Not in the least. It's like they're polite strangers. It's 'please' and 'thank you' at every turn. Jerry brings her coffee in the morning, and she makes sure the newspaper is just so for him."

"That sounds like the routine of a long married couple."

"I suppose," he said, but it didn't look as though he were reassured. If anything, he seemed convinced of the opposite.

"You think it's for show, don't you?"

His grin was slightly off center. "Yes, that's exactly what I think. It's like they're playing this game, making it seem that there couldn't possibly be anything wrong with their relationship."

"But you think there is."

"I know there is."

She didn't ask how he knew. "Then why would they go through this pretense?"

"I don't know. Possibly because it's close to Christmas and they don't want to upset the twins. Or because of me." He rubbed a hand down the side of his face and glanced guiltily at her. "Then again I've been distracted by a certain travel agent of late and wouldn't know my head from a hole in the ground."

Happiness filled her heart. "It's an honor to be considered a distraction."

He chuckled. "If only you knew."

"Tell me." Her ego could do with a few strokes.

"You tell me what sent you running to me like an injured rabbit after having dinner with your mother."

Reba glared at him, then smiled. "You don't play fair."

He didn't respond, merely seemed content to wait until she'd satisfied his curiosity.

"Vicki will be with my family Christmas Day." From the emotionless look in his eyes, she could tell he didn't understand. "There appears to have been a breakdown in communication between my mother and me. Since I'm the chair for the Christmas program, I can't attend dinner Christmas Eve, and apparently my sister is obligated to attend some shindig with her husband's family."

"You don't want to be with your parents at the same time as your sister?"

"I won't have anything to do with her. I already explained that, remember?" She knew she sounded defensive, but she couldn't help herself.

"Spend the day with me and the kids," Seth invited her.

She hadn't come seeking an invitation. She shook her head. "No, but thank you."

"Why not?"

"It's a pity invitation."

Seth chuckled. "Hardly. I'd like it more than you know. Come, please."

Pride should have been enough to keep her from accepting, but pride was cold comfort. For the first time since the disastrous day of her near wedding, she had someone in her life.

"Reba?" Seth coaxed.

"I'll come." Such a little thing. She had no right to be this happy.

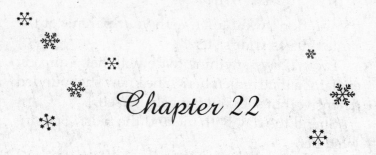

Chapter 22

You have to wonder about humans.
They think God is dead and Elvis is alive.

—Shirley, Goodness, and Mercy,
personal friends of Mrs. Miracle

The irony of it was that Sharon had gotten along with Jerry better in the last several days, since they'd agreed to a divorce, than in the previous twelve months. She sat next to him in the movie theater and forced her attention back to the screen. Agent 007 was back in action. James Bond had returned to save the world from the latest fiend.

She reached for a handful of popcorn, and Jerry angled the bucket toward her, granting her easy access to the buttery-topped kernels. A time not so long ago and they wouldn't have been able to agree on which movie, which theater, what night, or anything else. She wasn't entirely sure how they'd managed it this time. It was as though the decision to separate had freed them, and they could once more return to the congenial couple they'd once been.

The temptation was to forget the troubles of the past and enjoy this newfound accord, but Sharon knew this "honeymoon" wouldn't last. They'd agreed to make the best of it until after Christmas—it made sense not to ruin the children's holidays with the distressing news of their failed marriage.

The action-packed movie involved almost everyone else in the theater, but Sharon had a difficult time keeping her thoughts on the characters on the screen.

It wasn't supposed to happen like this. With the two of them sitting in a movie theater as if nothing were amiss, as if they were as deeply in love as the day they'd married. Or more so.

The heavy weight of her failure pressed down on her, until she felt as if she were slowly being lowered into a pit of despair. So many questions remained unanswered. Sharon wasn't sure what she'd do with herself. Or where she'd live. Or even what she'd tell her friends.

In retrospect, she wished she'd paid more attention to what other women she'd known had done

following their divorces. As far as she could remember, few, if any, had turned out to be friendly
divorces. They'd all started out that way, but
somewhere along the line animosity had taken
control. It was all so terribly depressing to see
what could happen between two people who'd
once professed to love each other. Soon it would
be happening to her and Jerry.

The movie credits started to roll across the large
white screen and Sharon realized, with some surprise, that the film was over. She hadn't realized
how close the plot was to the end, which was a bit
like her marriage, she mused. The credits were
about to scroll down the once white screen of her
life with Jerry.

"Whatever happened to Anita Perkins?" Sharon
asked her husband. Jerry wore a puzzled look as
he stood and led the way out of the theater. Anita
and her husband had been Elk members, and Earl
had routinely played golf with Jerry. A couple of
years back they'd divorced, and now Sharon
couldn't recall what had become of her friend.

"I don't know," Jerry admitted.

"Don't you see Earl anymore?"

"No." Her husband frowned and shook his
head. "I can't say that I do. It must be six months
or longer since he was out at the golf course. He
just drifted away." He paused and then asked,
"What about Anita?"

Sharon shrugged. "The last I heard she'd moved to Oregon to be closer to her daughter."

They remained unnaturally quiet as they made their way out toward the parking lot. Seth had loaned Jerry the family car. They were both sitting inside, the engine running and the defroster blasting hot air against the windshield, before Jerry spoke again.

"It won't be that way with us."

Sharon prayed he was right, but life held few guarantees. "What went wrong with Anita and Earl?" she asked, thinking Jerry might have some insight to share, something that would help see them through this difficult time.

Jerry shrugged. "Earl never said. What about Anita?"

"Not much, just that they'd grown apart the last few years."

"The same as us, then." For the first time since she'd mentioned divorce, a note of sadness entered Jerry's voice. "Like I said earlier, it'll be different with us. We'll make it different."

Sharon knew he believed that now. But once the attorneys started casting accusations and blame like poison darts, they'd react the same way their friends had, and all their good intentions would get tossed out the proverbial window. Despite their talk about making this a friendly divorce, it would eventually turn into something ugly, the same as it had with other couples they'd known. By nature the dissolution of marriage was ugly and painful.

Jerry pulled out of the parking lot and into the street. "Do you want to stop and have dinner?"

"No, thanks. The popcorn filled me up." A small white lie.

"Me too," Jerry muttered.

But it wasn't the popcorn, and they both knew it. Their appetite had been ruined by the reminder that soon they would be like their friends. A year from now one of Jerry's golfing buddies was going to ask what had ever happened to Sharon or Jerry and say how sad it was that they hadn't been able to work matters out.

The house was dark and quiet except for a thin slice of light coming from beneath Seth's study door. Sharon heard softly mumbled voices and suspected her son-in-law wouldn't appreciate an intrusion. Reba had apparently come to help him watch the kids.

Jerry raised his eyebrows when he heard a soft giggle. He didn't say anything until the bedroom door was closed. "What's going on with Seth?"

"He's got a woman friend." Sharon wasn't entirely sure how much she should say.

"The same one who stopped by last night?" Jerry asked with meaning. "It sounds like they might be getting serious."

"It's been four years."

Still her husband frowned. "He's not going to marry her, is he?"

"How would I know?" Sharon removed her sweater and hung it up in the closet. She ran her hand along the soft texture of the knit fabric. A gift from Jerry, one he'd purchased a couple of years earlier for her birthday.

"Do you like her?"

Sharon sighed. "I only met her once, briefly. She's a nice girl, what can I say? The twins seem to like her."

Jerry sat on the edge of the mattress, his shoulders sagging. "It shouldn't come as a shock. Seth's young and healthy. I didn't know he was dating. He hasn't before now, has he?"

"I wouldn't know."

Jerry looked away, as if the subject were an uncomfortable one. "It's not that I object, mind you, it's just that I've always thought of Seth as Pammy's husband."

"I did, too, but it's time. Past time. Like you said, Seth's young and healthy. From what he's told me about Reba, meeting her was like a gift from God. It's the same for her, apparently, although he didn't mention why."

"You say the twins like her?"

"Very much." It was one thing to accept this other woman as part of Seth's life and quite another to view her as a possible stepmother to Judd and Jason. Since she'd taken over Pamela's role until the last four months, Sharon had suffered more than one qualm. The fact that the children were eager for their father to remarry was confirmation that she'd done her job well.

"If the kids like her, then that's good enough for me." Jerry tended to see things in black and white. As far as he was concerned, the matter was settled in his mind.

"It is for me, too," she added with only the slightest hesitation.

Jerry removed his clothes and climbed into bed, then sat up, with his hands braced behind his back, his elbows jutting out at his sides. She'd been dressing and undressing in front of her husband for nearly forty years; it was ridiculous to be shy about doing so now.

Jerry studied her as she self-consciously removed her clothes. "You're a fine figure of a woman, Sharon."

Even more ridiculous was the wave of color that flooded her cheeks. "Thank you," she mumbled, embarrassed and eager to turn off the light.

"Will you remarry?"

The question came out of the blue and caught her by surprise.

"Remarry? Me?" she snapped. "Of course not, why would I do anything so foolish?" She didn't mean to sound waspish, but she was genuinely taken aback by the absurdity of the question.

"You're the one who asked for the divorce," he reminded her, his jaw tightening. "For all I know there might be someone else in your life right now."

For a moment Sharon was too stunned to respond. "Do you mean to say you've been living with me all these years and you still don't know me, Jerry Palmer?"

Jerry pinched his lips tightly closed.

Sharon tossed back the covers and climbed between the sheets—only this night she was the one who rolled onto her side and presented her back to her husband. She tucked the sheet more securely about her shoulder and held it tightly in place at her neck.

"I . . . I didn't mean that to sound the way it did," Jerry admitted gruffly a couple of moments later.

She heard his regret and sighed brokenly. "I know."

"I was curious, is all, but you're right, it was an insulting question." He turned off the light and hunkered down under the covers.

Sharon heard the even flow of his breathing.

"Who knows what the future holds for any of us?" he whispered.

"What about you?" She repositioned herself so

she was on her back. They lay side by side, each staring up at the ceiling, being careful not to touch one another. "Will you remarry?"

"I doubt it," he answered after a thoughtful pause. "I've loved you all these years. I . . . I can't imagine loving somebody else. . . . But then, like I said earlier, who knows what the future holds? Not me. Definitely not me."

Chapter 23

*Swallowing angry words is much more palatable
than having to eat them afterward.*

—Mrs. Miracle

*E*mily Merkle poured herself a cup of freshly
brewed tea and made herself comfortable at
the kitchen table. A slow, easy smile spread across
her face as she gave herself a mental pat on the
back. Everything was falling neatly into place. Seth
and Reba were thick as thieves; she glanced heavenward and asked pardon for the analogy. Certainly they had enormous problems to work out,
given Reba's troubles with her sister and Seth's ob-
session with the past, but her prayer was that love
would see them through all that.

She wasn't nearly as comfortable with what was

happening between Sharon and Jerry. Those two were stubborn, equally at fault, each willing to blame the other. But when Jerry showed up in search of his wife, Emily had hope. Sharon was mature enough to recognize that there was nothing going on between her husband and best friend. The love between those two wasn't as dead as they wanted to believe.

Harriett Foster . . . Well, Harriett still needed a bit of work. Nothing major, just a little heavenly illumination. It might take a direct message from the Almighty to reach the widow. The poor dear. She hadn't a clue of how she muddied the good name of God with her righteousness.

"Do you always wait to do your Christmas shopping until the last minute?" Reba asked Seth, who was pushing the cart through the impossibly crowded toy store. Music blared in the background, loudly enough to drown out her thoughts or, more appropriately, the cries of the children. High on sugar and excitement, kids ran helter-skelter down the aisles. With Christmas in the middle of the week this was the last weekend left to shop, and everyone in the Seattle metropolitan area, it seemed, had descended upon the toy store. There appeared to be a run on Barbie's playhouses. Reba saw several desperate parents waving fistfuls of money over their heads, hoping to persuade the clerk to be merciful toward them.

"I tell myself every year that I'm not going to do this," Seth said, maneuvering the cart down the bicycle aisle. He wove it around a little boy who sat in a wagon in the middle of the lane, waiting contentedly for some generous soul to hitch him to the back of a bike and tow him about the store.

Seth looped his arm around her shoulder. His eyes held hers, and everything else seemed to fade away: the noise, the children, the sense of panic and rush. The excitement remained, only now it seemed centered between the two of them. Reba was profoundly aware of Seth, profoundly aware of the strength of their attraction. In her pain and disappointment, she'd come to him. He'd comforted her with his words and his gentleness. And his kisses. If they hadn't been in his home, with family close at hand, Reba wondered where those kisses might have led them. She was glad she hadn't needed to make that decision. Seth was dangerous. He reminded her she was a woman. Any part of her that was sexual had been buried. He made her feel again, made her yearn for all that she'd been missing. The fear remained, but with nowhere near the intensity of previous relationships.

"I appreciate your coming with me," Seth told her, breaking the spell that had enveloped them.

"What, and miss all this?" she teased. Seth's in-laws had the children for the afternoon. Mrs. Merkle had sent them out with her blessing and the promise of a hot meal upon their return. Although Reba had teased him, she was enjoying herself. This was almost as good as being a mother herself. She loved Judd and Jason and the other children she'd come to know through the Christmas program. She paused as they turned down another aisle. She stood in front of the doll section. Ellen, Vicki's little girl, would be at the age where she'd love a baby doll. The urge to buy one was strong, but her mother was sure to take it as a sign that Reba wanted to mend the relationship, and nothing could be further from the truth.

Seth steered her farther down the aisle. "Say, did you hear they have a divorced Barbie?"

"No." Reba couldn't believe it.

"Yup," he said with a twinkle in his eye. "She's got all of Ken's things."

Reba laughed and elbowed him in the ribs, and Seth chuckled, too.

All in all, she felt good. Generally the holidays were an unhappy reminder of the problem between her and her sister, and this year was no exception. Although she'd agreed to spend Christmas Day with Seth and his family, a part of her resented that it was Vicki who'd be with her aunt

Gerty and uncle Bill. Reba would have liked to introduce Seth to her parents and her aunt and uncle, but that was out of the question now.

"Judd said something about wanting Power Ranger walkie-talkies," Seth said, breaking into her thoughts. "Do you have any idea where those might be?"

Reba knew next to nothing about the setup in toy stores. "Your guess is as good as mine. This is all new to me."

"New. You act like a pro with all those kids at church. One would think you'd been doing this for quite some time. You make it look easy. You know what's going to happen, don't you? You've talked yourself into a job for the next ten years."

Frankly, she wouldn't mind. The benefits from volunteering to direct the Christmas program had been an unexpected blessing. While her motives hadn't been pure, she'd reaped untold rewards. Sure, there was the hassle factor, but again the sense of accomplishment outweighed any problems.

The Christmas Eve program would be a wonderful success, and she'd like to think it was due in part to her efforts. Naturally Seth and his in-laws would be there for the performance. Reba would have liked to have her family there as well, and the knowledge that they would not be coming brought a twinge of disappointment.

Her spirits lifted again when she reflected on

yet other unexpected benefits of volunteering her time: she'd made friends with several of the other women, and she'd even picked up a number of new clients. It felt good to be an active member of the church family, contributing more than just her presence in a pew on Sunday morning.

For the first time in four years she was reaching out, charting new ground, planting seeds. She cast a glance at Seth, who wore a perpetual frown as he wandered aimlessly down one aisle after the next. Poor fellow. He needed her.

Next year she'd . . . Reba stopped herself, amazed at how she'd imagined them together twelve months into the future. She stood proudly at his side, happier than she could remember being in a very long while.

"Reba . . ."

The soft voice cut into her thoughts like the sharpest of sabers. Even after all this time, she recognized the speaker.

Vicki.

Reba tensed and slowly, deliberately, turned around. Seth must have sensed the way her muscles tightened because he turned with her.

Reba said nothing. She couldn't.

It felt as if her tongue had frozen to the roof of her mouth. The old, familiar resentment rose like bile in the back of her throat. Her gaze slid from her sister to the tall, good-looking man at her side and the little girl in his arms. So this was Ellen, the much-loved grandchild. Vicki and Doug's daughter. She was beautiful, sleeping contentedly on her father's shoulder, her blond hair spilling down his back. Reba's heart softened with an instant flow of love for this child she'd never seen.

"I talked to Mom this morning," Vicki said, her delicate voice shaking slightly. "She explained that there's been a misunderstanding about Christmas Eve."

"There was no misunderstanding." Her mother had sided with her sister, the way she had from the beginning. Seth must have realized who Vicki was because he moved closer, protectively, to her side. She was grateful for both the physical and the emotional support.

"I want you to know that I feel bad about that."

"Yeah, I bet," Reba muttered.

"I talked it over with Doug," Vicki continued, and glanced up at her husband, "and we decided it wouldn't be that much of a problem to change our plans."

"Don't worry about it." Reba made her voice as cold and as unfeeling as she could. She was horrified to feel a lump form in her throat. "I've already made alternate plans for Christmas. You go on ahead and visit with Aunt Gerty and Uncle Bill."

"But they're your godparents."

It was on the tip of her tongue to remind Vicki

that John had been her fiancé and it hadn't stopped her from sleeping with him. Hadn't stopped Vicki from ruining her life.

"We've already phoned Doug's grandmother and explained," Vicki said. "Please, Reba, it's a small thing. I want you to be home for Christmas."

"I appreciate the effort, but as I said I've already made other plans." Her sister must have noticed the way Reba's gaze fell on the sleeping child. The photographs that filled her parents' house didn't do the little girl justice. Reba's heart felt tight, as though a vise were constricting her chest. She didn't want to feel anything for Vicki's daughter, but she couldn't help herself. The desire to hold little Ellen herself was overwhelming. Forcefully she moved her gaze elsewhere.

"Ellen's a lot like you," Vicki said, "I don't know if Mom told you. . . ."

Reba shook her head, not able to bear hearing it. She was about to turn away when Vicki's husband stopped her.

"Reba," Doug said sharply. Her sister's husband looked at Seth and appeared to be asking for a few moments' indulgence. "I know what happened with Vicki and John. It's in the past—everyone makes mistakes. I have. You have. Wouldn't it make life less complicated if you could forgive your sister and get on with your life?"

Reba laughed, the scratchy sound as full of sarcasm as she could make it. "No way. If she's miserable with the way matters are between us, all the better. It's what she deserves."

"Doug, I told you it wouldn't do any good." Vicki reached out and touched her husband's arm. A look of hopelessness came over her face, and she was about to turn away when she stopped and raised her gaze to meet Seth's.

Reba bristled. Her sister had already stolen one man from her, and she wasn't about to let her take another. She was about to say something ugly when Vicki spoke, only this time her comment was directed to Seth.

"Make her happy," she whispered. "Make her forget." With tears glistening in her eyes, she walked away.

Doug remained a moment longer. "You're a fool," he said.

Again Reba was forced to restrain herself from reminding her brother-in-law that he'd married a woman who was as likely to betray him as she had her own flesh and blood. If he wanted to talk about fools, perhaps he should take a close look at his own life.

Not until her sister and family were out of sight did Reba lower her guard. The starch went out of her then, and all at once her knees felt like mush.

She exhaled slowly and lowered her head, struggling to regain her composure.

"Are you all right?" Seth asked.

She lied and nodded. Her fingers tightened about his arms, cutting into his flesh. "Thank you," she whispered.

"For what?"

"For not saying anything, for standing at my side." If she'd had the strength and the wherewithal, she would have turned and walked away the instant Vicki had spoken to her. Even now she couldn't explain why she hadn't. She'd stood and talked to her sister the way some people linger, fascinated, with the morbid.

Seth's arm tightened about her as if he'd instinctively recognized her need. He kissed the top of her head and whispered something she couldn't hear. Something about sincerity. That was when the trembling started, so badly that she was sure others could hear her knees knocking.

"Maybe we should find someplace to sit down," he suggested.

She nodded, barely conscious of what she'd agreed to. "That might be a good idea."

By luck the toy store had a small snack bar and a few tables. Seth found her a seat, left her momentarily, and returned with a cup of hot, steaming coffee. "Can I get you anything else?"

"I'm fine." She refused to allow her sister to ruin

this special time Christmas shopping with Seth. Every minute they could squeeze out of their already tight schedules to be together was precious.

Seth stood behind her and rubbed her tired, tense shoulder muscles. "Are you going over to your parents' on Christmas?" he asked.

"No," she stated emphatically, stunned that he would ask. Despite Vicki's assurances, she didn't trust her sister, couldn't. Vicki had proved exactly how untrustworthy she could be. "I'm spending the day with you, remember?" she added, turning to smile up at him.

"I'd enjoy meeting your family." The suggestion was made in gentle tones, as though he feared upsetting her.

He wasn't making this easy. "Another time."

"Okay," he agreed softly.

She'd thought he'd understood. Thought he'd appreciated her reasons for having nothing to do with her older sibling. Reba had carried the shame of her sister's betrayal while her family had gathered around Vicki as if she were the injured one. The old hurts, the old pain, returned.

Seth reached for a chair, positioned it in front of her, and straddled it. "Reba, don't you see? You're the one who's suffering. You're denying yourself the pleasure of visiting your uncle and aunt."

"I'll see them another time," she returned tightly.

"That wasn't what you told me after the dinner

with your mother. As I recall, you were upset because this may well be the last time you have a chance to visit them. They're getting on in years, remember?"

Reba longed to place her hands over her ears and block out his words. It wasn't what he said. She had no defense because common sense told her he was right. She had no argument; she stood on sinking ground and knew it.

This grudge she carried against her sister had hurt her and would continue to do so. Her sister, the wife and mother. Her sister, the wonderful, generous daughter, the mother of her parents' only grandchild. Always so perfect, always so good.

The traitor.

"Perhaps you should head toward the checkout stand," Reba suggested, looking blindly into the distance.

Seth hesitated. "I'm not siding with your sister against you," he said after a moment. "You're the one I care about; you're the one I don't want to see hurt."

"Again," she added, "hurt again." He hadn't a clue. If he had, he wouldn't have asked her to work matters through with Vicki. All her hopes for the future, all her dreams, came crashing to her feet and shattered like crystal.

Unlike any man she'd met since the broken engagement, Seth had led her to believe he understood. He didn't. He couldn't possibly comprehend what he was asking of her.

Reba joined him just as he was finishing up at the checkout stand and helped him carry the bulky purchases back to the car. She smiled, hoping that they could put this matter behind them.

Soon they were on the road again, heading back to Seth's house. The silence that stretched between them was like the rubber strand of a slingshot. The pressure so strong, it all but vibrated.

"Reba, I know it's none of my affair, but you've got to let go of this bitterness or you'll pickle in it."

If he meant to be amusing, he failed miserably. "I don't want to talk about it."

"You can't live in the past."

Furious that he of all people would say that to her, she refused to respond. He was the man hung up on a dead wife, the man who'd buried himself in his grief. Vicki was about to do it to her again: she was going to lose Seth, and all because of her sister.

"You've let what Vicki did jade your entire outlook on life. Don't you think this whole thing has hurt Vicki, too? It probably has and in ways you've never imagined. Have you ever really talked it over with her?"

"As I said before, I don't have anything to say to my sister, and furthermore I'm not willing to listen to anything she has to tell me." If he thought he was helping, he was wrong. Every time he opened his mouth he made matters worse. Much worse. All he did was repeat what other well-meaning friends and family had said to her. His attitude was one of the sorriest disappointments of her life. She'd expected much more of him.

"But—"

"Seth, don't," she pleaded, and closed her eyes. "Please don't say another word."

The rest of the drive was completed in dark silence. He parked his car in his driveway. Despite her unhappiness, she had to smile when two small faces appeared in the window. Judd and Jason battled for the best vantage point to check out the Christmas goodies, hoping for the opportunity to catch a glimpse of what presents they'd find under the tree on Christmas morning.

"It looks like we have a welcoming committee," Seth said.

"So I see."

"If I know Mrs. Merkle, she's cooked up a feast to tempt the saints. I don't know about you, but I'm starved."

"I can't stay," she said, eager to get away. She opened the car door, anxious to make her escape. Anxious to sort through what had happened.

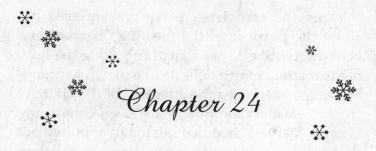

Chapter 24

There's a reason a dog has so many friends.
He wags his tail instead of his tongue.

—Mrs. Miracle

Harriett Foster decided she couldn't delay her talk with Pastor Lovelace any longer. This matter with Ruth Darling wasn't the only problem, either. God had graced her with a knack for details, and she'd noticed a number of other good Christians flirting with sin.

Since she hadn't been able to accidentally-on-purpose bump into the minister, she scheduled an appointment through the church secretary.

"It's vitally important I speak with Pastor Lovelace at his earliest convenience," she'd told Joanne Lawton.

When the church secretary had quizzed her about the purpose of the meeting, Harriett had been vague. She'd said something along the lines of the matter being a delicate one that in her humble opinion required the attention of the church's spiritual leader. She must have been convincing because Joanne scheduled her for an appointment first thing Monday morning, three days before Christmas.

Harriett dressed carefully, choosing her best outfit, the one she generally reserved for formal occasions: playing the pipe organ at baptisms and weddings, that sort of thing. Her new black pumps were a tad snug and uncomfortable but would loosen with a bit of wear, she decided.

Generally she avoided studying her reflection in the mirror. She allowed only one small hand mirror in her home; anything larger would be flirting with vanity. And while other Christian women were spiritually comfortable wearing cosmetics, Harriett had never used anything but a light shade of lipstick.

Jewelry was another matter of concern. Her only adornment was a plain gold wedding band and a locket that had once belonged to her grandmother. One day she would pass it along to her niece. To her way of thinking, a woman in the service of God would choose to don only what would enhance a meek and humble spirit. Harriett cringed whenever she saw a woman wearing large, looped earrings. And she'd nearly fainted the first time she'd seen an earring on a teenage *boy*. In his *nose*. The mere thought was enough to cause her to grimace, even now, months later.

She arrived promptly, as always, for her appointment. Cleanliness wasn't the only personality trait that was next to godliness.

"Pastor Lovelace will see you now," Joanne said when Harriett entered the office. The other woman led the way into Pastor Lovelace's private study.

The minister was a good man who preached straight out of the King James version of the Bible. Harriett approved of his choice and had let it be known early on. Although young, he possessed a healthy appreciation for the traditional view of such important matters.

He stood as she entered the room and motioned to the chair on the other side of his desk. "Good morning, Mrs. Foster. I understand you wanted to see me."

Harriett sat and folded her hands primly in her lap. "It's a matter of some importance."

"That's what I understand."

He sat down and waited for her to continue. Harriett had hoped to exchange small talk and ease her way into this burden on her heart. She inhaled slowly, thinking the direct approach was probably for the best. A soul couldn't ease into a discussion about sin.

Pastor Lovelace waited silently, and Harriett plunged right in. "As you're probably aware, I've been a member of this congregation for well over twenty years."

"It seems longer."

"My husband's family was one of the founding members of this congregation." She bowed her head out of reverence for the dead. "May God rest his soul."

"You've served our church community with great vigor," Pastor Lovelace admitted graciously.

Harriett had always been fond of the man. He showed a keen insight into the many personal sacrifices others had made on behalf of the church.

"Tell me, how is the pageant coming along? Have you enjoyed working with Reba Maxwell?"

"Well," Harriett said with a heavy sigh, and scooted closer to the edge of the cushion. "I understand that when Milly's husband was transferred, the church was in something of a bind, but personally—"

"From all indications," Pastor Lovelace interrupted, "Miss Maxwell is doing an excellent job, working long hours, and putting a great deal of time and energy into the project."

"Yes," Harriett admitted reluctantly. The Maxwell woman had done everything he said, but the church had taken a risk by allowing a woman, one with spotty attendance at best, to step in at the last minute. Luckily there hadn't been *too* many problems.

"I apologize, Mrs. Foster, I've sidetracked you."

Harriett cleared her throat. "As I was saying earlier, I've attended this church for several years now and am familiar with many of the families."

Pastor Lovelace relaxed on his chair.

"It's because I know the parishioners as well as I do that I feel I can speak freely about their concerns."

"As you see them?"

"Yes." There were things she could tell him that would turn his hair prematurely gray. If he showed any indication of wanting to know the levels of depravity some of the upstanding members of this very church had shown, she'd be happy to tell him. Only as a matter of prayer, of course.

"There appear to be a number of areas of deep concern," she said, meeting and holding his gaze.

He arched his eyebrows. "I'm afraid I'm not following you."

"First off, let's discuss Emily Merkle." She could tell by his blank look that he hadn't placed the name. "Seth Webster's new housekeeper."

"Ah, yes." A smile quivered at the edges of his mouth.

Harriett wondered what he found so amusing. "The woman's a busybody." And an old biddy besides, but she feared Pastor Lovelace would find her words unkind She didn't want to alienate him before she zeroed in on the real reason for her visit.

"I find Mrs. Miracle . . . I mean, Merkle . . . to be a woman of unique faith."

"Perhaps." Harriett was willing to grant the woman that much. "She certainly has found a way to ingratiate herself with the women of this church in short order." Harriett, however, wasn't as easily taken in by a smooth tongue and slick manners. The woman was trouble with a capital T. Baking cookies for the women's bazaar and contributing the recipe for winter fruit dip. Why, it was pure indulgence, that's what it was. Pure indulgence.

"Don't you agree?" Pastor's gaze narrowed as he looked at her. "Mrs. Merkle is a woman of unique faith."

"Faith, perhaps, but I see very little religion in her."

"How do you mean?" the young minister pressed. Something in his attitude changed; she noticed it in his eyes and believed he was keen to hear her response.

"Well, it's difficult to explain . . . with words.

It's as if the woman isn't quite like the rest of us, if you catch my drift."

"You mean she isn't of this world?"

"Something like that," Harriett agreed. "When she looks at me I'm left with the feeling that . . ." She didn't dare voice the truth, not with the opposite sex. The fact was, she'd been left feeling exposed, as if Emily Merkle had the power to know things she had no business knowing.

Once several years ago, shortly after her husband had passed on, Harriett had purchased a pair of silk underpants. She attributed the minor decline in common sense to her overwhelming loss and grief. She'd worn them only once and had hidden them in the back of her drawer ever since. For reasons she couldn't explain, Harriett felt Emily Merkle knew about those black silk panties.

"The feeling that . . . ," he prompted.

"Frankly, Pastor, I'm not here to talk about the Websters' housekeeper. It's Ruth Darling who concerns me."

"Ruth Darling?" He sounded surprised. "Ruth's the delicate matter you wish to discuss?"

Harriett sat up on the chair, stiffening her spine. She was so close to the edge of the cushion that she was in danger of falling butt first onto the floor.

She didn't expect this to be a comfortable conversation, but she considered it her Christian duty.

If she could save one lost lamb from stumbling into the den of wolves and being trapped in iniquity, then she'd completed her task.

"What I say must stay in this office," she warned, glancing over her shoulder to be certain the door was completely closed. She didn't know Joanne Lawton well, but she wouldn't put it past the church secretary to listen in on conversations that were meant to be private.

"But of course."

Once she'd been granted the assurances she needed, Harriett felt free to continue. "I fear for the spiritual well-being of my dear, dear friend." Unable to meet his gaze, she stared at her clenched hands. "I've discovered that . . ." She closed her eyes, hardly able to voice it. "That my friend has"— she paused for effect—"lusted after another man."

"Ruth Darling?" Pastor Lovelace leaped to his feet, then quickly sat back down. "I'm sure you're mistaken," he continued in a less boisterous manner.

Harriett had feared it would come to something like this. She reached for her purse and withdrew an envelope. "I've kept a list of my observances," she said, wanting it to sound as if the task had been repugnant to her. With a show of reluctance, she handed him the envelope. "You'll discover that the first occurrence happened several months ago. In September . . . September seventh, to be exact, and right here in this very church."

Pastor Lovelace lowered the envelope to his desk without opening it. Harriett had hoped that he'd read the mounting data for himself and save her the necessity of having to spell out what could only be the truth. The evidence was overwhelming, the conclusion simple.

"I'm afraid it's Lyle Fawcett," she said. "He's the man who's tempted her to this fall from grace."

"This has to do with Ruth Darling and Lyle Fawcett?" Pastor Lovelace sounded incredulous.

"Why, yes." His shock was what she'd expected. Apparently she was the only one diligent enough to recognize what was happening. To his credit, Lyle had been an innocent bystander, unaware of the course to sin his presence had wrought.

"It pains me to inform you that Ruth has eyed Lyle like a bird of prey every Sunday for weeks. It's most disconcerting to find a woman married to a man as good and kind as Fred Darling ogling another man."

"And you've discussed your concerns with Ruth yourself?"

Harriett's back went ramrod straight. Discuss the situation with Ruth herself? She'd never heard anything so ridiculous in her life. One didn't go about confronting people about sin.

That was a minister's job. While it was true that some less-than-charitable Christians might find it their duty, Harriett most certainly did not.

"Surely you're not suggesting that I speak to Ruth about this? Why . . . I couldn't. It wouldn't be right."

"That's exactly what I'm saying. It might surprise you to learn that matters are not always what they seem." Although Pastor Lovelace's eyes were kind, his words carried a sharp edge. "You might learn something."

"There's a link between the two, isn't there?" Harriett had suspected as much from the first.

"I believe you're right about that."

"Aha!" She raised her index finger toward the ceiling.

Pastor Lovelace laughed outright and then had the good grace to look repentant. "I want you to promise me that you'll discuss your concerns with Ruth Darling yourself."

It was unthinkable. "I . . . I don't know that I can."

"It's my feeling that if any of us has a question about one of our brethren, instead of asking others, we go directly to that person."

Harriett didn't like what she was hearing. It was the last thing she'd expected the good pastor to suggest. "Surely you don't condone Ruth's behavior?"

"It isn't for me to condone or condemn."

Harriett couldn't believe her ears. The woman was flirting with the worst form of sin. Surely Pastor Lovelace recognized as much.

The pastor stood, indicating their time together was at an end. "You'll do as I ask?"

Harriett's mouth opened and closed a number of times. "If you're sure . . . if you think I should."

"I do."

He seemed to be waiting for her to leave. Harriett fumbled in her purse for another slip of paper. "There are two others whom I'd like to report . . ." Flustered now, she unfolded the sheet. "Barbara Newton and Oliva Sanchez, and—"

"Have you spoken directly to them?" he interrupted.

"Ah, no, but I assumed . . . I thought you'd want to do that yourself." That he suggested she would was nothing short of shocking.

"As I said, it's been my experience that whenever one hears something unkind or negative about another person, the best course is to ask that person." He paused and seemed to wait for Harriett to respond.

"But . . ."

"I know that you have a kind and generous heart for the people of this church."

Harriett relaxed. "Indeed I do. I care deeply

about the spiritual welfare of every soul who walks through these doors."

"I felt you must. I know that you'd be the last person to want to create gossip."

She planted her hand over her heart. "Never. That's why I came directly to you with these matters."

"All I'm saying is that perhaps it would be best to talk to these individuals yourself, in a spirit of love, naturally."

"Naturally."

"Ask if there's any way you could be of help. Offer them your friendship."

She had so few real friends, and she wasn't entirely sure why. Her shyness was a problem, and she'd had Abigail, but now that both her sister and her husband were gone, it felt as if the entire world had shriveled up and died. For the first time in her life she was truly lonely. No one wanted to be friends with her. No one invited her to their homes. She was good enough to play the organ for all their special functions, but not good enough to be a friend. Never that.

"Thank you for seeing me," Harriett mumbled on her way out the door. She had achieved nothing. Her visit to Pastor Lovelace had failed. Ruth Darling would continue her flirtation with Lyle Fawcett and all the church would look on with horror as another family was destroyed.

Trapped in her musings, Harriett walked outside the church without watching her step. When she stepped on a thin patch of ice in the church parking lot, her feet went out from under her. Arms flailing, she let out a bloodcurdling scream that was loud enough to hail the Second Coming.

From her peripheral vision, she saw Joanne Lawton's face wide with shock and horror from the office window overlooking the parking lot.

The next thing she knew the pavement was rushing up to greet her. She closed her eyes and prayed for mercy.

She must have blacked out because when she opened her eyes, she saw two men leaning over her. Both wore the familiar uniform of paramedics. Carefully they placed her on a mat and wheeled her toward the aid car. It was difficult to focus on which part of her body hurt the worst. Her head felt as though someone had taken a sledgehammer to it. Her arm had to be broken, for the pain there was dreadful.

In her agony, she groaned.

"Try not to speak," one of the men said to her. "It looks to me like your jaw's broken."

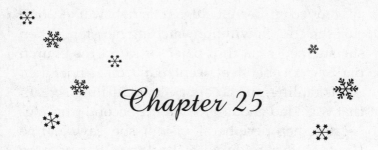

Chapter 25

Love looks through a telescope, not a microscope.

—Mrs. Miracle

"Good morning," Emily Merkle greeted as a bleary-eyed Sharon walked into the kitchen.

Sharon smiled back wanly. She hadn't slept well, and from the way Jerry had tossed and turned the night away, she knew he hadn't either. When she'd slipped out of bed she'd suspected he was awake, but he hadn't spoken, so neither had she.

After their frank discussion about their two divorced friends, they hadn't said much of anything to each other. But, really, what was there to say? Their conversation had been comment enough.

They'd get along better once they were divorced, Sharon suspected. Just making the decision seemed to have slackened the tension. They'd spent time with the children, attended a movie, and had spoken barely a cross word to one another in days, which she had to admit was something of a record of late. It was a sad comment on their life together.

"Would you like a cup of coffee?" Emily asked, and without waiting for a reply promptly poured her one. She carried it to the table and set it down for her. "The children are with their father this morning," she said companionably. "I believe they went Christmas shopping. Leave it to a man to put it off until the last minute." She chuckled to herself and returned to the task at hand. The large electric mixer hummed softly in the background, and the intoxicating scent of curry filled the kitchen.

"What are you making?" Emily was a fabulous cook, good enough to open her own restaurant if she wanted.

"It's a fruit dip," the housekeeper answered absently, reading over the recipe. "Delicious with winter fruit. Pear, apples, and the like." She knocked the lid on a jar of mango chutney against the edge of the counter to loosen it, then twisted it open with all her might. "Here, read over the recipe. You'll see what I mean."

"It sounds wonderful," Sharon said when she'd finished reading.

"If you think it sounds good, just wait until you taste it." Holding the mixing bowl in place under her arm, Emily scooped the fruit dip into a plastic container, then sealed it with the lid and placed it in the refrigerator. "Letting it set overnight is best, but if you can only chill it a couple of hours, that's fine, too."

"I'd need to eliminate the walnuts," Sharon said, glancing over the recipe again. "Jerry doesn't like them." She stopped, realizing she'd spoken automatically, without remembering that she no longer needed to concern herself with Jerry's likes and dislikes. From this Christmas forward she had only herself to please.

The knowledge should have delighted her; a few days ago it would have. Instead it depressed her. In her heart of hearts she recognized that the recipe would be tucked away, forgotten in the pages of a cookbook, like a good intention. It would be too much of a hassle to go to all that trouble just for one person. It wasn't worth the effort.

"Something smells good," Jerry said as he walked into the kitchen. "I love the scents of Christmas." He poured a cup of coffee for himself, then opened the refrigerator for the milk and spied the large turkey thawing inside.

"Christmas evokes memories for me," Mrs.

Merkle said conversationally. "They must for you, too, after all these years together."

"The first year Sharon and I were married, she baked a turkey," Jerry said. "She'd never done one completely on her own, and we couldn't afford for her to call her mother long distance and ask questions."

"It wasn't a turkey," Sharon corrected him, laughing softly, "just a large chicken, but I stuffed it and fretted over it with all the nervousness of a young bride wanting to impress her husband."

"How'd it turn out?" Emily asked.

"Wonderful," Jerry answered without looking at his wife. "One of the best Christmas dinners Sharon ever cooked."

"Jerry, it was a disaster." Sharon couldn't believe his memory was so short. "The bird was as tough as shoe leather, and the dressing was soggy and bland. I kept telling you how sorry I was that I'd ruined everything, and you insisted on eating it anyway." She'd loved him for it, loved him until her heart ached with the memory of it.

"The dinner was bad?" He looked genuinely surprised. "That's not the way I remember it."

"It wasn't much of a Christmas as Christmases go," Sharon murmured. "We had so little."

"Ah, the good ol' days. They bring back memories, don't they?"

"True," Jerry added, sitting on the chair next

to his wife. "As I recall, we couldn't afford a Christmas tree, so Sharon made one by sticking toothpicks into those foam balls till she had a stack of porcupines and then sprayed them all with that snow that comes out of a can. Then she decorated that with tiny glass balls, all blue."

"It wasn't that we couldn't afford the tree," Sharon explained. "Those were the days before the sheared trees were the fashion. We could have probably picked one up for a buck or two, but there wasn't room in our tiny apartment for anything more than the two of us."

"Three months later we made room. Our first Christmas, Sharon was six months pregnant with Clay and we needed every penny we could to save for the baby."

Her husband's gaze held hers and softened. Those had been frugal times, but some of the happiest of her life. She wouldn't trade one of those years for all the diamonds in the world.

Her mind wandered back to those early days and the one-bedroom apartment. They'd lived in an old, dilapidated building in San Francisco, away from family and friends for the first time in their lives. Her pregnancy had come as an unexpected surprise. It didn't help matters that her employer wouldn't allow her to work past six months, not even part-time, so their limited budget had been stretched even further. Somehow they'd made it, with love and laughter. Their finances might have been tight, but they'd held on to each other.

"It was one of our best Christmases," Jerry mused aloud.

"Yes," Sharon agreed. A hard knot filled her throat and she feared if she spoke again, Jerry or Emily would hear the tears in her voice, so she stood, mumbled an excuse, and hurried back to the bedroom.

She was sitting on the edge of the bed when Jerry came into the room. He didn't say anything as he sat down next to her.

The silence between them was long and profound.

"What went wrong with us?" she asked in a whisper.

Jerry leaned forward and braced his elbows against his knees. "I wish I knew."

Silence again as they mulled over the question neither of them could answer.

"I never suspected we'd end up like this," Jerry murmured at last.

"Me either," she said sadly, then stood and dressed. Jerry didn't want this divorce any more than she did, but neither wanted to go on living the way they had been. Their lives had become a constant tug-of-war, a battle of wills, in which they'd both become the losers.

Their marriage was a lose-lose proposition. The answers were more complicated than the questions.

What she needed, Sharon suspected, was a bit of fresh air and some time alone. With that goal in mind, she promptly finished getting ready for the day. "I'm going for a walk," she announced, and reached for her jacket.

Jerry looked at her as if seeking an invitation to join her. She didn't offer him one. She needed to mull over her future, what she intended to do with the rest of her life without a husband.

When she stepped outside she found the wind was strong and cold, cutting through her. Aimlessly she strolled along the sidewalk. She buried her hands in her pockets and bent her head against the force of the weather. Having had no real destination in mind, she was pleased when she happened upon a small park about a mile from Seth's house.

A large gust of wind tossed and tumbled multicolored leaves across the lush green grass as Sharon walked across the lawn and sat on a bench next to the merry-go-round and swing set.

All that talk about their first Christmas together had awakened her fears and regrets. She hadn't wanted to think about the past. Moving on with her life should be utmost in her thoughts. Just doing what needed to be done, purging Jerry from her life once and for all. Progression was what was important. She couldn't allow herself to dwell on all the good times or remember the love they'd once shared. A love so deep, it had defied their circumstances. All the reminiscences wouldn't help her deal with the reality of what she faced now.

That first Christmas, the two of them together alone, Jerry's weekly paycheck had been a whopping ninety dollars. Their rent had been a hundred and fifty dollars a month, and that had been the cheapest apartment they could find. What there was of their furniture had been a mixture of what their families had given them and the television, their pride and joy, which Jerry had won in a phone-in radio contest.

They hadn't been able to afford to exchange Christmas gifts, not with a baby due and the two of them living on one income. Nevertheless, Sharon had bought yarn, and while Jerry was at work, she'd knitted him a sweater. Her neighbor, Mrs. Grayson, had helped her read the pattern.

Despite the endless hours of effort she'd put into the project, one sleeve had turned out longer than the other. The neckline had sagged and the entire effort had been amateurish at best. No one would have seriously considered wearing that sweater. But Jerry had. He'd loved her enough to praise her efforts. She remembered when he'd opened the box. From the look of pride and wonder one might have thought she'd spun it from pure gold. He'd worn the sweater every night after work for years, and in all that time he hadn't once noticed a single flaw. She'd made it for him, and that was good enough for him.

Sharon's gift to her husband hadn't been the only one under the toothpick tree that Christmas. She'd awoken early Christmas morning to the sound of music and Jerry cooking breakfast, singing at the top of his lungs. It was a wonder their neighbors hadn't complained. Jerry, for all his other talents, was completely lacking in the area of voice. The eggs had been runny and the toast burned, but it might as well have been ambrosia for all the notice she had paid. He'd escorted her to their kitchen and sat her at the card table with the mock Christmas tree in the center. Beneath it there'd been a small wrapped box. She remembered the bow was red, the most beautiful red bow she'd ever seen.

Jerry had sat down beside her and, his eyes bright with love, handed her his gift. She'd unwrapped it carefully and found a pearl necklace. One pearl. He'd gone without lunches for two months in order to pay for it and the gold chain. He'd promised that someday he'd buy her an entire strand. Each pearl would be as beautiful and as perfect as she was.

He'd kept his word, too. For their twentieth

wedding anniversary he'd given her an eighteen-inch strand of pearls. She'd worn it a number of times since, but that single pearl had been a part of her for years and years, until it had become scratched and flawed and dented.

Like her marriage.

Sharon remembered she'd cried when she'd opened the necklace. Jerry had kissed the tears away, and then he'd romantically carried her into the bedroom and they'd made love until they were both exhausted.

Now it was over. Whatever they'd shared, whatever they'd loved about each other, had left them. It wasn't what she wanted. If she could turn back the clock, she would have given everything she owned to recapture the love.

The years had destroyed it. Dealing with life's complications. Children. The trying teenage years. The challenges of financing three kids in college all at the same time. Burying a child and rearing two grandchildren for four years. Retirement.

Somewhere along the path they'd fallen into a rut, one so deep that they hadn't been able to crawl out. Eventually the joy, the adventure, the enthusiasm, had gone out of their marriage. Out of their lives. The day-to-day routine had become filled with pettiness and trivial arguments. A duel of words and deeds.

A death knell.

Her steps grew sluggish as she walked back to the house. Her thoughts were heavy and full of self-recriminations. So many things she would do differently now. Her pride wasn't worth this agony, or was it? She'd thought she knew what she wanted, but now she wasn't so sure. She was confused and unhappy.

They were both so stubborn. So obstinate and unreasonable. She was to blame, but then so was Jerry. He hadn't made this easy.

She was tired, depressed, and about to make one of the most important decisions of her life.

The house was quiet and empty when she let herself inside. Not until she hung up her coat in the entryway closet did she realize she wasn't alone. A faint sound, the television, she surmised, could be heard from the family room off the kitchen.

Jerry and his football games, she thought, amused. She never had understood football or men's fascination with the game. The season seemed to last all year, August to January.

Jerry loved to watch the games. College. Professional. Pee-Wee League. The same with baseball and basketball.

For more years than she could count she'd sat at his side and knitted (her skills had improved over time) while he relaxed in front of the television, cheering on his favorite team. She hadn't understood the complexities of the game but had enjoyed just being with Jerry, sharing these quiet moments with the man she loved.

"I'm back," she called, unexpectedly cheered, knowing Jerry was in the other room. She had some things she wanted to say. Until that moment she hadn't realized it, but the need to speak to him burned within her. It had all started with Emily's comment about memories, and Sharon had soon found herself caught up in the years she'd shared with Jerry.

"Is that you, Mrs. Palmer?" Emily Merkle called back.

Sharon found Seth's housekeeper in the family room, her bare feet propped up against the otto-man. She grinned and wiggled her toes. "These dogs are barking," she said.

"Where's Jerry?"

"You mean to say he didn't meet up with you?"

"No." A small sense of desolation took hold of her.

"Why, that's strange. He left a few minutes after you did. I assumed . . . I thought he intended to join you."

Winter Fruit and Chutney Cream Spread

    1½ pounds cream
    3 tablespoons dry sherry
    3 tablespoons brown sugar
    1 tablespoon curry
    1 tablespoon ginger
    1 teaspoon dry mustard
    3-4 green onions, minced
    ⅔ cup chutney
    6 ounces shredded sharp cheddar cheese
    6 ounces chopped walnuts

Whip cream cheese with sherry, sugar, and spices. Fold in onion, chutney, cheese, and nuts. Chill overnight. Serve with fresh sliced apples and pears to scoop up the dip.

Chapter 26

It's all right to sit on your pity pot every now and again. Just be sure to flush when you're finished.

—Mrs. Miracle

"What do you mean your aunt Harriett can't play the piano for the Christmas program?" It was all Reba could do not to clench Jayne by the collar and demand an explanation. "This is some kind of joke, right?"

Jayne retreated one small step. Reba didn't blame her. She could feel the hysteria rising. The Christmas Eve program was scheduled in less than forty-eight hours. While she was confident that any number of volunteers were qualified to replace Mrs. Foster, Jayne's aunt was the only one who'd practiced the routine with the children.

The only one who knew the program backward and forward.

"She's taken a nasty fall," Jayne repeated. "She has to spend the night in the hospital and have her jaw wired. Her arm's broken, too."

Reba didn't mean to be callous about the older woman's injuries, but she was the one responsible for the performance. All week she'd heard how much this Christmas pageant meant to the church family. How pleased people were that she'd stepped in and taken over for Milly Waters. How grateful they were. Friends and family were planning on attending, people of other faiths. The pressure was on her and the children to give the performance of their lives.

And now she was without a pianist. Without hope.

Reba sank onto her chair and resisted the urge to bury her face in her arms. She didn't know what she was going to do.

"I realize this isn't the best time to ask, but would you mind terribly if I left a few minutes early?" Jayne asked, her words soft and cautious as if she were tiptoeing across a freshly polished floor. "I'd like to stop off at the hospital and visit my aunt. I know I complain about her a lot. She drives me crazy at times, but she is my aunt, and the only living relative on my mother's side of the family."

"Of course." Having Jayne leave an hour early wasn't nearly the catastrophe of not having a piano player for the church program. "Give her my best while you're there. Tell her not to concern herself about a thing." No need to heap more trouble on the woman's shoulders. She had enough on her mind without having to worry about the Christmas program.

Something like this was bound to happen, Reba thought as Jayne silently gathered her things and left the agency. She glanced over her shoulder on her way out the door, and Reba managed a brave smile.

"Don't worry," Jayne said, "everything will turn out the way it's supposed to."

Reba didn't believe that for an instant. She was supposed to go through this agony? Supposed to conjure up a piano player at the last minute? If she believed that, she'd have to accept that her sister was supposed to have ruined her wedding and her life. This was one of those clichéd comments she'd come to hate. It made no sense.

"Just remember, God doesn't close a door without opening a window."

The door closed, and Reba muttered, "Yeah, right." She closed her eyes and sighed deeply, releasing her pent-up frustration.

It never failed. Just when she was beginning to see the light at the end of a tunnel, she discovered it was an oncoming train. Just when she was beginning to believe that she'd found a man who would love and accept her with all her faults and foibles, Seth revealed his true self.

He was like all the others, preaching love and forgiveness, telling her how much better it would be if she forgave Vicki. It hurt—far more than she cared to admit. She'd been so hopeful with Seth. She'd started to believe again. And trust. Still, she hadn't said anything yet about ending their relationship. All the emotional strength she possessed would be focused on getting through Christmas and New Year's. Afterward she'd deal with the situation with Seth, although there really wasn't much to say or do. As far as she was concerned, it was over between them. Over before it started.

Their brief relationship wasn't all that different from the others she'd had in the last four years. Only this time her heart had gotten involved. She cared about Seth, cared about his children.

Working with Judd and Jason, getting to know them, love them, would make parting all the more painful.

The bell over the door chimed, indicating that she had a customer. She looked up, expecting another last minute walk-in desperate for her to part the Red Sea and book Vegas on New Year's. But it was much worse than that.

It was her mother.

"Hello, sweetheart." Joan Maxwell strolled inside, as cheerful as a canary. "Merry Christmas."

"Merry Christmas," Reba returned with a decided lack of enthusiasm.

Her mother's face fell. "What's wrong?"

"Have you got a year?"

"As a matter of fact, I do." She pulled up a chair beside Reba's desk and plunked herself down as if she intended to sit right there until all was right with the world once again.

"The piano player fell and broke her arm." No need to mention that her jaw was out of commission. It was her arm that mattered. At her mother's blank look, Reba continued, "The Christmas program, remember?"

"I'm sure there are other people in the church who're qualified."

"It's not that simple, Mother." Such matters rarely were. "First off, no one else has practiced with the children or knows the songs. It's more than just pounding out a few numbers on the keyboard. It's knowing when to play, giving the children their cues, and playing the background music. It's . . . everything."

"Oh, dear, you do have a problem, don't you?"

For the first time in recent memory her mother wasn't trivializing her troubles. Reba was grateful enough to comment. "Thanks, Mom."

Joan suddenly looked unsure and flustered. "Thanks for what? I can't help you. I would if I could, you know that, but I don't have any musical ability. Why, I don't even know where middle C is on a piano."

"Thank you for understanding," Reba explained.

"Oh." She sounded disappointed, but Reba forgave her that.

"Can I help you with something, Mom?" She didn't think this was a social call.

Her mother smoothed out her skirt, brushing her hand down the length of her thigh. "I understand . . . actually Doug was the one who brought it up . . . that you bumped into your sister."

"Yes," Reba answered shortly. She'd been hoping the conversation wouldn't turn to Vicki, the way it always did when she was with her mother. Just once she'd like it if they could talk without involving her sister. Just once. It shouldn't be too much to ask.

"Vicki said you looked well and happy."

"You know what I look like," Reba returned, unable to disguise her irritation.

"It was the happy part that pleased her."

"Why don't I believe that?"

"Oh, Reba, don't you know how eager your father and I are to resolve this? All we want, all everyone wants, is for you to be happy. Meeting Seth has been the best thing to happen to you in years, and—"

"I won't be seeing him again after the holidays." She might as well get that out in the open now.

The sadness and regret that filled her mother's eyes were immediate. "But why? I thought . . . we all did. You two are so good together. . . ."

"You don't know that," Reba challenged. "You've never even met him."

"I don't need to. I saw the difference in you."

"I'm sorry to disappoint you," Reba muttered.

"Oh, Reba," her mother murmured sadly, "there are so many things you don't know."

"Then tell me," she challenged, waving her arms in the air. She was tired of hearing it, tired of having her mother throw it in her face, as if any excuse she offered would change the way she felt.

"It involves your sister." Her look was skeptical, as if she expected Reba to stop her. The assumption was a fair one. Her mother had attempted to talk some sense into her plenty of times before, and Reba had refused to listen.

"Doesn't everything?"

Joan briefly closed her eyes, as if praying for patience.

"Are you going to tell me again how very sorry Vicki is?"

"No," she responded, pressing her lips together tightly. "There's no denying Vicki did something foolish."

"There are a number of other adjectives I'd like to add, but won't."

"Good. I appreciate that. She's paid dearly for her mistake. . . ."

Reba sighed. "If you're going to tell me she's suffered enough, I don't want to hear it."

Her mother ignored the comment. "After you found Vicki with John she came to your father and me and told us what she'd done. She blamed herself, was sick with regret."

"Yes, well, it wasn't exactly a picnic for me, either."

"No, but you dealt with it in an adult manner. In the beginning at any rate," she amended.

Reba's head came back with surprise.

"Vicki didn't. I don't know what happened that night, but I strongly suspect, as does your father, that John seduced her."

There it was again, the willingness to offer excuses for her sister.

"I know what you're thinking," her mother announced stiffly, "but we were the ones who dealt with the aftermath of that night, as far as Vicki's concerned."

Reba couldn't believe her ears. Her mother made it sound as if canceling the wedding had been some kind of picnic for her. True, she'd left town almost immediately, but who could blame her?

"Your sister ended up in the hospital." The words were low and filled with pain. "She attempted suicide the day that was supposed to have been your wedding day."

Reba's breath jammed in her throat. Vicki had attempted suicide? "Why didn't you tell me this before?"

"Only a handful of people know about it. Vicki made me promise that I'd never tell you, and until now I've kept my word. I wouldn't discuss it now except that I'm desperate. Your sister isn't the same person she was back then. Not anymore."

"We all change," Reba said, unwilling to allow this information to influence her attitude.

Joan sighed. "You can be so stubborn, Reba. I'd like to blame your father for that obstinate streak of yours, but I fear you get it from my side of the family as well." She smiled sadly, acknowledging her lame joke, then went on.

"Vicki was in counseling for a long time afterward. You refused to forgive her, and she had to learn to deal with that along with everything else. With time, therapy, and a sympathetic counselor, she was able to forgive herself. Shortly afterward she met Doug."

The silence that followed was unwelcome. Apparently her mother was looking for her to make some charitable comment, but unfortunately she was all out of charity. "Okay, you've told me, and I've listened, but it changes nothing."

The sadness and dejection in her mother's eyes was almost enough to make Reba capitulate. "Somehow I didn't think it would," Joan mumbled. She reached for her purse and stood. "Actually the reason I stopped by was to tell you that your father, Gerty and Bill, and I plan to attend the Christmas Eve program. They want to be able to spend some time with you, no matter how limited."

Reba nodded. Terrific. The pressure to put on a memorable pageant had just increased a hundredfold.

"I hope everything works out for you, sweetheart." Joan paused at the door. "And I'm not just talking about the Christmas program."

Reba desperately needed someone to play the piano. Someone who knew the routine. Someone who'd attended the practices and knew the nuances of timing as well as she did.

Seth.

The instant his name flashed into her mind, Reba knew it was divine inspiration. He'd been to almost every practice. He'd sat in the back of the church activity room and had even helped out backstage a time or two.

More important, he played the piano. He hadn't

in some time, she remembered, but he'd been good. He'd said so himself.

Heart pounding, Reba flipped the pages of her personal directory until she found the work phone number he'd given her. She punched it out so fast and hard, she bent a nail.

"Seth Webster."

"Seth," she breathed, relieved he'd answered the phone himself. "I need you."

"Now? I mean, I'm perfectly willing to give you my body, but—"

"Not sexually."

"Oh." He pretended to be terribly disappointed.

"Mrs. Foster, you remember Mrs. Foster, don't you? She fell and broke her arm, and now I need a piano player. Not just anyone, either, but someone who knows the program. Someone who's been there practice after practice. You." She spoke so fast that the words all but ran together. The silence that followed left her feeling as though she were standing on a precipice, ready to tumble over a cliff.

"Surely there's someone else more qualified," he said finally, breaking the tension.

"No, there's only you." Her hand squeezed the telephone receiver tightly. "You told me you play, remember? I wouldn't ask if this wasn't important. There's no one else who knows the program. No one."

She felt his hesitation once again. "I'm sorry, Reba. I hate to let you down, but I told you before, I gave up playing the piano after Pamela died."

"Are you saying you won't help me?"

The delay before his response said it all. "That's exactly what I'm saying."

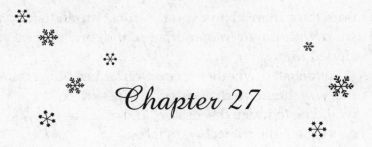

Chapter 27

*You'll notice that a turtle only makes progress
when it sticks out its neck.*

—Mrs. Miracle

Seth hated to turn Reba down, especially now. He knew he was already in her bad graces following the meeting with her sister. It hadn't taken a crystal ball to read the pain in Vicki's eyes or the anguish in Reba's. She had to force herself to hold on to her grudge, had to work at feeding her anger toward her sister. Seth had sensed that all it'd take would be a few words of encouragement for her to give in to what she actually wanted.

While his intentions were good, he'd realized the minute he'd opened his mouth that he'd traipsed onto treacherous ground. Reba had closed up tighter than a bank vault. Almost immediately she'd withdrawn into another world, one that excluded him.

He debated whether to stop off at her office on the way home and decided against it. To do so would be to invite discussion, and as far as he was concerned, the subject was closed.

He'd told Reba early on in their relationship the reason he'd given up music. He hadn't touched a piano since the day Pamela had died, and he wouldn't. At the time she'd been so understanding, sensitive to his grief. She hadn't lectured or offered him any bits of well-meaning wisdom, but had silently accepted his decision. She'd suffered a loss of her own and could empathize—until she had a reason to show him the error of his ways.

She'd gotten to him, Seth realized, frowning. He found himself wanting to help her and angry that she'd put him in an impossible situation. A vow was a vow. The music had gone out of his life, and he wasn't going to let Reba talk him into doing something he knew he'd later regret. All for a silly Christmas program.

His heart was heavy as he drove home. He didn't want matters to be like this between them. They were struggling, and this complicated everything.

His mind wasn't on the road, and when he

pulled into the driveway, the thirty-minute drive had completely escaped him. He could remember none of it. Early on after Pamela's death, it'd been like this. He'd find himself at the cemetery and not remember how he got there. It shocked him that this kind of thing would repeat itself at this late date.

Carrying his briefcase, he opened the door leading from the garage into the kitchen. Mrs. Merkle was busy with dinner preparations. Her meals were culinary masterpieces, but he had little appetite this evening.

"You have company waiting in the study. Ms. Maxwell," the housekeeper announced, and then lowered her voice. "I thought you two could do with a bit of privacy."

Seth smoothed the hair away from his brow. "I suspect you're right." He wasn't looking forward to a confrontation with Reba, and there was sure to be one. He hated to disappoint her. Hated to let her down.

Reba was pacing the room and turned to stare at him when he entered.

"Hello, Reba."

"Seth."

Her eyes held his, and he felt the burden of her frustration, the weight of her disappointment. He longed to help her, but she didn't seem to realize what she was asking. His stomach clenched with dread. He'd never expected to fall in love again. Finding her was one of the biggest surprises of his life. Love had taken him by storm, and it was all about to be ruined. And he'd have no one to blame but himself.

"I came because I had to talk to you once more about helping me out." Her eyes implored him, and he found it impossible to look away. The urge to take her in his arms and soothe away her worries nearly overwhelmed him, and at the same time he found himself fighting his anger. He'd already told her no, and he resented her pressing the issue. This had to do with Pamela and him, not Reba.

"You don't know what you're asking." He sat on the ottoman and buried his hands in his hair, holding on to his head. "Music was something I shared with Pamela."

"She's gone," Reba reminded him gently. "But you're still here."

"You don't understand."

"The music didn't go away with Pamela."

"It did for me." He struggled to keep from shouting.

"You're using this thing with the piano to hold on to your grief. You've got to let go if you're ever going to get on with your life."

Her timing was all too convenient, he noticed. "So I can play the piano in some church program because you want me to? Isn't that just a tad self-serving?"

She exhaled sharply, and he realized his words had hit their mark. "The Christmas program isn't the only reason I'm asking."

"I don't believe you."

"All right, all right. I wouldn't have asked if it wasn't for the Christmas program, but—" She stopped abruptly, and he noticed that her hands trembled as she clenched them and raised them to her lips.

"You're saying that I'm clinging to my grief."

"Yes!"

"You might take a look in the mirror. You don't have any right to talk. If anyone's clinging to anything, it's you. I saw the look in your sister's eyes the other day, and it was a reflection of what you were feeling. Everything in you longs to make peace with Vicki, but you're clinging to your anger with both hands, because heaven help you if you ever let go."

"I don't know what you're talking about," Reba insisted.

"You don't have a leg to stand on," he continued. "The truth is, if you settled your differences with your sister, you'd have to take a long, hard look at some things in yourself. Like maybe the real reason you agreed to marry John in the first place. You told me your sister made a play for him because he was yours, but admit it, Reba—wasn't it more the other way around? That maybe you wanted him because of how your sister felt about him? . . . That was the big attraction, wasn't it? Walking off with something just so your sister couldn't have it."

The blood drained from her face, and she knotted her hands into tight fists.

"For the first time in your life you had something your sister didn't."

"Stop it!" she shouted, and covered her ears. "That's ridiculous. I didn't come here to talk about Vicki, I came to ask for your help with the Christmas program."

"You have my answer."

She stiffened, grabbed her purse, and swung it over her shoulder. "You're right, I do." She started toward the door as if she couldn't escape him fast enough, then stopped abruptly and glanced over her shoulder. Her eyes were bright with unshed tears, and she offered him a sad smile. "I apologize, Seth. I should never have come. Good-bye."

The finality of her words didn't strike him until she was gone. An immediate sense of sorrow seeped into his being, saturating his head and his heart. The pain was familiar, the feeling of loneliness, of facing life without friends, without a partner. Alone again. Terribly alone.

Part of Seth longed to run after her, take her in

his arms, and tell her that he'd do whatever was necessary to make things right between them. But he didn't. He couldn't, because that would mean he'd have to give her something he wasn't ready to relinquish: his grief. He was perfectly content to live with a foot in both worlds; the land of the living and the valley of death. Content to hold on to both women, refusing to release one and give his heart to another.

Fine. If that was what it took, then so be it. He'd loved Pamela first. She was his wife, the mother of his children. His heart. Now she was gone, and giving up the piano was his testimonial to their love.

Reba had made it sound as though he were a candidate for therapy. It'd angered him, and rightly so. She had no room to talk. None whatsoever.

It was over. She'd said as much on her way out the door. That was the way he wanted it.

"Excuse me," Emily muttered, standing in the middle of her kitchen, and raised her expectant eyes heavenward. "Is anyone listening up there? . . . Anyone? . . ." She didn't anticipate a response, but she would have appreciated one. "We've got trouble down here. Real trouble, and I'm not talking about the gelatin not setting in my salad recipe, either."

She reached for the wooden spoon and, tucking the bowl under her arm, whipped the cake batter with frenzied effort. There'd be high-tide warnings in Arizona before she'd agree to use an electric mixer. One didn't get the feel of batter or gauge consistency with any newfangled machine.

"In case no one's noticed, there's been a major screw-up here," she said. "Reba just walked out the door, and it doesn't look to me like there's going to be a piano player for the Christmas program, either." She expelled her breath heavily. "There's only so much one person can do." Once again she glanced heavenward. "Housekeeping and cooking are one thing, but sorting out people's lives, well, that's an area I prefer to leave to the experts."

The so-called experts seemed to be on coffee break. Wouldn't you know it! She was going to be left to deal with this mess on her own, and by heaven, someone was going to hear about it.

"I don't like this one bit," she muttered, setting the bowl back on the kitchen counter with a bang. "I don't play the piano," she reminded the powers above, "so don't expect me to step in and rescue the day." She clamped her mouth closed. "You might have given me some warning, you know!"

Spraying the cake pans, she glanced toward the other room and caught a glimpse of Sharon. "I'm not entirely pleased with what's happening with the Palmers, either. Not one bit. Forty years down the tubes. Something's got to be done, I say, and fast before it's too late. What's going on up there, anyway?" She wiped her hands on a fresh towel from the drawer. "If I didn't know better, I'd say the entire heavenly realm was out to choir practice."

It seemed to her that what heaven really needed was a wake-up call. Well, she was just the one to give it!

Harriett Foster had rarely been more miserable. Her jaw was wired closed and her left arm sported a thick white cast. Her niece had spent the better part of an hour with her, but Jayne had family and other commitments and couldn't be expected to hang around the hospital with a sick old woman.

This certainly wasn't the way Harriett had intended to spend the holidays. Now she'd miss the Christmas program, and Reba would be left to find a last minute replacement for the piano. She closed her eyes and let her mind wander over a list of possibilities. It would be tough finding someone, almost impossible. She was irreplaceable and knew it. The entire Christmas Eve program would need to be canceled.

"All things are possible with God."

Harriett's eyes flew open. She looked around to see who'd spoken, but no one was there. It was the medication, she decided. She was hearing voices. She'd heard others speak of such matters, and she'd scoffed, but this was very real, drugs or no drugs.

"Trust."

This time her eyes were wide open, and it most definitely was a voice. One loud and clear. Precise. There could be no dismissing it.

Next time I won't be so quick to judge others claiming to hear voices, she thought.

"Exactly my point—don't be so quick to judge others."

Although it caused her considerable discomfort, Harriett twisted her head to look about a second time. It was uncanny, as if someone were standing in the room, reading and commenting on her thoughts. Someone who—"Here you are." The hospital door banged open and Emily Merkle sauntered into the room. "My oh my, you've gotten yourself into a fine mess, haven't you?"

Harriett had never been fond of the other woman, but she was grateful for a familiar face. Perhaps now the voice would fade, and she could bask in the glow of well-deserved sympathy. Every part of her body ached, despite the pain medication.

"I only have a minute," Emily said, coming closer to the hospital bed. The housekeeper sighed and tucked a stray strand of hair around her ear. "I needed to escape, so I thought I'd drop in and visit my friend Harriett." She dropped herself down on a chair next to the bed. "I take it Pastor Lovelace told you about Ruth's brother?"

Ruth's brother? Harriett didn't know Ruth had a brother.

"Matters are in a tither at the house. I don't understand it, either," she said, and Harriett wasn't sure she was speaking to her. Her eyes held a faraway look. "I suspect I'll be missed if I don't get back soon. I'm sure you'll be feeling better before long, so don't you fret." She frowned. "But then, the way matters are developing at the Websters', I might be speaking too soon."

The woman actually planned to leave. Swoop in, make a few candid comments, and then leave? With her one good arm, Harriett reached out and grabbed the other woman's sleeve, then stopped. Because she was unable to speak, she reached for a tablet and pen.

Ruth has a brother? she wrote out quickly.

Emily Merkle grinned from ear to ear. "Lyle Fawcett."

Harriett felt as if someone had hit her along the side of her head with a two-by-four. Lyle was related to Ruth. They were brother and sister. No wonder Pastor Lovelace had reacted the way he had. Her heart sank at the memory of what she'd said and done. Of the things she'd been thinking about Ruth.

"Don't worry about it, we all make mistakes," Emily said. "It comes with having to deal with the human side of ourselves. A real nuisance, if you ask me."

Frustrated because she couldn't speak, Harriett waved her good hand about, not even sure what it was she wanted to say. She wasn't sure if Emily was reading her thoughts or the expression in her eyes. As far as she was concerned, there'd always been something peculiar about the Websters' housekeeper.

"You okay?" Emily asked.

The answer was far too complicated, so Harriett penned the words *As well as can be expected,* but when she glanced down at the tablet she found the words *I feel like an old fool.* She looked at the sheet again, certain there must be some mistake. Perhaps more was wrong with her than just a few broken bones.

Emily chuckled and patted her hand. "Don't worry. Most of us are guilty of making assumptions now and again. It helps when we decide to resign as general manager of the universe. Personally, I don't need the headache." She laughed again and was gone.

This time the door didn't so much as open. Harriett was sure of it. The door didn't budge an inch, yet Emily had disappeared.

One moment the Websters' housekeeper was there and the next she was gone.

Something very weird was going on. Harriett Foster pressed the button to call the nurse. She needed help; clearly she'd had a reaction to the pain medication.

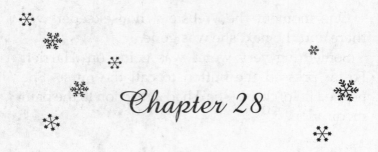

Chapter 28

If the grass is greener on the other side of the fence,
you can bet the water bill is higher.

—Mrs. Miracle

Sharon didn't see much of her husband the entire day. Her stroll to the park had helped her sort through her feelings about the divorce, and she'd been eager to share her thoughts with her husband. But he'd disappeared—and when he returned late in the afternoon, he didn't even offer an explanation of where he'd been or what he'd been doing.

If it wasn't for the twins' enthusiasm for Christmas, dinner would have been a glum affair. Seth had apparently had a falling-out with Reba and looked about as cheerful as a cadaver. Jerry wasn't much better. Emily appeared to be in a rare bad mood as well. If it hadn't been for Judd and Jason, who rattled on like chatterboxes, Sharon would have suggested they all meet later for a mass suicide.

The evening wore on, and knowing that the following day, Christmas Eve, would be full, Sharon opted to retire early. When Jerry joined her shortly afterward she was already in bed, propped up against several pillows and reading.

"Where were you this afternoon?" she asked. Considering that they'd agreed to divorce, she had no right to pry into his business. Nor did he have any responsibility to report his whereabouts to her. "You don't need to answer that," she added quickly, embarrassed.

"I don't?" He sat on the end of the bed and untied his shoes.

"Unless you want to, of course." Every time she opened her mouth she seemed to make it worse.

"I went to the movies."

"Oh." She would have enjoyed going with him, but it was senseless to admit as much.

"To think," he added.

"Oh." Apparently her entire vocabulary had shrunk to words of one syllable.

He twisted around to look at her. "Aren't you going to ask me what I was mulling over?"

"Do you want to tell me?" Clearly he did, or he wouldn't have prompted the question.

"I was remembering our first Christmas in San Francisco and comparing it to this year . . . the last one we're likely to spend together."

"I went for a walk and couldn't help wondering at what point we stopped being good to one another?"

"I wish I knew," he mumbled. His right shoe landed with a clunk onto the floor, then his left. He undressed and pulled back the covers on his side of the bed and slipped inside.

Sharon continued to read, or pretend to read. Jerry lay on his back and stared at the ceiling.

"I had Chinese food for lunch."

He'd never been fond of Chinese, but it was her favorite. She had to bite her tongue to keep from reminding him that he complained every time she suggested Szechuan. It used to be—when they lived in San Francisco—that he'd take her to Chinatown. It was such a rare occasion when they could afford a meal out, and Jerry loved to treat her to a dinner he knew she'd find special. She recalled that back then they could eat dinner for two for under five dollars. How times had changed!

"Funny how a dish of chow mein can bring back the memories," Jerry added.

"We were happy then." The lump in her throat felt as large as a grapefruit.

"Yeah," Jerry agreed on a sad note.

Giving up the pretense of reading, Sharon removed her reading glasses, set them on the end table, and turned off the lamp. The room went dark. For the last several nights they'd slept side by side, each as close to the edge of the mattress as they could manage. They'd acted as though touching each other would be akin to pulling the plug on a hand grenade and tossing it into a crowd.

Sharon lay on her back now, too, staring blankly up at the ceiling.

"Remember our first real Christmas tree?" he asked unexpectedly.

"Of course." Clay had been barely two, and Neal had been a year old. Two babies within two and a half years. Living on one income, they'd had no money for luxuries like tree ornaments.

"You strung popcorn and cranberries."

Sharon laughed softly. "Which the boys promptly ate."

"We ended up putting the tree inside the playpen, remember?"

She laughed again. "Neal was so excited to open a gift, he ran around it three times and then tore into it like a Tasmanian devil."

Soon Jerry was laughing, too. "Remember the time Pamela stuffed a bead up her nose and we had to take her to the emergency room to get it out? That bead cost us a fortune."

"And ruined my favorite necklace."

They were silent for a while, each caught up in the rich texture of their years together.

"Remember the time in church when some poor unsuspecting elderly woman sat down in the middle of a song?"

"And I was holding Clay on my hip and somehow he got hold of the woman's wig and started shaking it like a dog with a dead rat."

"You were mortified."

"And you kept trying to put it back on the woman's head, and her hands kept getting in the way."

"Didn't we change churches shortly after that?"

"I don't remember, but I bet that woman did."

Sharon started laughing, and soon the tears ran unrestrainedly down her cheeks. For the memory, true, but mingled in with the laughter was sadness and regret.

"Are you going to tell the boys?" Jerry asked a moment later.

"I thought we should do it together."

"That would be best," he agreed.

The silence was back, but neither of them rolled onto their sides as they had previous nights.

"We had some really great years."

"Yes," she whispered, and to her horror her voice cracked.

"Sharon?"

She didn't answer, fearing she'd dissolve into tears if she did.

"Come on, Sharon," Jerry said, tossing aside the covers as if he couldn't remove them fast enough. "I don't want a divorce. I never did, but I was too proud to say so. Enough is enough. I've loved you all these years, and I'm not going to stop now."

Wide-eyed, Sharon sat up, clutching the covers to her breasts.

"If you want to fight me on this, fine, but I'm telling you right now—"

Sharon ran her hand down his back. He jumped at the unexpectedness of her touch, then twisted around, moved in closer, and lowered his mouth to hers.

The kiss was filled with frustration and anger and need, and it took Sharon by surprise. It had been so long since her husband had showed her any physical attention that she momentarily shied away, but Jerry wouldn't allow it. He deepened the kiss, and, sighing, she wound her arms around his neck. "Jerry?" she whispered when he buried his face in the curve of her neck.

"Are you surprised the old man's still got some life left in him?"

"No. Oh, Jerry . . . I love you so much. I don't want the divorce, either, but I can't go on living the way we have been."

"Me either." She heard and felt his sigh, which

came from deep within his chest. "I've been a stubborn fool."

"Me too. I was the one who decided to sleep in the guest bedroom."

"But I knew that you didn't want that Panama Canal cruise. I was being selfish and pigheaded." He raised his head just enough to meet her eyes. To her surprise, she found his beautiful dark eyes bright with unshed tears.

"Jerry," she whispered, and gently pressed her palm to his cheek. "I'm so sorry. I don't know why we let this happen."

Tenderly he held her hand to his face and kissed her fingers. "There's never been anyone but you. I wouldn't know how to love anyone else." He reached down and unfastened the buttons to her pajama top. His hands shook with eagerness.

Smiling to herself, Sharon completed the task for him and then looped her arms around his neck. "Love me."

"I do," he murmured between deep, satisfying kisses. "I do."

He took his own sweet time proving how very much he did love her. The years fell away and it was as though they were young again, their eagerness for one another as strong as it had been in the early years.

Some time later Sharon lay in her husband's

arms, her head cradled against his chest. "Do you think anyone heard us?"

"I don't see how they could help it," he teased, and kissed the side of her face. "You never could keep from making those little love noises. Thank heaven the twins are asleep."

Sharon felt herself blush and groaned with embarrassment. "What will Seth think of us?"

"He'll think I'm the luckiest man alive, and he'll be right."

"Oh, Jerry, we've been such fools."

"No more. We're both going to have to work at this. It isn't a fifty-fifty proposition with us. It's a hundred percent and nothing less. Talking about when we were young and first married was the kick in the pants I needed. If you want to cruise to the Orient, then that's what we'll do."

"Thank you, but I insist we go through the Panama Canal first. You've been talking about it for years. You deserve this, and I want to share the experience with you."

He rubbed his jaw along the top of her head. "There's no shopping in the Canal," he reminded her.

"I'll survive." She could live without buying T-shirts and pottery, but she couldn't live without Jerry. "Now what was all this business about you having Chinese food for lunch?"

He went still and quiet. "I'm not entirely sure myself. I guess in my own way I was looking for a way to be close to you again. I had a miserable afternoon. The movies weren't nearly as enjoyable without you sitting there with me. I didn't even buy popcorn."

Sharon smiled to herself.

"While I'm at it, I might as well confess that I don't dislike walnuts nearly as much as I made out. I prefer almonds and cashews, but a walnut isn't as repugnant to me as I let on."

"Then why . . . ?"

"I'd had a bad game of golf and was sick and tired of sleeping alone."

"I overreacted," Sharon conceded. "It was a bit dramatic of me to insist you cook your own meals."

"It taught me a lesson," Jerry said, and rubbed his hand down her bare arm. "I won't complain again for a long time."

"Good thing."

He chuckled, then grew serious. "If we've decided to make a go of our marriage, we can't be tossing the option of divorce in each other's faces again. It's too dangerous."

Sharon agreed. Bringing up the subject had been like opening a Pandora's box, creating more problems than it solved. Once she'd started thinking of leaving Jerry, her mind had justified her decision. Everything he said or did was further evidence that their love was dead.

"I love you, Jerry Palmer." The tears were back in her voice, only this time they were evidence of her happiness.

"I love you, Sharon Palmer. Forever."

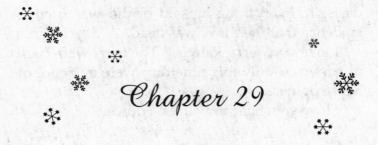

Chapter 29

God gave the angels wings and humans chocolate.

—Mrs. Miracle

The twins were down, and Sharon and Jerry had headed for bed at a ridiculously early hour, and now Seth was left alone to deal with his thoughts. Try as he might, he couldn't forget the look of hurt and disillusionment on Reba's face when she'd walked out the door.

But what she'd asked of him was impossible. He hadn't touched a keyboard in four years. She seemed to believe he could pick up where he'd left off and play in public with less than twenty-four hours' notice. Talk about unrealistic. Talk about absurd. She wasn't even making sense.

He refused to think about it any longer. Having

nothing better to do, Seth sat down in front of the television and reached for the remote control. He'd started to surf through the channels when Mrs. Merkle waltzed into the room with a feather duster.

"Don't pay me any mind, Mr. Webster," she said as she breezed past him. "With so much to do tomorrow, I want to finish up what housework I can this evening. I'll be out of your way before you know it."

Seth leaned his head against the cushion and waited patiently while she dusted off the top of the television. He noticed that she stood directly in front of the screen, blocking the view.

"Christmas Eve is almost upon us. My oh my, how the days fly by. I don't suppose you've noticed how excited the twins are to be a part of the church program. They're going to be the best little angels on God's green earth. It would be a terrible letdown to them if the pageant had to be canceled."

Seth frowned. He heard the censure in his housekeeper's voice but didn't know if it was real or imagined. He did notice that it seemed to be taking her an inordinate amount of time to dust.

"I feel so bad for Reba. I don't know how she'll ever find someone to play the piano at this late date." She turned and looked deliberately at him.

"Emily, stop."

She hesitated, the feather duster clenched in one hand. "Stop? You want me to stop dusting?"

"Yes." His wishes were simple and direct. He'd suffered enough recriminations without his housekeeper adding to his guilt. "I'll finish up myself later."

"As you wish."

She left, and Seth heaved a sigh of relief. He soon realized that he'd underestimated the woman the children called Mrs. Miracle. Before he could refocus his attention on the TV, Emily returned, this time with the vacuum cleaner in tow.

Without a pause she plugged it in and ran it across the carpet in front of him with the determination of a woman intent on wiping out the plague of household dust in her lifetime. It amazed him that the carpet remained glued to the floorboard.

"Emily!" he shouted.

She turned off the vacuum and cast him a look of pure innocence. "You wanted something, Mr. Webster?"

"How about some peace?" he said between clenched teeth.

"Peace," she repeated as though this were a foreign word she couldn't translate. "If you're looking for peace, then I suggest you search for it within yourself."

"Oh no," he said, wagging his index finger at

her. "You aren't going to start in with those crazy sayings of yours, not to me. Don't try to tell me silence isn't always golden, that it's sometimes just plain yellow."

"Oh, excellent," she said, her entire face brightening, "but I never said that. Dear Abby did, or perhaps it was Ann Landers."

"You know what I mean," he challenged, in no mood to lock horns with the housekeeper.

Arms akimbo, Mrs. Merkle stood squarely in front of him. "She needs a piano player, and furthermore she needs you almost as much as you need her. Now, what are you going to do about it?"

He glared at the woman, wishing he had the courage to fire her on the spot. It was what she deserved for interfering in his personal affairs, but he wouldn't last a week without her and he knew it.

"If you let Reba down now, you'll regret it the rest of your life."

She sounded so sure, so self-confident. He hesitated, and she closed in for the kill. "Ask yourself what Pamela would want you to do."

Seth squeezed his eyes closed. Pamela. This sacrifice had been for her—in her honor, a tribute to what they'd shared. It was a way of forever remembering his wife. A way of hanging on to his fears.

The moment the words went through his mind, Seth recognized the truth of them. His vow over Pamela's grave had been a convenient excuse to offer Reba. The truth was that he was afraid: only a fool would step in and play the piano for the Christmas pageant at this late date.

"Or someone with little to lose and lots to gain," the older woman said, cutting into his thoughts.

Seth looked at Mrs. Merkle. "Excuse me?"

"I didn't say anything," she said, and pushed the vacuum into the next room.

"I thought—"

"Are you going to help Reba or not?" she demanded impatiently. She planted one hand against her ample hip and glared at him.

"I . . . don't know."

"Well, you'd better decide soon. You don't have all day, you know." Having had her say, she disappeared. At last Seth had the peace and quiet he'd asked for, but it didn't help. He was more agitated now than he'd been with Emily waving a feather duster under his nose.

Now there was no help for it. Pamela would have been the first person to encourage him to step in and help, for the children's sake, if for no other reason. He wasn't happy about it, but he was also aware there would be no rest for him until he agreed.

The decision made, he decided to phone Reba.

Few things could have surprised him more than to find she wasn't at home. He waited until the answering machine clicked in and then said with a complete lack of graciousness, "All right, you win. I'll do it. Get the sheet music to me as soon as you can."

Seth's accusations burned like branding irons in her mind as Reba sat in her car outside her sister's home. She'd never spoken to her sister about what happened that fateful night. She certainly hadn't given either John or her sister an opportunity to explain. It wasn't in her to listen to their excuses, their justifications. The minute she'd found her sister with John, she'd blocked out all feelings for both of them.

Or so she wanted to believe.

Then she'd run into her sister at the toy store. What Seth had said was true: they were both in anguish, both hurting, both miserable. It was seeing Ellen for the first time—the niece she'd never held, never laughed with or cuddled—that had done it. For so many years Reba had begrudged Vicki happiness, at the cost of her own. Then she'd found Seth . . . a miracle, a gift from God. And now, once again, for the sake of perpetuating her resentment toward her sister, she was about to throw away everything she yearned for.

Perhaps what Seth had said was true about the

real reasons she'd agreed to marry John. Reba didn't want to examine his accusations too closely. Assigning blame was far too tiring. She was through with it.

It demanded a great deal of courage to walk up to the front door and ring the bell. An eternity passed before the porch light went on and the door opened. Doug stood on the other side.

"Reba?" He held open the screen door for her.

"I'd like to talk to Vicki," she explained.

Her brother-in-law hesitated, as if he weren't sure he could trust her. "Is there a problem with your parents?"

She liked Doug and the way he acted to protect Vicki. "No. The problem's between my sister and me. I need to talk to her."

"Doug, who is it?"

He glanced over his shoulder, waited a moment, and then announced, "Your sister."

Vicki appeared from the hallway almost immediately. Ellen rode her hip, dressed in Minnie Mouse pajamas, her wet hair combed back, her eyes filled with simple joy and laughter.

It looked as though Doug were ready to stand guard over his wife and daughter, protect them both from her, if necessary.

"Reba." Vicki's round, dark eyes revealed her surprise. "Could you give us a few minutes alone?" she requested of her husband. She handed him the child and walked quietly into the living room.

Reba followed. Now that she was here, now that she'd crossed the bridge and was facing the woman she'd actively resented for four long years, she found all she could do was weep. The years of keeping her anger alive, of feeding her resentment and pain, left her feeling as though she were drowning in emotion. Tears welled in her eyes and spilled down her face, despite her almost frantic efforts to keep them at bay. Her throat felt raw. She'd wasted so much time feeding her pain, when the person she'd hurt the most had been herself.

For years she'd been telling herself how much she hated Vicki. For years she'd closed herself off from her family and friends. For years she'd tabulated the wrongs committed against her, when all along she'd missed her sister desperately. Her best friend. Her own flesh and blood.

When she found the courage to look toward Vicki, she found her sister sitting across from her, tears running unrestrainedly down her cheeks. She offered Reba a gentle smile and then bit into her lower lip as if she were afraid to speak.

"Ellen is a beautiful little girl," Reba whispered. It was all the voice she had, and it came out choked and breathy.

"I named her after you. Ellen Louise." Vicki

rubbed the heel of her hand down her cheeks and sniffled. "Oh, Reba, I'm so sorry, so very sorry." She lowered her face. "You have every reason to hate me. . . . What I did was despicable. You don't know how I hated myself afterward . . . how . . ."

"Don't," Reba said, her voice surprisingly strong.

Vicki looked up to meet her eyes.

"I know you're sorry, it's unnecessary to say it again. The reason I've come is to apologize to you. My unwillingness to forgive you has hurt everyone. You. Mom and Dad, and probably most profoundly, me. I came because . . . because I need you to forgive me!"

Vicki stood, walked over to where Reba sat, and got down on her knees.

With a soft cry of joy Reba wrapped her arms around her sister, and the two hugged and openly wept.

Chapter 30

Fear not for I bring you tidings of great joy.

—A personal friend of Mrs. Miracle

*S*eth sat down at the church piano, poised his fingers over the yellowed ivory keyboard, and hesitated. He had studied the music, and the notes rang loud and clear in his head long before his fingers struck the keys. The first song, "Joy to the World," was one of his favorites, one he'd often played during the holidays because Pamela had loved it, too.

The last time he'd played the carol had been the Christmas before the accident, while his wife had sung the solo in front of the church.

He forced the memory from his mind and pressed his fingers upon the keys. Convinced his

talent would be rusty following a four-year sab-
batical, he'd arrived two hours early to practice.
The music flowed. From his heart and from his
soul. Joy mingled with sadness, and to his wonder, the joy drowned out the sorrow. It was as
though he'd sat and practiced hours every one of
those days away from the piano.

He wasn't the only one who noticed. Reba
stepped out from behind the painted manger
scene, paused, and stared. The joyous notes filled
the church, resounding through the building, am-
plified until the music swelled and echoed like a
chorus of angels.

"Oh, Seth," she whispered when he'd finished,
awe in her voice. "That was lovely. I don't know
when I've heard the carol played more beautifully."

Her praise embarrassed him, and he fumbled
with the sheet music. "You'll be able to cue me,
won't you?"

"Of course." She walked to the far edge of the
stage. "I'll be standing here. Emily and a couple of
other volunteers are seeing to everything backstage. They'll get the children where they're supposed to be. The others are seeing to the costumes
and everything else backstage. My job is to cue
you when to play and usher the actors and ac-
tresses on and off the stage."

Seth ran his fingers up and down the scales,
marveling in the sense of freedom and joy he ex-

perienced. If not for practical reasons, he would have sat at the piano all day. What Reba had said about him letting go of his grief was true. He felt as if the shackles had lifted from his heart, and his spirit soared in jubilation.

"I don't know how to thank you," Reba said when he'd finished.

He grinned. "I'll think of something," he said, and then lowered his voice. "Preferably something that involves leather and lace."

She smiled and lingered, then walked around the piano. Although they hadn't known each other long, he was beginning to understand and appreciate her. Something was on her mind. He also knew that she'd tell him in her own good time.

"My sister's coming this evening," she said shyly.

Seth noticed the slight tremble in her voice.

"What you said hit home."

He regretted that now, because he'd spoken in anger. "It wasn't my place to berate you, and you were right: it was a prime example of the pot calling the kettle black."

"Vicki and I talked half the night; she didn't make any excuses for what happened, but I know in my heart that John seduced her. She's changed so much, and she says I have, too." Her eyes misted. "Thank you for giving my sister back to me."

He reached for her hand and raised it to his

lips. "Don't credit me with that. You're the one responsible."

"But I never would have gone to see her if it hadn't been for you. I was terribly afraid."

"It was a courageous thing to do after all this time."

"Ironically, going to see Vicki wasn't what frightened me," she said. "Losing you was." This last confession was followed by a noticeable gasp, as though she'd said more than she intended. "You were the first man who didn't run to hide at my obvious emotional problems."

"Two wounded souls reaching out to help one another," he added. "My guess is that we were brought together for a specific purpose."

"The Christmas program," she suggested tentatively, moving to stand behind him. She looped her arms around his neck.

"For the pageant? Perhaps, but I have the distinct notion that we were meant to be together for a lifetime. You've brought sunshine into my shade-filled existence." He wasn't a poet, and he didn't know the words to express all that was in his heart. Of one thing he was confident: they were meant to be together. God had brought this incredible woman into his life. He was grateful for the years he'd had with Pamela and the two children she'd borne him. He loved her and always would, but the love he felt for his dead wife was different. Loving Reba took nothing away from Pamela. Having loved Pamela increased his ability to reveal his devotion to Reba.

He brought his hands back onto the keyboard. A smile came to his heart.

Judd readjusted the belt and sword and squared his shoulders as he raced off the stage and back to Emily's side.

"How'd we do?" Jason asked, his face bright with happiness, his aluminum angel wings flapping behind him.

Emily clasped her hands together. "You were wonderful, both of you." She was going to miss these two munchkins. This happened every time she got involved with children. She'd go and leave behind a piece of her heart.

"Grandma and Grandpa are in the front row, sitting next to Reba's sister and her family."

"So I saw." Emily placed her hands over their shoulders and steered them back to where they could remove the angel costumes. "I have something to tell you both. Something important." She sat them down and then did so herself. This was the most difficult part. "I'm afraid I'll be leaving shortly."

Jason's face crumpled. "No way."

"You can't," Judd cried, his dark eyes imploring her.

She'd expected the protests, would have been offended if they hadn't put up some fuss. The human side of her had deep concern for her employers.

"Now, now, it has to be this way, and really, it won't be so bad. The agency is sending over another housekeeper, but she's only temporary."

"Why can't you stay?"

"Because the agency needs me elsewhere," she explained patiently.

"Tell them you won't go."

"We need you with us."

"I'm afraid I can't do that, but you needn't concern yourself because—"

"But we want you, not some other housekeeper."

"They might send Mrs. Hampston back," Judd muttered, folding his arms over his chest and pouting.

Emily laughed softly. "As I said, you won't be needing one for long since your dad's going to be marrying shortly." Oh dear, she'd done it again, spilled the proverbial beans. This time she feared she was going to hear about it from the powers above.

"Dad's going to marry Reba?" Jason's eyes grew as round as bowling balls. "Wow. When?"

"This will be our secret, all right?" Emily said, doing her best to cover her small faux pas.

Both of the children nodded.

"Soon you'll forget all about me," she said,

wanting to reassure them. She'd be upset if they did, but that was beside the point.

"Never," Judd insisted.

"Is Reba going to have any babies?" Jason asked.

Oh, dear, she'd gotten herself into a fine kettle of fish. "I believe that is highly possible."

"Girls or boys?"

"One of each," she said, and then pressed a finger to her lips. "Remember, this is our little secret."

"My lips are sealed." Jason pantomimed zipping closed his mouth. Judd did, too.

"We're going to miss you," Judd said, bowing his head. "Are you sure you have to go?"

"Very sure."

Soon the sound of applause was the cue to send the children back on stage for the final curtain call. Judd and Jason hurried out with their friends to sing a rousing version of "We Wish You a Merry Christmas."

Emily Merkle stood in the wings and smiled at her young charges. It was time to move on. Mission accomplished.